INTERROGATING SOCIAL CAPITAL
The Jharkhand Experience

INTERROGATING SOCIAL CAPITAL
The Jharkhand Experience

Anirudh Prasad

LITHOUSE
2019

Interrogating Social Capital: The Jharkhand Experience — Published by Lithouse, 1654, Madarsa Road, Kashmere Gate, Delhi-110006.

© Anirudh Prasad (Author), 2019

(dr.anirudhp1949@gmail.com)

ISBN: 978-93-88945-26-4

Laser typeset by
Lithouse, 1654, Madarsa Road, Kashmere Gate, Delhi-110006
• *Tel:* 23866323

Contents

Preface

In developing countries, people historically managed both the natural as well as the social resources (CPRs Social Capital) through collective action. But development assistance has paid too little attention to how CPR Social Capital affects environmental outcomes and ensures individual empowerment. Recent years have witnessed remarkable growth of community-based resource management groups for forest, watershed, micro – finance, irrigation, integrated pest management, tree growers' cooperatives, grazing societies and for farmer's research.

Broadly speaking, social capital refers to the actual or potential resources, such as trust, information, effective social norms (Coleman 1990; Lin, Cook, and Burt 2001; Putnam, Leonardi, and Nanetti 1993), and a propensity to undertake mutually beneficial collective actions (Krishna 2002), that are linked to a durable social network of more or less institutionalized relationships of mutual acquaintance and recognition (Bourdieu and Wacquant 1992). Thus, social capital, unlike other forms of capital, is not depleted with use but actually increases in value with its use (Ostrom, 1999).

Both the common property resources (natural sciences) and the social capital resources (social sciences) are the precious gifts of the Lord nature. Although the Governments, NGos and the Corporate do recognise the revolutionary potential of 'CPR Social capital' as a viable livelihood and poverty alleviation mechanism, particularly for the forest-dwellers communities (Prasad, 2001, 2016), but neither the Government nor the NGOs or even the Corporate have been paying their due and full attention in such issues. It is argued that the social capital resources, which are inherent in CPRs help the rural poor to survive in moments of extreme crises by relying on the solidarity of their social networks and community organisations. This is because the rich have far more access to 'social' as well as 'political capital' than the poor and thus the problem of inequality, let alone poverty, persists in the tribal communities till today.

This study gives an exploratory report on the government of Jharkhand's efforts on the issue and about the Church-inspired development of tribal Jharkhand, India. When I joined Xavier Institute of Social Service (XISS), Ranchi as a Professor of Rural Management, and HOD of Research and Publications in 2002 from the A. N. Sinha Institute of Social Studies, Patna, Bihar (India), I knew virtually nothing about the contributions of Christian Missionaries in rural development although I had an opportunity to study a few Church-centered developmental organizations of Jharkhand, and later on these studies were published in the book form under different titles: (i) *Alleviating Hunger: Challenge for the New Millennium* (book 2001); (ii) *The Catholic Church In Jharkhand: A Mediator of Change* (edited book 2003), and (iii) *Christians of Tribal Origin in Jharkhand: Implications on Demography and Development* (article 2010). I had studied a fair amount about Indian society, economy, culture, polity, and history, and I had some personal experience with other rural development works too, but I was not much aware that Christian Missionaries in Jharkhand have been demonstrating a vibrant dynamism variously operationalised by them through supplementing and complementing government's development efforts, even though they will be financially independent of the government. I was indeed not aware that the Christian Missionaries functioning in the field of tribal development have also been engaged in Natural Resource Management, System of Rice Intensification (SRI), System of Wheat Intensification (SWI) methods, and more particularly engaged in the field of **social capital** projects.

I came to know about the functioning of the SIGN where I had certain academic requirements to fulfill and set out to find some **"CPRs social capital"** projects to study. It was not difficult. Rev. Fr. S. Christu Das, Director of the SIGN at Ranchi suggested a number of projects I might be interested in, and he invited me to address a workshop on 'Social Capital and Sustainability' in Development' on 24th September 2017 at the Social Development Centre, Ranchi. 60 persons participated in the workshop allowing a restricted participation from 18 partners. The workshop was an inspiration for all, and they decided to generate social capital to accomplish sustainability through the various project interventions in their operational areas. I was indeed inspired by the workshop and the deliberations of the action-partners committed to the cause of the indigent community forest management and the disadvantaged. Ultimately, I decided to write a book related with common property resources and social capital after a good deal of fieldwork research. From a large number of choices, I arbitrarily selected SIGN and its nine partner-organizations in order to capture the maximum extent of universe of the research areas on the objective study with the differing patterns of methodologies at work. Methodologically this exercise is necessary to compare the contributions of SIGN that with its partner-organizations working in the same geographical location.

It had been, for me, exciting explorations. I visited one project after another, interviewing different social groups among the tribal and non-tribal population in the sampled villages of Jharkhand and reading whatever literature and documentation I could find. The data for this book is from interviews, case studies, surveys and written material in the form of annual reports of the organizations available at the project offices and very little of them have been subjected to cross-referencing through other sources.

The studied organizations were namely: Social Initiatives for Growth and Networking, Ranchi; Catholic Charities, Jamshedpur; Catholic Charities, Ranchi; Hoffman Social Service Society, Khunti; Jan Vikas Kendra, Hazaribag; Vikas Kendra, Simdega; Samaj Vikas Sansthan,

Chandwa, Latehar; Dumka Social and Educational Society (DSES); Gram Utthan Kendra, Gumla; and Snehadeep Holy Cross, Hazaribag. These organizations naturally tend to highlight facts which show them in a favorable light, and to avoid presenting their own weaknesses. During my field visits and interviews many approximate figures were given to me, some of which may be generous approximations. Also, I did not become fluent enough to interview in respondents-languages and some of the contacts were not adept at communicating in *Kurukh/Santhali/ Mundari/Ho/Sadri*. Therefore, I stress that this is an exploratory report and not an evaluation. I hope that I have conveyed a living sense of the social capital movement and its revolutionary potential, and of some of the issues in indigent community forest management.

There are far more people who should be thanked than editorial discretion permits. I am leaving out many who were indispensable to the completion of this book, but still I would like to list a few names of people who helped me out in one way or another: Rev. Fr. Mark De. Brower; Rev Fr. S. Christu Das; Rev. Fr. C. R. Prabhu; S.J.; Rev. Fr. Tomy; Rev. Fr. Sonatan Kisku; Rev. Fr. Regi Pymattam; Rev. Fr. Sebastiyan Ekka; Rev. Fr. Xavier Topno; Rev. Sr. Britto H.C.; Rev. Fr. Preamchand Tirkey and Fr. Anil Kujur. I am also deeply grateful to Late Most Rev. Bishop Charles Soreng S.J.; Most Rev. Bishop Binay Kandulna; Most Rev. Bishop Anand Jojo; Dr. Sr. M. Grace Toppo; Daughters' of St. Anne's Mother General Rev. Sr. Mary Linda Vaughan; Prof. Ramesh Sharan; Dr. Prashant Verma (Scientist KVK, Haz.); Mr. Birbal (Manav Vikas, Haz.); Rev. T. S. Cyril Hans; and Mr. Gladson Dungdung for their intellectual stimulation. To all these people and more, thank you very much.

This book would not have been possible without the material help extended by the villagers, beneficiary-respondents, and members of the *Gram Sabhas*, SHGs, *Gram Pradhans*, and government officials of different departments of Jharkhand. I would like to thank Ms. Martha Hansdak, Ms. Chanchal Jyoti Bara, Miss Reena Soreng and other staff-members of the SIGN for their secretarial support.

My wife, children and the grand children – Saanvi Sinha, Nevaan Sinha, Aaryav Aayansh have paid a heavy price for the writing of this book, in absences and silences; but I cannot begin to speak of what I owe to their affection. The Lithouse, Delhi (India) agreed to publish the Script. I am grateful to the publisher.

Ranchi 1st July, 2019.

Prof. Anirudh Prasad

A Distinguished Social Scientist

Formerly: Professor & HOD (XISS);

Chair Professor, JRD Tata Chair of Tata Steel;

SRF, ICSSR (Ministry of HRD, Govt. of India)

Glossary

Adivasi	indigenous people of India, also known as tribals.
Akhara	village dancing place
Andolan	people's movement
Anghan	courtyard
Badhya	professional herbalist
Bari zamin	homestead land
Bhagat	ghost finder
Bhagat	an honorific term, usually used by Oraon men who belong to the Tana Bhagat faith
Bhaktain	an honorific term, usually used by Oraon women who belong to the Tana Bhagat faith
Bhuinhar	Oraon pioneer settler
Bhut	ghost or spirit
Coupe	a system of forest management which usually involves the annual felling of a certain amount of the forest area so that by the time the 'coupe rotation' has been completed, the first coupe to have been cut is ready for felling again

Chaala Pachcho	the 'old lady of the grove': the principal village deity in the Sarna pantheon. Also known as *Jakra Burhia or Sarna Burhia*
Churil	the spirit or ghost of a woman who died during pregnancy or childbirth
Danda Katta	'cutting of the evil teeth' ceremony
Dain	witch or wizard
Dal	lentil
Dawai	medicine or (usually when the term is used ironically) liquor
Dharmes	the supreme deity in the Sarna pantheon
Dhumkuria	youth dormitory
Dhuwan	incense
Don	relatively wet and fertile lowlands
Dowli	a sickle-shaped tool for cutting wood
Diku	an abusive Jharkhand term for (exploitative) 'outsider'
Garmajurwar	common land
Garmi paddy	summer paddy
Gite	song
Gora paddy	upland paddy
Gotra	clan
Gram	village
Hanria	rice beer
Hat	village market

Hisingar	jealousy
Hul	rebellion or uprising
Jagirdar	traditional rent collector
Jakra	sacred grove
Jakra Burhia	the 'old lady of the grove': the principal village deity in the Sarna pantheon. Also known as Jakra Burhia or Chaala Pachcho
Jaree bootee	herbs or other small plants
Jarru	sweeping brush
Jatra	fair
Katat	a system of land use whereby villagers had unrestricted use of local forests upon payment of a fixed 'tribute' to the zamindar.
Kattiyan	a village-level record of rights that contains details of local land holdings (Kattiyan Part I) and fuelwood, timber and minor forest produce allowances (Kattiyan Part II)
Kharif	the monsoon season (June-November)
Khuntkattidar	Munda pioneer settler
Kurukh	the name by which Oraons call themselves and their language
Lac	shellac
Latha Kunta	a pivot device used for drawing water from wells and ponds
Lunghi	an item of men's clothing consisting of a cloth that is wrapped around the waist
Madal	help or assistance

Mahto	the secular headman of an Oraon village
Maidan	an open stretch of grassland
Mandar	a special type of clay drum which is particularly popular with the Oraons
Manjhihas	land owned by the village community
Mukhia	elected Panchayat leader, also known as a Sarpanch
Nagpuri	a common tribal lingua franca, also known as Sadri
Otanga	someone who hunts people for human sacrifice
Padam Shri	A civilian award provided by the President of India
Pahan	the main religious leader in Oraon villages
Panch	village committee
Panchayat	village-level local government
Parha	a traditional Oraon form of village administration run by village elders and consisting of up to 21 villages
Parha Raja	a Parha chief
Puja	worship
Pujar	Pahan's assistant
Purdah	seclusion
Raag	tune
Rabi	the winter season (November to March)
Rajhas	land reclaimed from the forest

Rakhat	a system of landuse whereby villagers' rights to forest produce were subject to certain restrictions imposed by the zamindar
Sadan	'artisan' or 'service' castes which have developed reciprocal relationships with the Adivasis and share a common cultural (and often religious) outlook
Sadri	a common tribal lingua franca, also known as Nagpuri
Samiti	committee
Saran	a semi-Animist faith to which most Oraons and Mundas in the research area subscribe. The term also means 'sacred grove'.
Saran Burhia	the 'old lady of the grove'; the principal village deity in the Sarna pantheon. Also known as Jakra Burhia or Chaala Pachcho
Sarpanch	elected Panchayat leader, also known as a Mukhia
Sikar	hunt
Soussar	Pahan's assistant
Sup	winnowing basket
Tangiya	axe
Tanr	relatively dry and poor quality uplands
Tola	hamlet
Zamin	land
Zamindars	traditional rent collectors who were made into landlords by the British Permanent Settlement Act

CHAPTER – 1

The Problems: Property Rights, Common Property Resources, and Social Capital

Many negative effects of human use of resources do not become visible until after lengthy periods of time, often even centuries. Over time, and in particular since the middle of the twentieth century, the term 'common property resources' (CPRs) has been used in many ways. Previously, in the historical documents 'CPRs' referred to common land, often in the form of pasture, or meadowland. CPRs in the historical sense refer to land that was used and managed by several people or households during a certain period, in distinction to land that was used by only one person or household throughout the whole year. The CPRs as a physical phenomenon started to be used repeatedly by scientists from other disciplines to indicate collective property. Though she (Ostrom) was not the first to 'conceptualize' the historical CPRs, Ostrom's 'Governing the Commons: The evolution of collective action' can be considered as a bench mark in the evolution of the discourse on the CPRs (presently known as 'commons'). Hardin's 'the tragedy of the commons' caused considerable confusion by giving a false account of the historical functioning of the commons. The 'commons' 'Hardin described was 'Land' whereupon no property rights rested, thus making it very easy for everyone to overuse it (De Moor, 2007).

This chapter is divided into three sections. In the first section, we examine the subject matter of the study. i.e. 'property rights', 'common property resources', 'social capital' (CPRs social capital), and their direct hunch on individual/household poverty status. What follows does not depend upon precise definitions of these terms; nevertheless some comment on their meaning may be helpful. In the second section, the evolution of the Jharkhand policies on environment- forest, lands, tribal welfare programmes, their current status; how these policies are relevant for CPRs management in the state; whether these policies provide incentive for the people to protect CPRs, etc., have been discussed. In the final section epistemological and methodological issues relating to the design of this research work are considered. This provides the philosophical underpinning, or credibility, which legitimizes knowledge, as well as the framework for a process that, through the use of a rigorous methodology, produces valid results (Sumner and Tribe, 2004).

SECTION - I

The Property Rights Debate

Definition

The term, common property rights resources (CPR) has four ingredients namely: (i) common, (ii) property, (iii) property rights, (iv) resources, and their inter-linkages. Firstly, I would like to discuss the concept of 'property', and 'property rights' theory. The study of property rights is still important because there is a growing emphasis on questions of governance, participatory processes, and trust (social capital).

The key concept of CPR theory is 'property': and property is seen as a social relation (social capital), not an object, which defines the property holder with respect to something of value i.e. the benefit stream, against all others (Bromley, 1992:4). In fact, the CPR management thinking is rooted in the debate sparked by Hardin's 'tragedy of the commons' thesis, which advocated either state intervention or private property to resolve the tragedy.

The property rights school sees private property as the most appropriate way to make individuals 'internalize the externalities' generated through resources exploitation; 'efficiency considerations dominate the property rights school arguments' (Baland and Platteau, 1996:36-37).

Thus, the concept of 'property rights' itself, it is noted, has been multifaceted and difficult to understand, leading to enormous conflicts and debates among the social scientists, environmentalists including CPR management theorists. The purpose of this section is, therefore, to elucidate briefly the various meanings, nuances and applications of property rights theory down the ages and show its meaning and relevance in 'CPR social capital' study.

Broadly speaking, a 'property'[1] is a benefit (income) while a 'property rights' is a claim to a benefit. Property has broadly four categories, namely: (i) *private or exclusive property, (ii) state (public) property, (iii) common property,* and (iv)*non-exclusive* or *nobody's property.* 'Exclusive property' and 'non-exclusive property' are the two extremes on a continuum of property rights (Singh, Katar, 1994). However, the present study is concerned with the study of 'common property' resources i.e. resources jointly owned by more than one individual or a group of people who have co-equal use rights of the village resources. These resources may be community pasture, village-forest, wastelands (state-property), common dumping and threshing ground, watershed drainage, village ponds, rivers, etc. Even when the legal ownership of some of these resources rest with another agency, such as wastelands belonging to the state property, in *a de facto* sense they belong to the village communities as a common property resource (Jodha, 1994).

The second important ingredient is 'resource'. Resource is an economic good or a valuable service, and it is a dynamic one in the sense that changes technology, information, and relative scarcity that previously had no value (Randall, 1981). Resources shrink as human and animal population multiply and they lead to economic pressures. A resource becomes common property only when a group of people who have right to its collective use is well-defined, and when the rules that govern their use of it are set out clearly and followed universally (Chopra, Kadekodi and Murti, 1990).

Economists have long recognized the concept of public goods in terms of resources. Ordinary goods, such as automobiles, are generally purchased by one household, and only the purchaser enjoys their benefits. Public goods, in contrast, benefit many people, often the whole society. Public goods are said to be non-exclusive, – that is, they are available to all for consumption – and no rival, because their use by one person does not reduce their availability to others[2].

Broadly speaking, the 'common property' is that what is not 'private property' is CPR property but, this definition overlooks the importance of institutions that may exist to manage it. In other words, we may say that such definitions of CPR are without pre-existing rules or clear institutional arrangements. Another possible definition of CPR is resources accessible to the whole community to which no individual has exclusive property rights (See Jodha, 1986 for this definition and its use in an empirical context).

CPR is a resource (be it physical, spatial, conceptual) that is managed by the community, for the welfare of the community. The question is 'who is the community'. The answer invariably depends on the resource in question (Hepburn, 2005). Certainly, the definition of the CPR varies with the type of resource at hand. The CPR literature, however, illustrate that most people approach the CPR as a positive resource, but the negative behavior in a CPR, such as 'free riding' is considered 'CPR problems' or social dilemmas (Ostrom 1990; Anderson and Simmons 1993). However, these authors have no unified definition of the CPR commons but there are some family resemblances in their usage of the term. The understanding that the CPR commons is the 'shared heritage of us all' is fundamental to much of the CPR literature.

In traditional or tribal societies, private property rights over resources are rare. Resources important to the life of the tribe are either held in common (as with a common grazing ground), or are not owned at all (as with animals hunted for food). In this regards, both Kelkar and Nathan have rightly pointed out that for tribal community whether to gather/hunt forest products or to bring forest land under cultivation, was an unhindered right. However, the economically developed societies have generally evolved elaborate systems of property rights covering most resources as well as most goods and services. But even modern industrialized nations have resources, goods, and services difficult to categorize as 'property'.

Thus, it appears that the term common property resource is full of ambiguity and rarely defined. Most traditional commons research has focused on common-pool resources, common property, or the tragedy of the commons. Ostrom's (1990) *Governing the Commons* focuses on common pool-resources, resources that are subtractable and difficult to exclude. Ostrom also emphasizes the importance of distinguishing between common-pool resources and common property. Common property is a formal or informal legal regime that allocates various forms of rights to a group. Schlager, Ostrom and Singh illustrate that there can be different types of 'rights' involved in commons property: access, extraction, management, exclusion, and alienation rights. The types of rights are determined not only by the regime but by the nature of the resource. Hardin's (1968) "Tragedy of the commons" conceives of a common as an unregulated, open-access pasture- quite the opposite of real-life institutional arrangement in shared pastures. All of these new types of rights and arrangements require rigorous study and analysis in order to better grasp the institutional nature of these beats.

Private-Public-Commons=
Continuum of Property Rights- Institutional Arrangements:
A conundrum for contemporary CPRs
(Barring Conceptual Variations)

In my view 'property rights' refers to a basic concept with a strong core speaking to and being understandable for most people, but without clear conceptual boundaries. While most people will be able to point to a property right they readily recognize, any two persons from different institutional contexts may have to discuss at some length to agree on similarities and differences in the classification of their favourite 'property rights' or CPRs. It would seem reasonable to call it a fuzzy concept.

My concern in this study is with '*de facto* CPRs' in this sense that the resources like land, forest, water, fishing etc. are accessible to and used in common by the villages in whose (village) jurisdiction they lie. These resources could be privately owned cultivated fields; common property (village panchayat grazing lands); state property (revenue lands), or no body's property. Thus, the present study is, by and large, based on Ostrom's framework of CPRs. This framework provides the clues of CPrRs and community based institutional solution to manage CPR on a sustainable basis. Therefore, my proposed definition of CPR is: A CPR is a resource - the resource needs to be monitored, protected, and managed by an indigent group in order to sustain it. This study also discusses the challenges of defining CPRs, and suggests a possible definition. It also proposes future area of research: how people come to understand or recognize that a resource is a CPR- that is, the entry point into the CPRs. Both outside and within the academy, there is growing numbers of people today who think of CPRs as a '*movement*'. However, many contemporary CPRs are not just academic areas of study but also '*movements*' aimed at changing the way people think and behave.

Social Capital

In economic terminology, the term 'capital' is used for any wealth producing assets. Economists recognize two forms of capital namely, physical and human capital. Physical capital refers to tangible assets like equipment, buildings, real estate, etc., which help in generation of income. The human capital, on the other hand, refers to the knowledge, skills, creativity, etc., of individuals which contribute to the economic life.

Like physical and human capital, a new form of capital has been recognized by the French Sociologist Bourdien[3] with the name social capital. It is defined as the aggregate of the actual or potential resources which are linked to possession of durable network of more or less institutionalized relationships of mutual assistance and recognition.[4] Another definition refers to inclinations that arise from social networks to do things for each other.[5] The World Bank defines social capital as "the institution, relationships and norms that shape the quality and quantity of a society's social interaction".[6] Simply, social capital can be defined as the advantage created by a person's location in a structure of humans relationships.[7]

Social Capital is categorized as formal and informal social capital. Formal social capital refers to "to formally defined patterns of behavior, norms of exchange, networks and institutions".[8] On the other hand, informal social capital refers to informal networks like individual, families, groups and kinship. It is easy to measure and estimate the extent of the first kind of social capital while estimation of second type is problematic and complicated. The interdependence of social capital becomes obvious when social capital is measured using the three generic criteria of productivity, equity and sustainability.[9]

Why social capital is important?
Economic problems involve making choices under conditions of uncertainties and scarcity. Public goods share two characteristics important for collective choice: (i) they are under product; and (ii) collective actors would be better off if more are produced (Coleman, 1987). A crucial cause of underproduction are incentives rewarding the maximization of short-term self-interest while leaving all participants worse off in aggregate than feasible alternatives (i.e. individual tend to free ride).

If optimal levels of public goods are to be produced and trade gains are fully exploited, shared understandings and patterns of collective action need to be developed beyond immediate kin. Various research findings suggest that humans are more predisposed to social exchange through reciprocity than is expected under narrowly defined rational choice levels (Barkow et al., 1992; Ostrom et al., 1994; Hoffman et al., 1998). Cognitive science holds that a variety of heuristics (Heiner, 1983; Simon, 1996) and reciprocity (Ostrom, 1998) are hard- weird by evolutionary selection, resulting in a propensity to co-operate with others not perceived as foes, even if functional mechanism of reciprocity vary between societies. Collective action is facilitated through the inhibition of short-term self-interest behavior via a self-reinforcing cycle of trust and reciprocity. At the individual level, a norm of trust and reciprocity lead to the formation of reputation thereby reduces transaction cost of interaction (Ostrom, 1998). In the aggregate level, increased returns are achieved via increased levels of generalized trust (Putnam, 1993; Fukuyama, 1995) and by institutionalizing mechanism of trust, reputation and reciprocity both of which reduce transaction cost (North,1990).

The concept of capital derives from economics in which it refers to money, property, and anything of monetary value (Bourdieu, 1986). According to Bourdieu the social world is accumulated history, and capital is accumulated labour – in its materialized or its 'incorporated' embodied form. He proposes that capital presents itself in three fundamental guises; as economic capital, directly convertible to money and institutionalized in the form of property rights; as cultural capital, institutionalized in, for example, educational qualifications; and as social capital[10], comprised of social obligations and networks, and for example institutionalized in the form of a common name, a social group, or a class. Such groups are seen to be able to concentrate the totality of their social capital in the hands of a single or group of actors, to represent the group. Some goods and services can be immediately accessed with economic capital, whereas 'others can be obtained only by virtue of a social capital of relationships…which cannot act instantaneously, at the appropriate moment, unless they have been established and maintained for a long time, as if for their own sake….' (Bourdieu, 1986:252).

Specific definitions of social capital can be clubbed into three broad categories: (i) the view that social capital is 'generalized trust', formed largely as the byproduct of the activities of individuals interacting with each other within voluntary or informal associations (Putnam, 1993; Fukuyama, 1995); (ii) the view that social capital consists of the norms and social networks that facilitate collective action for instrumental and collective benefit (Granovetter, 1985; Coleman, 1987; Nee and Ingram, 1998; Ostrom, 1999); and (iii) the view that social capital consists of the institutional infrastructure that facilitates the development of trust, co-operation and trade between individuals who would otherwise remain socially isolated (North, 1990, 1998; Williumson, 1994).

In the light of the above discussion, I will now examine the relationship of core factors of social capital – (i) trust; (ii) reciprocity and exchange; (iii) institutional arrangement; (iv)social network; (v) leadership; and (vi) community characteristics. Besides these, I will also examine what type of state – community relationship may be required to promote social capital and whether external intrusion can boost the CPR management. In the present study, I will assume the technological inputs used for raising natural resources are conductive that for the sake of understanding the importance of social and political issues in CPR regimes vividly.

Ostrom (1994) argues that neither government nor market institutions but, the community-based institutions such as social capital, networking, trust, collective action, and reciprocal behavior are capable of managing the CPRs. This is because the individuals do not intend to sacrifice their own welfare for promoting others but, there is an incentive for them to manage the resources in order to maximize their own benefits (income). This is possible because of reciprocal behavior, and other rules designed by the community.

CPRs Social Capital: Way out of Poverty?
In the last decade or so the concept of social capital has become fashionable. At first it was being used by sociologists and anthropologists but soon it was also appropriated by economists being widely propagated

by the World Bank.[11] While in some respect it is a useful extension of the concept of capital, as was the case with the notion of human capital, it can also lend itself to divert attention from other sources of capital, such as the capital embodied in natural resources (land, water, forests, minerals, etc.), infrastructure (roads, buildings, etc.), machinery and equipment, and finance. These other forms of capital are generally more important than social capital and the latter usually has only meaning when it is able to activate or lead to access to these other forms of capital.

The concept of social capital is seen by some analysts as offering the possibility for a better understanding of poverty which may even lead to a new paradigm.[12] Many of those who use the concept of social capital find that it allows them to highlight the agency and 'capabilities' of the poor. It is argued that while admittedly the poor have few if any access to the other capital resources they often do have substantial social capital, such as social networks and connections through membership of organizations, clientelism, and so on, which allows them to weather subsistence crises and might even afford them the possibility of capital accumulation and a way out of poverty. While the notion of social capital has its uses it should not detract from focusing on the issues such as the concentration of ownership and the unequal distribution and access to assets and other forms of capital. It is an illusion to think that by attempting to mobilize via public policy, or other means the social capital of the poor, a way can be found out of poverty.[13] I do not deny that under certain circumstances such as with a progressive reformist or revolutionary State it is possible to develop a positive state-society synergy which benefits the rural poor. However, proponents of social capital generally do not advocate the radical political mobilization of the rural poor.[14] Quite the opposite, policies or measures of social capital mobilization are often used for preventing, or and tackling the far more important problem of the unequal distribution of assets and other forms of capital. [15] By attempting to find an intermediary position between neoliberalism and statism the notion of social capital is in fact disregarding issues of political power, social conflict and the wider political economy.[16]

Thus the terms 'CPR social Capital' can be useful for a number of reasons. Unlike a term such as "environment", it conveys more immediately a physical resource-human being connection. With "environment", people often visualize flora and fauna detached from human existence. This is despite the fact that research has repeatedly demonstrated that environment problems cannot be solved without addressing people's problems (social regime)- the needs of those who live by, manage, use, or harvest those resources. With the term 'CPR social capital', on the other hand, one automatically thinks of people; people sharing a resource.

Tribals Outlook on Social Capital

Tribal farmers approach the money they have saved as they would do with a piece of *'jungle'* which they preserved from destruction. They cut a couple of trees from this *jungle* only when they need some beams to repair the roof of their house, but for the rest they leave the *jungle* in pieces. They would never think of exploiting this 'standing capital' systematically, or optimizing it as an economic resource. Occasionally they cut and sell large trees when they are faced with short-term cash deficits.

The concept of 'standing capital' forms an integral part of the age old experience of tribal people of surviving in rather inhospitable environment. It motivated them to keep the forests and their subsistence agriculture sustainable. Thus, the tribal concept of social capital can be seen in the form of 'standing Capital'. Chapter – 3 provides a framework which helps to deal with problems of different kinds of standing capital and explains how does (CPR social capital) or (CPR standing capital) stimulates development in tribal communities of Jharkhand.

Figure 1
Relationship among social capital, CPRs and poverty alleviation

Close link between CPRs, social capital, and poverty

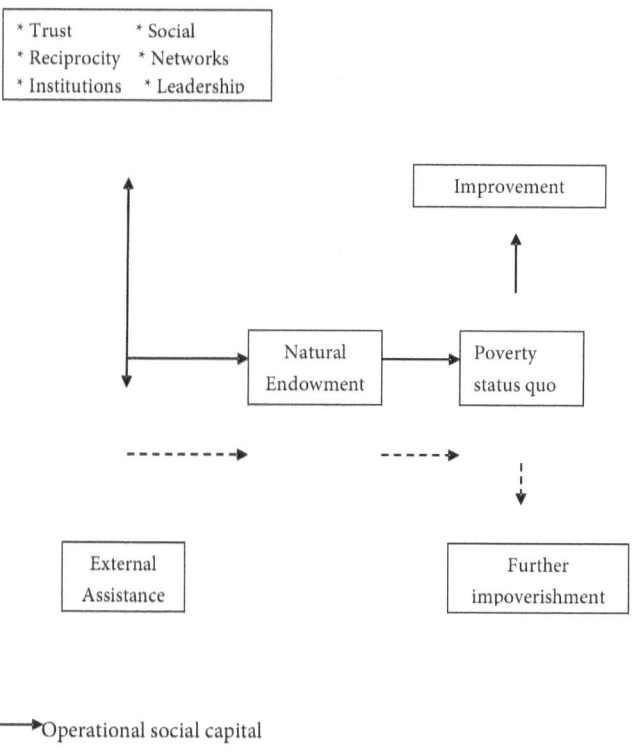

* Trust	* Social
* Reciprocity	* Networks
* Institutions	* Leadership

Improvement

Natural Endowment

Poverty status quo

External Assistance

Further impoverishment

————▶ Operational social capital

------▶ Non-operational social capital

The discussion on the meaning and various theories of CPRs Social Capital has been long, varied and complex.

The links between property, property rights, common resources, social capital with poverty thinking, the extent of externality, and the consequent appearance of 'free rider', the process of conflict resolution and tragedy of the commons types of problems as reviewed can help in providing clues to a theory of property rights and common property resources. This has been discussed in a greater detail in chapters 2 & 3.

Section – II

Evolution of Jharkhand Policies on Environment

There have been a number of discussions on the subject: natural resources, environment[17] population and development are indeed interrelated. The objectives of the present study are to focus discussion on the evaluation of state policies on environment and the way corrective action could lead to sustainability in CPR social capital management. This has to be done in relation to state policies on social, cultural and economic milieu.

Historically, we have been serious minded about environment and the basic philosophy has been one of "harmony with nature" as against western concept of "domination over nature". This worldview has been a legacy of our civilization and tradition. It got sharpened, however, during the recent centuries. Today the whole world, particularly the developing countries, is facing a near-crisis situation, both the economic and environmental terms. Policy makers find it difficult to formulate programmes that would work under the present situation of escalating population on the one hand and diminishing resources on the other (Prasad, 2016, p XV)

Keeping this perspective in view, this section provides background information on the evolution of state policies on environment, forests, tribal development programmes and their current status of the Jharkhand State. How these policies and programmes are relevant for CPR management in the state; whether these policies provide incentive for the people to protect CPRs, etc. have also been discussed in this section.

Environmental Composition of Jharkhand

The State of Jharkhand, earlier more known as a geographical entity of *Chotanagpur,* and *Santhal Pargana*, was created on 15th November 2000. Since 1936, it was part of the State of Bihar when Odisha was separated during the British Rule. The demand for Jharkhand State was rejected by the State Reorganization Commission of 1955 on the ground that it didn't have a common language. A large number of tribal dialects, regional language along with Hindi and Bengali are spoken in Jharkhand.

In the early 2000, a slogan was raised: *First Food Then Industry,* just when the Jharkhand, the 28th Federation State of India, came into existence on November 15, 2000 after cutting off the umbilical Cord from the mother State of Bihar and the government was planning for industrialization of the state on a massive scale. The twang was similar to the outcry in the late 18th – early 19th centuries of the forest dwellers: *First Forest Then Civilization,* when intensive village settlements based on an agrarian economy was in the progress. This happened in the early days of the British East India Company's rule in the province of Bihar: When a map published in a historical narrative showed that large tracts of the present districts of Jharkhand were arboreal and hilly regions. Villages in the map were scattered, towns were sparse, and cities were few and far between.

Yet ruralisation of Jharkhand took place, feeding emerging towns and growing cities, despite the cry: *Save Forest from onslaught of Civilization.* This was one of the demands of local revolts in the province of undivided Bihar such as the *Santhal* and *Mundari* people in early 19th century. But according to Government statistics, in 1939-40 "forests" claimed only 36 per cent of the total surveyed area of Bihar (Bihar Gazetteer, 1961).

Up to 1940s the villages subsisted overwhelmingly on forest and agriculture, and agriculture was engrossingly concerned with one crop a year. Inputs to agricultural production were from the readily and locally available primary sources: water from nearby river, canal, tanks and ponds: fertilizer as cow dung, black- soil from dried up tanks and ponds, etc. implements like self – or locally – made wooden plough, harrow, leveler, husker (*dhenki*), etc.; seeds – the stored grains from last year's production; and so on. In sum, rural and tribal Jharkhand lived at an elementary stage of agriculture as the mode of production, characterized by primeval state of productive forces: and thus, depended entirely upon the employment of kinetic energy of human and animal labour, namely that of the peasants tilling the land and that of the draught cattle employed for the task.

Meanwhile from the 2000s and particularly since 2015s, various inputs to agricultural production have been increasingly available from beyond previously accessible natural and local sources; such as irrigation projects leading to water supply to peasants-land by means of electricity – driven mechanical motor pumps, fertilizer production – both organic and chemical high – yielding seeds for diverse kinds of crops, portable husking machine reaching individual households, etc. Energy in mechanical and electrical forms had thus reached farm lands and farmer's households, and was being harnessed for agricultural production beyond manual labour of human and animals. As a result, on the one hand, land – holdings began to yield 2- 3 crops a year in place of only one in most cases; on the other, especially the input of large – scale brought preciously fallow land under cultivation.

In sum, the rural and urban folks of Jharkhand are being less and less identifiable as distinctive entities – culturally and politically, just like the obliteration of earlier distinction between *gramya* (The rural folk) and *banya* (The forest dwellers). However, a difference is there: the rural could extend by pushing back the hilly/ arboreal to the periphery of Jharkhand and, thus, agriculture reduced forestry into a marginal; whereas agriculture, presently, needs industry to survive and prosper and, therefore, the rural pulls the urban towards it. Simultaneously, the urban can survive and prosper only by evermore industrialization – from small to heavy industry without limits so long as the ecological balance is maintained.

Some attention is paid in recent times to cry of *Save Forestry for Survival,* along with the Slogan of *Save Land for Agriculture or Save Land for Industry and Agriculture.* Notice is taken of restoring the ecological balance; but the issue of enforcing a balance among the hilly/ arboreal, rural, and urban sectors of Jharkhand seems to have lacked drawing a precise attention from a very vocal section of the milieu and the media. The calls for optimizing the share of land among forestry, agriculture, and industry – which, in theory, is accepted by all while, in practice, they sharply differ on how to meet this basic social need.

However, a few paramount questions may be posed in the context of present – day Jharkhand: Are the share of natural resources like land, forest, water, and so on in the same stage contemporarily as they were at the time Elwin wrote "The Story of Tata Steel" (1957) and after two years later he wrote "Philosophy for NEFA[18]" (1959), in which he argued in favour of a policy of 'National Park' where the tribal people could be left alone to manage for themselves with least outside interference[19].

There are many accounts that refer to a so called forest 'golden age' prior to the period of British colonial rule when local people apparently enjoyed unrestricted access to and use of forests. Even though the *de jure* ownership of most forests rested with various local rulers, many were managed *de facto* as common property resources (see for example: Guha, 1983; 1989; Tiwari, 1983; Prabhu, 1983, Kulkarni, 1983; FAO, 1085; Falcorner, 1987; Shiva,1988 Mehrotra and Kishore,1990; Kany *et al*, 1991; Ghate, 1992).

For tribal societies, in particular, forests have traditionally been so important for subsistence, cultural and religious purposes that many *Adivasis* consider themselves to be the true owners of local forest. Ghate (1992). For example that from 'times immemorial the tribal people have enjoyed freedom to use the forest and hunt its animals, and this has given them a conviction that remains even today deep in their hearts, that the forests belong to them" (p17).

The reservation of certain forests for commercial purposes followed soon afterwards with the introduction of the Indian Forests Act of 1878. By empowering the government to "declare any land covered with trees, brushwood or jungle as government forest by notification" (Ghate , 1992 p33) , this Act established the colonial state's monopoly right over India's forest lands which were to be divided thenceforth into four categories: 1) Reserved Forest ,2) Protected Forest, 3) Private Forest, 4) Village Forests. Of these, only Village Forests were available for unrestricted use by villagers. Reserved Forests were out of bounds to local people except for the collection of certain types of minor forest produce such as fruit. In protected forests, villagers were allowed the 'privileges' of grazing their cattle and of collecting wood for domestic needs.

Much of the research on autonomous forest management in Jharkhand and Odisha has been done by Mehrotra and Kishor, 1990 and Kant *el al* (1991), as part of a project on community based forest protection and management funded by ISO/Swed Forest, the Swedish International Development Authority, the Indian Institute of Forest Management, Bhopal and the Bihar Social Forestry Project. Their work suggests that the forest protection committees tend to become established in areas affected by large scale deforestation, by communities that are unified, homogeneous and which have a high degree of dependence on and equal access to local forests.

In the early 1970s, for example, a student in the predominantly *Adivasi* Karandih Panchayat, Jamshedpur, mobilized 'local villagers' about forest degradation and the problems of fuel wood shortages, local climatic change, soil erosion and water tangle lowering, etc. Realizing that it was pointless waiting for the state to intervene, a forest protection committee was established and villagers started to guard their local forests and to limit their own use of forest produce. Forest regeneration was rapid and the committee gained the support of the Forest Department. Now, Thirty five villages are protecting their forests and many committees have also taken on board wider issues such as health and education (Mishra, 1993).

The establishment of community-based forest management has been particularly common in *Adivasi* areas of Bihar and Odisha, where there is a strong tradition of village level administrative institutions (Gadgil and Guha, 1994). There has also been a history of socio-cultural and political emphasis upon such instruction as part of a demand, in the Jharkhand region. To increase *Adivasi* autonomy and economic determination through the creation of a nominally tribal Jharkhand state. Indeed, it may be significant that a number of forest protection committees date from the early 1950s when the 'Jharkhand movement' was politically very strong and the full impacts of forest nationalization; increased commercial exploitation of forests and widespread illegal dwellings by contract cutters were first felt.

It is apparent from the above statements that the question of land and control over it is dealt with many different ways at various levels in Jharkhand. Approaches based on political, economic, security and environmental considerations are adopted by actors like political parties, social movements, development specialists and NGOs. Each one of these approaches tends to exclude the others, treating them as mere externalities which need to be addressed and not as a part of the main issue while dealing with land and its control. Discourses based on these approaches are working against each other as a result of which it becomes difficult to get a holistic picture, making it difficult to understand the situation and prepare a roadmap for the future.

The case studies show significant reliance on CPRs by rural communities. Such dependence extends across community, class and regional distinctions, though the type of activity may vary. For instance, most *Adivasi* communities depend on minor forest produce for a significant part of their livelihood.

Jharkhand also depends on CPRs for grazing, fuel wood and water. In all these areas, the loss of CPRs is a major blow to the livelihoods and survival of rural communities. CPRs are under constant threat.

Takeover of land has two primary forms. The first is the reclassification of land under regulatory regimes intended to restrict use, which effectively curbs or destroys the rights of those who using the land. The most common form of such takeover is conversion of land to forest land.

The second form of state – driven take over is better known and far more discussed – the forced annexation of private and common lands for large projects. There are no consolidated figures available for such takeover at the national (or even at the State) level.

Why does it appear so much easier to take over CPRs particularly to common lands? The obvious answer – that they lack sufficient legal protection – is only half true. For, on paper, several laws exit that purport to provide such protection. Common lands in forest areas are exclusively protected by the Forest Rights Act; common lands in Fifth Schedule Areas are meant to be covered by the governance, provisions of the Panchayats (Extension to Scheduled Areas) Act (PESA) and by the Fifth Schedule itself; and several State laws exit with similar provisions. Yet, in practice these laws hardly seem to matter. The discussions in the case studies (chapters- 3 & 4) reveal some strong indicators of the processes that are at work.

There is a distinction between institutions of control that vest power in the state machinery and those that vest it in local democratic institutions. This difference emerges clearly between the FRA, the PESA Act, the Chhotanagpur Tenancy Act, etc., on the one hand, and the forest laws and most revenue laws on the other.

Consolidating *gram sabhas'* powers over CPRs through uniform and clear procedures established by Central and State governments for operationalising PESAs provisions that empower *gram sabhas* to manage water bodies, community lands, grazing areas, others community resources and *Adivasi* lands.

Jharkhand's Common Lands and Forests

The State of Jharkhand is spread over an area of 79,714 sq. kms. The state is rich in terms of natural resources, comprising two distinct hilly regions namely: (i) *Chotanagpur,* and (ii) *Santhal Pargana.* The state is an "Ethnological Museum" with 32 different tribes including nine primitive tribes[20] with non-uniform socio-economic condition, different culture, and economic development. The total population of the State is 3.29 crore spreading over into 24 districts. The tribal population of the State is 85.44 lakhs (26.1 per cent) of the total population, which is the third largest scheduled tribe population in the country (Census, 2011) after Chhattisgarh (149.99 lakhs) and Odisha (95.32 lakhs).

The question of common land and control over it is dealt with many different ways at various levels in Jharkhand. Approaches based on political, economic, security and environmental considerations are adopted by actors like political parties, social movements, development specialists and NGOs. Each one of these approaches tends to exclude the others, treating them as mere externalities which need to be addressed and not as a part of the main issue while dealing with land and its control. Discourses based on these approaches are working against each other as a result of which it become difficult to get a holistic picture, making it difficult to understand the situation and prepare a roadmap for the future.

However, Land is one of the important components of the life support system and has been overused and abused. The Table below shows that about 2.4 million hectares (32.4 per cent) were under net area sown. The common pool lands in Jharkhand include most of the 2.9 million hectares of land classified as cultivable waste, permanent pastures, grazing lands, land under miscellaneous tree crops and groves, fallow land, barren and uncultivable land, etc. The following Table 1 gives the detail:

Table 1
Common Pool Lands in Jharkhand as Compare to India

Classification	(In Million ha)	
	Jharkhand	India
Total Geographical Area	7.9	328.73
Reporting Area for Land Utilization Statistics (1 to 5)	7.4	307.80
1. Forests	2.1	71.83
	(28.4)	(23.4)
2. Not available for cultivation (Barren and Uncultivable Land, Non-Agriculture Uses)	1.2	43.86

	(16.2)	(14.3)
3. Other uncultivable land excluding fallow land (Permanent Pasture, Grazing Land, Cultivable Waste, Misc.)	0.5	25.83
	(6.8)	(8.3)
4. Fallow land (Fallow Land, Current Fallow)	1.2	24.85
	(16.2)	(8.1)
5. Net Area Sown	2.4	141.43
	(32.4)	(45.9)
6. Cropping Intensity*	4.7	142.02
	(63.5)	(46.2)

Note: *Cropping intensity is percentage of the gross cropped area to the net area sown.*

Figure in parentheses indicate percentage share to reporting areas

Sources I: Agricultural Statistics at a Glance 2015

II: Department of Agriculture, Animal Husbandry and Cooperative, Government of Jharkhand, 2016.

Table 1 shows that Jharkhand has a reporting land area of nearly 7.4 million hectares in which about 2.1 million hectares (28.91 per cent) were under forests of different categories and the remaining 5.3 million hectares (71.09 per cent) were uncultivated, permanent pasture, fallow and other than fallow land, etc. Most of the uncultivable land is owned either by the government or village panchayats and therefore a CPR (Singh, 1994). The district wise forest areas and the forests covered under river valleys projects in Jharkhand are shown in Tables 3 and 4.

Table 2
Forest Coverage in Jharkhand (Area in percentage)

Reserved Forest Area	29.45
Protected Forest Area	37.67
Unclassified Forest Area	32.88
(Tree covers Area and Miscellaneous)	100%

Source: Forest Summary, Government of India (Jharkhand Chapter) 2013.

The above Table shows that out of the total forest areas (2.1 million hectares) in Jharkhand about 32.88 per cent were unclassified forests, which were basically of very low productivity, were always open to use. In the estimates given in Table 2 protected and unclassified forests are treated as forming a part of CPRs, keeping in mind that this may yield an over-estimate of land to which, common property rights exist. Thus, CPR area so defined comes to 19.33 per cent of the total geographical area, keeping in mind that not all protected forest and common pastures form CPRs, this estimate can be an over estimate. However, it is interesting to examine the results and their implications.

Table 3
District-Wise Forest Area Covered in Jharkhand (In ha)

S. No.	District	Total Geographical Area	Total Forest Area	Percentage of Forest Area to Total Forest Areas of Jharkhand
1.	Dumka	551800	140989	6.52
2.	Godda	211000	16231	0.75
3.	Deoghar	69257	10544	0.49
4.	Jamtara	178643	13000	0.60
5.	Sahebganj	340600	8254	0.38

6.	Pakud	69300	14027	0.65
7.	Hazaribag	304900	180904	8.37
8.	Ramgarh	200000	42000	1.94
9.	Chatra	370600	166154	7.69
10.	Kodarma	241000	89038	4.12
11.	Dhanbad	207400	26380	1.22
12.	Giridih	488700	188930	8.74
13.	Bokaro	292700	39355	1.82
14.	Ranchi	457000	100454	4.65
15.	Khunti	300400	79000	3.66
16.	Lohardaga	773300	36573	1.69
17.	Gumla	195900	80835	3.74
18.	Simdega	100000	50000	2.31
19.	East Singhbum	542800	168240	7.79
20.	West Sighbhum	501200	113000	5.23
21.	Saraikela-Kharsawan	300000	100666	4.66
22.	Palamu	497400	180133	8.34
23.	Latehar	300000	143000	6.62
24.	Garhwa	477500	172840	8.02
25.	Total	7971400	2160547	100

Sources: 1) Forest Summary, Government of India Jharkhand Chapter – 2013

2) Department of Agriculture, Animal Husbandry and Cooperation, Government of Jharkhand.

In Jharkhand, CPRs include community pastures, community forest, wastelands, common dumping and threshing grounds, watershed drainages, village ponds, rivers and their banks, etc. Although the legal ownership of watersheds in Jharkhand rests with the state, but in a *de facto* sense they belong to the village communities and continue to be a significant component of their land resources base. These resources contribute to the production and consumption needs of the tribals in Jharkhand in some critical ways. We have discussed these issues in detail in the third chapter.

Table 4
Forest Covered Under River Valleys of Jharkhand State (In ha)

S. No.	Name of the Valley/Basin	Area covered
1.	North Koel	439,822
2.	Damodar	337,386
3.	South Koel	248,238
4.	Suvarnarekha	237,036
5.	Barakar	232,448
6.	Khadkai	139,387
7.	Maurakshi and related	71,809
8.	Gumani and koyabhena	62,486
9.	Shankh	61,118
10.	Ajay	56,588
11.	Rivers emerging outside Jharkhand but flowing through it.	54,072
	Total	19,40,390

Sources: Forest Department, Government of Jharkhand, 2017.

Jharkhand is famous for its subtropical forest resources. Famous *Saranda* Forest is one of the Tourist attractions. Tribal population of the state had waged war against British to protect their forest. Colonial as well as post independent 'Indian forest policy' never recognized the 'local tribes right' over forest. As a result, tribal people lost interest in forest protection. Outside contractors took full advantage of the tribal disenchantment and caused the mass destruction of the forest. However, many tribal leaders tried to stop this destruction by reviving their forest related cultural values and thereby mobilized the forest protection activities and subsequently many Indigent Committees of Forest Management (ICFM) groups were formed. It is noted that the total reporting forest areas of Jharkhand (2.1 million ha) have been classified into three categories:

Jharkhand is also called for a '*Tasar* State' of India. Production of Tassar raw silk is increasing gradually which is shown in the following Table.

Table 5
Production of Tassar Raw Silk in Jharkhand

Year	Production in MT
2007-08	143.00
2008-09	296.00
2009-10	403.70
2010-11	766.00
2011-12	1025.24
2012-13	1088.35
2013-14	2000.00
2014-15	1943.30
2015-16	2281.06
2016-17	2630.00

Source: Annual Report of the Central Tassar Research and Training Institute, Ranchi, Jharkhand, 2017.

Lac – a fauna based natural resin, is found in Jharkhand and the Jharkhand State ranks 1st in Lac production followed by Madhya Pradesh, Chhattisgarh, Maharashtra and Odisha. These five states contribute around 93 percent of the total Lac production in the country. The following Table describes the details of Lac production in the Jharkhand State of Eastern India:

Table 6
District Wise Lac Crop Production
in Jharkhand during 2017-2018

Name of District	Baisakhi	Jethwi	Katki	Aghani	Total production (in tons)
Bokaro	—	45.0	—	40.0	85.0
Garhwa	0.7	2.5	0.1	4.0	7.3
Gumla	2.0	55.0	4.0	47.0	108.5
Latehar	0.2	9.0	0.5	13.7	23.4
Palamau	2.5	20.0	0.6	12.0	35.0
Ranchi	0	85.0	—	764.0	849.0
Khunti	0	560.0	—	4060.0	4620.0
Simdega	5.0	110.0	10.0	103.0	223.0
West Singhbhum	40.0	168.5	14.5	292.5	515.5
Total	50.4	1055.0	29.7	5336.7	6471.8

Sources: *I. Lac and Resin Research Institute, Jharkhand, 2017.*

II. Annual Bulleting of Institute of Forest Productivity, Ranchi, 2017-2018.

The region has abundant rainfall (1250-1650 mm per year), which falls mainly during the monsoon months (June to September) and drain quickly along a series of small river valley that give the plateau an undulating appearance. Most of these valleys and hills or outliers that rise above the level of the main plateau were, until recently, blanketed with dense standard of *Sal-* dominated forest from which the Jharkhand – Literally 'Land of Forest' – got its name.[21] In addition to providing an important subsistence resource for the local human population, these forests also used to provide habitats for wild animals such as the tiger leopard, bear, wolf, wild pig, Nilgai (*boselaphus tragocamelus*), sambar (cervus unicoler) and antelope (Roy, 1984).[22]

Water Resources in Jharkhand

Damoder, Maurakshi, Barakar, North Koyel, South Koyel, Sankh, Subarnarekha, kharkai, and Ajay are major water resources in the State; the net sown area is 2.4 million hectare of which 8% is irrigated. There are a number of irrigation and hadro electric project in the State. The major Dam projects are Tilaya, Maithon, Mayurakshi, Panchet, Sanjay and Subarnarekha. According the Central Water Commission, there were total of 133 large Dames in Jharkhand in 2016 besides 7829 minor irrigation projects in the region.

Table 7
Availability of water resources
for irrigation purposes in Jharkhand

S.No.	Water resource type	Available water resources (mill m3)	Utilization of water resources Mill m3)	Available water resources utilized (%)
1.	Surface	23789	3964	16.7
2.	Ground water	4992	772	15.5
3.	Total	28781	4736	16.1

Source: GOJ, 2016

However, the Water Resources Department has planned a major programme, *Gram Bhagirathi Yojana,* for the development of minor surface irrigation in the state in a 'participatory' manner (Upadhaya, 2004); but the manner in which it has planned leaves no doubts about its possible success. This is further supported by the World Bank Report entitled 'Jharkhand: Addressing the challenges of Inclusive Development' promotes a view that "(i) in Jharkhand, irrigation coverage did not expand in the past largely because of under investment in the major and medium irrigation system" (World Bank, 2007: ix).[21]

Wild Life, National Park and Other Projects

A large number of the plant and animal species are found in these forests, some of them being considered as endangered by the forest department officials and environmentalists. In order to protect these species, the government has declared a total of about 10 Wildlife Sanctuaries, national Parks and Fossil Sanctuaries in Jharkhand. They occupy a total of 2045.50 sq km or 2, 04,550 ha of forestland, which is approximately three per cent of the total area of Jharkhand.[22]

Environmental Composition

Jharkhand is endowed with vast depository of mineral resources ranging from iron ore, copper ore, coal, mica, bauxite, fire clay, graphite, kyanite, sillimanite, lime stone, uranium and other minerals. The major mining activities are focused on exploitation of coal, iron ore, bauxite and minor minerals like limestone, china clay, kyanite, etc. By open cast mining method due to nature of the deposits as well as economic and technology considerations. The other minerals like uranium, copper, mica, and some coal resources are mined by underground method. The surface mining activities have regional distribution pattern in the state.The coal mining open cast projects are concentrated mainly in the Damodar Vally with subordinate mining centers in the Rajmahal and Palamu Regions. Bauxite mining centers are found in Lohardaga, Latehar and Gumla districts of Jharkhand Iron Ore mining centers are found in Western Singhbhum region. Besides these, small mining activities are scattered in the state for exploitation of minor deposits like Limestone, Kyanite, China clay etc. The magnitudes of environmental impact of open cast mining project are more widespread in comparison to underground method. In the state, coal mines are mostly of open cast type. The major coal companies in Jharkhand are Central Coalfield Ltd. (CCL) and Bharat Coking Coal Ltd. (BCCL).

Problems in Assessing the Land Acquired in Jharkhand

Jharkhand was one of the regions where development schemes were first started in the country, particularly in the mining areas of Dhanbad, Singhbhum, Ranchi and Hazaribag districts. The Jharia coalfields were started in the late 19th century, iron ore mines at Gurumahisni in 1911, at Badampahar and sulaipet in 1923, and at Noamundi in 1926, bauxite mines in Palamu and Lohardaga in 1940s and mica mines in Hazaribag and Koderma in 1930s to mention a few. Similarly, industrial development in Jharkhand was spearheaded by the Tata Iron and Steel Company (TISCO) in 1907. It was followed by the Indian Hume Pipes in 1921, Tinplate Company of India Limited in 1922, Indian Cables in 1923, Tatanagar Foundary in 1927, Indian Oxygen and Acetelyne in 1935 and the Tata Engineering and Locomotives (TELCO) in 1945. It is not known how much land they have acquired. But going by the number and size of the schemes it can be said that it would be substantial. It nevertheless indicates that the massive shifts in the land-use pattern caused massive dislocation of human populations already before independence. Other sectors like railways, roads and infrastructure that had started developing fairly well in the region before independence, also acquired much land.

Table 8

Total Land Acquired for Development Projects in Jharkhand

Category of Project	Private Land	%	Common Land	%	Forest Land	%	Total Land	%
Water Resources	364646.00	71.7	94808.00	18.7	48498.00	09.6	507952.00	34.0
Thermal Power	98525.59	56.1	63768.68	36.3	13435.91	07.6	175730.18	11.7
Mines	184169.00	37.7	156341.19	30.4	174614.40	33.9	515124.59	34.4
Defence Estd.	22543.61	20.1	11134.93	09.9	78610.57	70.0	112289.11	07.5
Misc. Schemes	152000.65	85.0	8941.21	05.0	17882.43	10.0	178824.29	12.0
Sub Total	824483.30	55.1	337528.39	22.6	333935.35	22.3	1495947.04	100.0
Missing Schemes	27550.00	55.1	11300.00	22.6	11150.00	22.3	50000.00	
Grand Total	852033.30		348828.39		345085.35		1545947.04	

Source: Ekka, A. and Asif, M. 2000.

Displacement and affected people in Jharkhand

During the pre-independence period, Jharkhand experienced substantial exodus of population especially of tribals to the tea gardens of Assam and to the Jute mills of Calcutta (Corbrige 1988; Sharma 1994). After independence, Jharkhand experienced intensive industrialization and urbanization accentuating the historical push forces for tribal out - migration from the region (Maharatna, Arup and Chikte 2004). The level of urbanization in Jharkhand was more than double of Bihar when it was created. The latest available data from NSSO 64th Round shows that the state of Jharkhand was a net out-migrating state (NSSO 2010), although it has received huge in-migration in the past particularly from Bihar and neighboring States. Also as a result of mining and start of heavy industries, a large number of people have been displaced since independence largely belonging to the tribal population. The figure of displacement varies from 1.5 million to 3 million people (Lok Sabha Secretariat 2013; Maharatna and Chikte 2014). It is estimated that nearly 500 thousand people from Jharkhand are circulating every year for a period of one month and more but less than six months during a year for seeking livelihood outside their place of origin mostly belonging to rural areas. These migrant workers mostly work as construction workers, domestic servants and in the transport and hotel industry mostly outside the state of Jharkhand.

Table 9

Number of the Displaced & Project Affected People in Jharkhand

S.No.	Type of Project	STs	%	SCs	%	Others	%	Total
1.	Water Resources	175127	75.2	17554	07.5	40287	17.3	232968 (15.5)
2.	Industries/Quasi Industries	22473 7415	34.0	15006 4950	22.7	28548 9421	43.2	66087 21809 (05.8)
3.	Mining: Coal Mining: Non-Coal	79568 3975	29.6	42268 21084	15.7	146752 73324	54.6	268588 134294 (26.7)
4.	Defense Establishment	237147	89.7	18529	07.0	8677	03.2	264353 (17.5)
5.	Wildlife Sanctuaries National Parks	80867	15.8	87601	17.1	339266	66.5	509918 (33.8)
6.	Infrastructure Development	13800	27.6	5900	11.1	30300	60.6	50000 (00.3)
	Grand Total	620372	41.2	212892	14.1	676575	45.0	1505017 (100.0)

Source: Ekka and Asif. 2000, p.95

Tribal Jharkhand Tops States in Rural Poverty

Despite abundant mineral and forest resources, an organized industrial sector and high level of urbanization, Jharkhand is India's second poorest state. In an assessment of rural India Jharkhand is ranked (with Bihar State) India's most food insecure State, and (separate from Bihar) as having India's richest percentage of population below the poverty line (MSSRF, WFP,2001)And the tribals, who form about 26 per cent of the state population, are far poorer than elsewhere in the country. The reasons are: (i) extremely poor status of agriculture; and (ii) scanty agricultural land.

According to the 55th Round of NSSO, the incidence of both rural and urban poverty is relatively higher in Jharkhand as compared to India as a whole. Interestingly, urban poverty in Jharkhand has increased during 1993-2000. The per capita GDP in Jharkhand was Rs. 11,103.00 which was almost three times higher than Bihar (Rs. 3,669.00) and almost equal to all India (Rs. 11,472.00). This indicates a very keyed distribution of income and greater inequality so far as weaker sections of society in Jharkhand is concerned. According to the NSSO, Jharkhand has the highest rate of poverty at 68 per cent, which is alarming indeed. And, if the same trends continue, we will not be able to resolve the problem of poverty in the foreseeable future.

The objective of the Tribal Sub-Plan of Jharkhand was primarily elimination of poverty and socio-economic development through elevation of infrastructure development to enable the weaker sections in general and tribal community in particular to cross the poverty line. Despite Tribal Sub-Plan, Special Component Programmes and many other development programmes launched by both the central (centrally sponsored schemes) and state government as well as the NGOs of Jharkhand for the development of weaker sections, hardly a couple of lucky ones have benefitted from the poverty alleviation programmes.

Broadly speaking, in Dumka, Jamtara, Sahebganj, Ranchi, Gumal, Simdega, West Singhbhum, Saraikela, Palamu, and Garhwa districts of

Jharkhand, more than 70 per cent of the families are living below the poverty line.

Both the scheduled tribes and scheduled castes of the families were associated with lower per capita consumption. They are highly vulnerable, voiceless and powerless. They also lack access to and influence over the institutions of the state and the resources and services it can provide. Social marginalization and social distance are often at the root of these problems. Their low-caste status operates as social barriers that exclude them from the benefits of social and economic fruits. Even today, people are reduced to eating the bark of trees, grass, leaves and plants. The true misery of the 18,292,000 persons (68 per cent) who live below the poverty line, or more than 40 per cent of the displaced persons by various projects, or the majority of the population who suffer from malnutrition, gets overlooked.

Tribal Development in Jharkhand through Self-Rule

In the independent India a new approach to tribal development was what Nehru termed as the *'Panchsheel of Development'*. The demand of statehood in the Jharkhand movements had this justification – that they be the masters of this own development and change. At the lower level of villages and panchayats, however, the self-rule in the tribal areas ascending to their traditional pattern has been reiterated by a new legislation called 'PESA' (Provision of the Panchayats: Extension to the Scheduled Area Act, 1996; The act endorses the traditional structures of *Gram Sabha* which is the policy and decision making body at the village level. It also gives to the tribal community the right of ownership of resources, sustains them on forest produce and non- wood forest produce and enables them to manage their forest and their day-to –day economic relations by word of mouth.

The state government has introduced many protective laws and administrative measures since independence with a view to prevent exploitation of the tribals at the hands of the powerful sections of the population. The state government has identified 112 blocks in the entire districts of Ranchi, Gumla, Lohardaga, Singhbhum, Dumka, Sahebganj and parts of Godda and Palamau districts as areas of high tribal concentration in which special protective measures under the scheduled areas regulations have been enforced. The most important piece of legislation relates to ban on transfer of tribal land to non-tribals. There are special provisions in the Chotanagpur and Santals Parganas Tenancy Acts, aimed at prevention of alienation of tribal land and for return of land to the tribal if such land has been transferred by fraudulent means. There are also special provisions to minimize the indebtedness of the scheduled tribes and to free them from the clutches of the unscrupulous money lenders who have been troubling them for ages. Freedom of the bonded labourers, special provisions in the excise and forest policy of the state government are some of the other measures introduced in favour of the tribals.

The strategy for development of the scheduled tribes must take into account the special features of the tribal economy and culture. In the Twelfth Five Year Plan tribal development blocks were opened in the predominantly tribal areas of the state to bring about an all-round development through community development approach.

But it was soon realized that the more advanced sections of the community took much greater advantage of these development schemes, resulting in making the gap wider between the tribals and non-tribals. The tribal development block approach proved to be ineffective in the absence of proper administrative set-up and protective aspects. A comprehensive view of the tribal problem was taken in the Seventh Five Year Plan and a new strategy called the Tribal Sub-plan Approach was evolved.

Due to a decline in the quality and quantity of forests that are open to a growing rural population, however, there has been a reduction in the availability of many of the forest products. For many tribal communities, traditional subsistence strategies must now be supplemented with incomes from activities such as seasonal migration, agricultural labour, small scale business, cash cropping and minor forest produce sales and (less so nowadays for *Adivasis*) mining and quarrying (Sachidananda, 1979; Munda, 1988; Corbridge, 1986; Pathak, 1994). For service and artisan castes with little or no land, the problem is even more acute as they have traditionally depended heavily upon forests both for raw materials and basic subsistence requirements (Kelkar and Nathan, 1991). As a result, a growing number of very poor families that can find no alternative source of employment are forced into destroying forest resources still further by selling firewood for cash.

Pesticide Use in Jharkhand and the Policy Environment

At the time of its formation in 2000 much of Jharkhand State – aside from certain pockets – was almost organic by default. Use of pesticide by farmers has increased in recent years for two reasons. In the one hand pesticides have been promoted by government policies and programmes, and by certain NGOs through projects.[23] In the past six years, there has been a 6-fold increase in consumption of pesticide in Jharkhand, from 84 to 541 metric tons. Jharkhand does not have an Agricultural Policy or an Organic Farming Policy unlike States like Sikkim, Uttarakhand, Karnataka, Kerala, MP, Bihar and Maharashtra that have announced their own organic farming policies.[24]

According to government data shows that in Jharkhand, consumption has risen from 2.2 to 13.9 kg per 1000 persons over the period 2010.11 to 2016-17. [25] A 2017 study of 493 farming households across the Jharkhand State found that 75 percent use chemical pesticides.[26] This increase in pesticide use is neither sustainable nor desirable. Most food production has been based on high- input and resource – intensive farming systems at a high cost to the environment, and as a result soil, forest, water, air quality and biodiversity continue to degrade.

Policy Initiatives of the State Government on Environment including Forest Wildlife and Pesticide Use

Following are the silent initiatives taken by the Government of Jharkhand to develop and conserve the forest, wildlife and environment:

1. Government of Jharkhand (GOJ) has issued a comprehensive joint Forest Management (JFM) resolution in September 2001 to ensure people's participation in protection, conservation and development of forest.

2. To enhance people's participation 35 Forest Development Agencies in all the Territorial and Wildlife division have been Constituted and registered under Societies Registration Act, 1860.

3. Entry – point activities have been made an integral part of all the plantation schemes to ensure people's co – operation in forestry activities.

4. Rehabilitation of degraded forest on large scale is being undertaken.

5. Large – Scale plantation of Bamboo has been taken up.

6. To increase Lac & Tasar production, plantations of Lac & Tasar host species have been taken up. Forest Department has been made the nodal Department for the development of Lac and Tasar in the state.

7. Forest Rights Act, 2006, empowers 4 acre land to all forest – dwellers.

8. Jharkhand Government is in process to formulate policy on organic farming.

Let me sum up the efforts that the Jharkhand Government will have to make: (i) entrepreneurship development should be given top priority because State's dignity and freedom through entrepreneurship work is highly valued. This would also be great encouragement to the unemployed; (ii) faster implementation of labour reforms and operationalising co-operatives; and (iii) strengthening infrastructure, especially that of social infrastructure, etc. (iv) The tribal and scheduled castes have special interest and aptitude for goat and pig husbandry.

The programme of   natural capital improvement with environmental priorities, breed improvement, development of fodder and feed for animals & birds, fodder seed farm, chick farms, milk chilling plants along with the development of road facilities can go a long way in promoting animal husbandry and poultry in the State. And, these can be achieved through the massive support and co-operation of the people in general and socially disadvantaged population of Jharkhand in particular.

From the above brief description of some of the Jharkhand's main characteristics, it is clear that the state is neither ethnically, socio-economically or politically as homogeneous as both the British and the post-colonial governments have tended to suggest. Quite obviously, this presented problems in terms of finding a fieldwork area that was both 'representative' (to enable my 'findings' to be generalized) and conducive to in-depth village level research.

Endnotes

[1] Most of the documents selected are journal articles, published books, as well as some well-established websites. All of the references in the paper, as well as many more, are contained in Katar Singh (1994) and Hess (2007) where there are usually abstracts and, when possible, URLs to the full documents.

[2] The formal definition of public goods is "a commodity or service which if supplied to one person can be made available to others at no extra cost" (Pearce, 1992). A "pure" public good is one that the producer cannot exclude anyone from consuming. Thus a pure public good demonstrates both no rival consumption and no excludability.

[3] Bourdieu, Pierre, The Forms of Capital.

[4] Bourdieu, Pierre, http://www.viet-studies.org/Bourdieu-capital.htm.

[5] Putnam, Robert, Bowling Alone: The Collapse and Revival of American Community.

[6] World Bank, Social Capital Initiative.

[7] Wikipedia, The Free Encyclopedia.

[8] Morris, Mathew, Social Capital and Poverty in India; IDS Working Paper No. 61.

[9] Mukherjee, Neela, Measuring Social Capital.

[10] Social capital was also theorized in the 1980s by Coleman, a 'rational choice' theorist (Harriss, 2001). The concept has been used in various frameworks, such

as the 'livelihoods' framework (Ellis, 2000) and the 'capitals and capabilities' framework (Bebbington, 1999). Harriss concludes that mainstream usage of the concept has blunted its critical edge, its presentation systematically obscures class politics and power, thus offering a way to talk about 'social relations' without seriously questioning existing power relations and property rights (2001).

[11] One of the first original thinkers to formulate the concept of 'social capital' back in 1980 was Pierre Bourdieu, see his chapter 'The forms of capital' in J. Richardson (ed.), *Handbook of Theory and Research for the Sociology of Education*, New York: Greenwood Press. Pierre Bourdieu's vision is radical and quite different from that espoused later by the World Bank. For a forceful and illuminating critique of the World Bank notion of social capital, see John Harriss, *Depoliticizing Development: The World Bank and Social Capital*, London: Anthem Press, 2002. For a reflexive and most enlightening analysis of the debate on social capital, see Anthony Bebbington, 'Social capital and development studies 1: critique, debate, progress?', Progress in Development Studies, 4 (4), 2004, pp.343-349; this is the first of three notes on this topic and the next two notes will be published in future issues of the journal.

[12] As an illustration of the uses of the notion of social capital within the Latin American rural context, see John Burston, El Capital Social Campesino en la Gestion del Desarrollo Rural: Diadas, Equipos, Puentes y Escaleras, Santiago: Naciones Unidas, Comission Economica para America Latina y el Caribe (CEPAL), 2002; and Raul Atria, Marcelo Siles, Irma Arriagada, Lindon J. Robison and Scott Whiteford (eds.), Capital Social y Reduccion de la Pobreza en America Latina y el Caribe: en Busca de un Nuevo Paradigma, Santiago: Naciones Unidas, Comision Economica para America Latina y el Caribe (CEPAL), 2003.

[13] For a forceful critique of the World Bank's interpretation and use of the concept of social capital as a model for action in the Post-Washington Consensus context, see Victor Breton Solo de Zaldivar, 'Los paradigmas de la "nueva" ruralidad a debate: el proyecto de desarrollo de los pueblos indigenas y negros del Ecuador', European Review of Latin American and Caribbean Stdues, No. 78, 2005, pp. 7-30.

[14] For a discussion of the literature on social capital that asserts that relations of trust and cooperation between state representatives and the rural poor result in positive state-society interactions, see Raju J. Das, 'Rural society, the state and social capital in eastern India: a critical investigation', *The Journal of Peasant Studies*, 32 (1), 2005, pp.48-87.

[15] For a critical examination of the concept of social capital, see John Harriss and Paolo de Renzio, "Missing link" or analytically missing?: the concept of social

capital: An introductory bibliographic essay, *Journal of International Development,* 9 (7), 1997, pp.919-937.

[16] This point is developed by Ben Fine, Social Capital versus Social Theory: Political Economy and Social Science at the Turn of the Millennium, London and New York: Routledge, 2001.

[17] Environment has been defined "as the sum total of all conditions and influences that effect the development and life of organism including human being."

[18] Elwin, V. 1959. Philosophy for *NEFA.* (2nd ed.) Shillong: Govt. of Assam.

[19] Elwin, V. 1968. "Do we really want to keep them in Zoo, the Adivasis," in L.P. Vidyarthi (ed.). *Applied Anthropology in India: Principles, Problems and Case Studies.* Allahabad: Kitab Mahal, p.125. Quoted by D.K. Panigrahi in *Social Change,* 23 (nos. 2&3 June-Sept.) 1993, pp.90-96.

[20] Tribe is essentially a politico-administrative category. In the 1931 census an attempt was made by the colonial administration to list the 'primitive tribe'. Shortly thereafter, the Government of India Act of 1935 registered them as 'backward tribes'. After Independence, special provisions for the administration of these peoples were mode under which they were listed in separate schedules of the constitution, this creating the term 'scheduled tribes'.

[21] The level of rural poverty ascending to the National Sample Survey (NSS) 55th round in 1999/2000 was 49%, the highest of all India States (followed by Orissa 48% and Bihar 44%).

At the village level irrigation system management appears to take place with little or no influence from the State or by legislation directed towards the water resources.

[22] Forest Department.1994. Annual Administration Report for the year 1989-90 to 1992-93. Compiled by the Statistical Section, Forest Research Division, Bihar, Ranchi; Govt. of Bihar.

[23] Hill, J. 2017 Agrarian crisis in Jharkhand: Results of a farmer survey. Ranchi: BIRSA MMC.

[24] Alvares, C. (2017). Who's the most organic country of them all? 19th IFOAM Organic World Congress, 9-11 November 2017, Souvenir and Guide., pp.38-43.

[25] Directorate of Plant Protection, Quarantine and Storage (2016-17 figures are provisional) http://ppgs.gov.in/divisions/pesticides-monitoring-documentation.

[26] Hill, J. 2017. Agrarian crisis in Jharkhand: Results of a farmer survey. Ranchi: BIRSA MMC.

CHAPTER – 2

Cprs Social Capital and Poverty: A Theoretical Perspective

Much interest has been shown in social capital in recent times both in academic and development activist circle (Granovetter, 1985; Coleman, 1988; North, 1990; Putnam, 1993; Fukuyama, 1995; Ostrom, 1998; Woolcock, 1998; Pretty & Ward, 2000; Rudd, 2000). The term captures the idea that social bonds and social norms are important basis for sustainable livelihoods. Social capital is the productive asset that enables individuals to fulfill their aspirations better through access to goods and services via their social network and through collective action (Castle, 1998). Social capital facilitates co-operations by lowering costs of working together. People have the confidence to invest in collective activities knowing that others will also do so. They are also less likely to engage in unfettered private actions that has negative impacts such as resource degradations. Social capital is deemed to increase production of both quasi-public and public goods by increasing levels of knowledge about production, transformation processes and trading partners, and by exploiting the gains through specialization. Transaction costs associated with trading are reduced via an increase in levels of trust between trading partners and the development of institutions that provide incentives for lasting co-operation (Coleman, 1988; North, 1990; Ostrom, 1999; Woolcock, 1998). Social capital, unlike other forms of capital, is not depleted with use but actually increases in value with its use (Ostrom, 1999).

Social capital refers to the actual or potential resources, such as trust, information, effective social norms (Coleman 1990; Lin, Cook, and Burt 2001; Putnam, Leonardi, and Nanetti 1993), and a propensity to undertake mutually beneficial collective actions (Krishna 2002), that are linked to a durable social network of more or less institutionalized relationships of mutual acquaintance and recognition (Bourdieu and Wacquant 1992). A growing body of research examines the role social capital plays in facilitating the economic actions of individuals (Granovetter 1985) and firms (Burt 1992) and the economic and political development of countries (Putnam et al. 1993). This research hotly debates whether social capital can be created or is predetermined by historical factors.

Much of the environmental movement concern then was with pollution, population growth and resource depletion- themes emphasized by the popular literature of the time such as Rachel Carson's "Silent Spring" (1964), Hardin's "The Tragedy of the Commons" (1968), Ehrlich's "The Population Bomb" (1966) and the Club of Rome's "Limits to Growth" (Meadows, 1972). These ideas all gained increasing popularity in the evolution of Ostrom's 'Governing the Commons' (1990), after which the concept of CPRs social capital within the resources management and sustainability in development thinking received a great deal of attention.

This chapter presents a conceptual analysis of social capital, and common property resources (CPRs social capital). The chapter deals with the meaning and interpretations of 'CPRs social capital' and their various uses for human development. Literary meaning of social capital is 'social skills' or 'social connections'. The concept has been used in various frameworks such as the 'livelihoods', the 'capitals', and the 'capabilities'. It has gained a lot of significance and is regarded as a vital component in development activities. This study, however, examines questions of 'CPRs social capital' practices interacting with natural resources notably land, forest and water (natural sciences); of trust, reciprocity, social ties and networking, reputation, livelihoods, and poverty alleviation (social sciences), and of development interventions in this case that of watershed technologies and conflict management resolutions (touching on management and engineering sciences). The research further examines the discourses and practices of actors at different levels in society; CPRs practices striving to make a living, NGO workers attempting to improve the lives of those CPRs households, and policy makers at various levels be they local government official or international level researches and donors. These actors have conflicting views, values and ontological assumptions.

Coleman (1990) argues that social capital can be created "when the relations among persons change in ways that facilitate action" (p. 304), however, "most forms of social capital are created or destroyed as a byproduct of other activities" (p. 317). While factors such as network closure, stability of social structure, and appropriate ideology facilitate social capital, factors that reduce mutual dependence, such as affluence and government aid in times of need, erode it. This generalization suggests that externally funded development projects hamper existing social capital to the extent that they reduce villagers' mutual reliance for resources and assistance. Depending on their characteristics, however, externally initiated development projects may actually generate social capital. For example, scholars have found that user-committees formed for watershed development and public land use projects (Krishna 1997, 2000), joint forest-management groups (Wijayaratna and Uphoff 1997), and farmer-managed irrigation facilities (Ostrom 1994) foster social capital by creating networks and inculcating attitudes that promote cooperation and collective action.

In social capital, norms and rule-ordered relationships are viewed as resources that individual can use to reduce risk, access services, obtain information, and co-ordinate collective action (Grootaert, 1998). Collier (1998) identified that overall capacity for co-ordination raises output in four potential ways: (i) social sanctions against opportunism by free-riding individuals reduce transaction costs; (ii) common pool resources can be effectively managed on a sustainable basis; (iii) public goods provision can increase; and (iv) society can take advantage of economies scale in non-market activities. Social capital can act as an input to the production function for individuals and organizations by constraining opportunism and thereby increasing the probability of collective action to deal with social externalities.

But is social capital really capital? The key characteristics of capital are that there is an opportunity cost required investing in it and that it permits people to become more productive in fulfilling human aspirations. In the case of social capital, both time and effort are indeed expended on transformations and transactions to build social assets-norms, rules, and institutions – today that increases income in the future through increased productivity (Bourdieu, 1986; Narayan and Pritchart, 1997; Castle, 1998; North, 1998; Ostrom, 1999). Changes in the level of social capital have economic and political consequences. In economic terms, the level of change in social capital can lead to – alteration in the terms of trade, individuals internalizing the externalities, change in the probability of successful collective action, change in the number of opportunities for specialization and gains from trade, changed personal income levels, and redistribution in income and social welfare (Robinson and Siles, 1997). Additional evidence that social capital is indeed capital comes from observing the tradeoffs between social and other forms of capital in the production of quasi-public goods like tradeoffs between market and social network mechanisms of social provisions (Frank, 1992, Grootaert, 1998, Castle, 1998).

Core Factors of Social Capital

Relations of Trust

Trust lubricates co-operations. It reduces transaction costs between people, and so liberates resources (Pretty and Ward, 2001). Instead of having to invest in monitoring others, individuals are able to trust them to act as expected. This saves time and money. It can also create social obligation – trusting someone engenders reciprocal trust. There are two types of trust: the trust we have in those whom we know; and the trust in those whom we do not know, but which arises because of our confidence in known social structures. Trust takes time to build but is easily broken (Gambetta, 1988; Fukuyama, 1995). If a society is pervaded with distrust, co-operative arrangements are unlikely to emerge (Baland & Platteau, 1998). Having all these facts in mind, it is yet to see if magnitude and nature vary with time in the collective action framework and how that contributes to the poverty alleviation at the individual actor's level.

Reciprocity and Exchanges

Reciprocity and exchanges also increase trust. There are two types of reciprocity-specific and diffuse (Coleman, 1990; Putnam, 1993). Specific (horizontal) reciprocity refers to simultaneous exchanges of items of approximately equal value. Diffuse (vertical) reciprocity refers to a continuing relationship of exchange that at any given time may be unrequited, but over time is repaid and balanced. This contributes to the development of long-term obligations between people, which can be an important part of achieving positive environmental outcomes (Platteau, 1997). Nature and magnitude of reciprocity in the different stages of CPR management in India would encourage other communities to take up natural resource management at the collective level.

Institutions

Institutions cover a wide array of phenomena – common understandings (beliefs, norms) that facilitate co-operation; hierarchic bodies like judges, village chiefs or even Panchayat for resolving disputes; money as standardized unit of exchange; family as a core arena for intense social interactions and mutual exchange etc. Institutions may have varying degrees of collective acceptance. Institutions are dynamic in nature and referred as process (institutionalization) than a state (Uphoff, 1993). The institutional environment includes social structures (organizations, networks, social relationships), rules (formal and informal), and culture (perceptions and identities). Depending on the type of social structure, different kinds of rules are evolved that governs exchange process of information and resources.

The nature of social interaction and its role in shaping common property resource regimes vis-à-vis household survival can be an important debate in social capital parlance. Social capital refers to the nature of social structures and rules and their effect on development. Institutional environment although largely a neutral concept, but within the concept of "capital" may facilitate individual development under CPR regimes/collective frame work.

Social Ties, Networks and Groups

Social ties, networks and groups and the nature of relationships are vital aspects of social capital. In common property resource management, it is essential to link micro level interpersonal ties with macro level networks –within the group, among the groups; and between groups and local governance, market, other agencies. Interpersonal ties refer to amount of time spent, emotional intensity, intimacy (mutual confiding), reciprocal services provided between two persons or among persons. It may be one way or two way, and may be long established (and so not responsive to the current conditions), or subject to regular update.

Macro level ties manifest themselves in different types of groups at the local level –from guilds and mutual aid societies, to sports clubs and credit groups, to forest, fishery, or pest management groups, and to literary societies, NGO network. They also imply ties/connection with other groups in society both at micro and macro level (Uphoff, 1993; Woolcock, 1998). Ties therefore, can have four elements in Indian CPR regime:

1. Local ties ties between individuals and within local groups and communities;

2. Local-local ties-horizontal ties between groups within communities, which sometimes become platforms for new higher level institutional structures;

3. Local-external ties – vertical ties between local groups and local level governance (Panchayat), external organizations or agencies, being one way (usually top down), or two way;

4. External-external ties – horizontal ties between external agencies, leading to integrated approaches for collaborative partnerships.

Even though some agencies may recognize the value of social capital, it is common to find that not all these ties are emphasized. For example, a government may stress on the importance of integrated approaches between different sectors/or disciplines, but fail to encourage two-way vertical ties with local group. A developmental agency may emphasise formation of local associations without building their linkages upward with other external agencies that could threaten the success.

Leadership

The basic question in organizing community based forest management is how and under what conditions can the community be mobilized and organized for CPR management. Any attempt to establish an organization must recognize that individual interest and organization's interest can be conflicting. Therefore, an effective mechanism for incentives and or sanctions is required to reconcile the conflicting interests and to facilitate group action. Individual participation in collective action is found to be based on four considerations (a) cost of participation in terms of money, time, and energy; (b) expected benefit from collective action; (c) probability of individual action/participation leading to the provision of the collective good; and (d) leadership viability and trust. Of these factors, leadership was considered as most important (Shah, 1991). Absence of good leadership is often found to cause non co-operation in co-operatives when other factors reported to be congenial. Good leadership having both credibility and capability can enhance the probability of success in providing collective good for the group. At the same time it also helps in reducing individual's apprehensions about (i) whether the expected benefit from common forest will accrue to them; (ii) whether the benefits will be distributed equitably among the contributors; and (iii) whether the non-contributors (free riders) will be excluded from appropriating the benefits. Olson (1965) identified leaders as constructive political entrepreneur for collective actions.

In the case of CPR management seven critical roles of leaders were identified (Shah, 1991). These are (i) generation of ideas; (ii) motivation and inspiration of people to implement the idea of participation; (iii) acquisition of land if necessary; (iv) holding negotiation with governmental and non-governmental organizations; (v) mobilization of resources; (vi) development of a management system; and (vii) settling the conflicts.

However, in Indian context often leadership is assumed only to monopolise power and control over a system with or without political suzerainty. Such leadership may not perform any of the roles mentioned above. Sometime leadership is also acquired through lineage or caste. How such phenomena contribute to social capital to manage resource base, and create an environment of economic welfare for all actors of CPR needs to be explored.

Community Composition

Why do some communities succeed and others fail in collective action? Does heterogeneity hinder collective action? Beneath an apparent consensus in CPR discourse, there are several unresolved questions. Particularly important among these is the question of size and heterogeneity and their effect on collective action and resource management (Baland and Platteau, 1995, 1996; Keohane and Ostrom, 1995; Blomquist and Schlager, 1998; Uphoff, 1998; Varughese and Ostrom, 2001).

Research findings showed less convergence. In India, different interests for man and women led to different perceptions of costs and benefits about the collective actions (Agarwal, 1994, 1997; Molinas, 1998). Dayton-Johnson and Bardhan (1998) while exploring the question of how inequality of assets affects the timing of harvest in fishery (thus affecting the conservation) found that increasing inequality in general, did not favour conservation. A study of Fulani, Mali, while unable to find a systematic relationship between heterogeneity and success in collective action, suggests that co-operation may possibly be enhanced by heterogeneous social structure except when such heterogeneity is 'tantamount' heterogeneity in economic interests and political power (Vedeld, 1997, p. 32). Varughese and Ostrom (2001) while examining the contested role of heterogeneity in collective action under community forestry programme of Nepal found that heterogeneity did not have a determinant impact on the likelihood or success of collective action.

State-Community Relationship

Robert Wade (1987) observed that in CPR regimes the less the state can, or wishes to, undermine locally based authorities, and the less the state enforce private property rights effectively, the better the chances of success. However, in most developing countries, governments have chosen to centralize management of all local –level natural resources, vesting it in administrative bodies and possibly granting medium – or long-term leases to private agents or companies. In India, entire forest reserves were brought under centralized rule during colonial period and legacy continued even in post independent era until recent times.

Recent experiences of community based resource management in India have shown much prospect. Government of India has also encouraged many decentralized resource management systems in recent times of which National Watershed Mission and Joint Forest Management are of prime importance. The importance of community based resource management are multifarious: (1) it allows community to take part in resource management and resource ownership; (1) it helps in rebuilding relationship of trust and reciprocity and network thereby reduce transaction cost; (3) it helps in downsizing the government bureaucracy and thereby helps in reducing overhead costs; (4) it offers more effective monitoring of natural resources; (5) it helps in utilizing diversified knowledge base for resource management; (6) it motivates local-community to strive for sustainable development.

However, it is not yet known clearly whether total transfer of power to community will ensure sustainable resource management everywhere or some governmental control still is essential. It is also not fully known what kind of state-community network would make the system more effective and that network can be developed.

External Intrusion

It is virtually becoming impossible for any community to remain confined and totally exclude outsiders. Due to increased social mobility, market exchange, external intrusion becomes inevitable in any communitarian system. In CPR, external intrusion can take place either as motivator or facilitator or technical expert or market agent (buyer or seller) or stakeholder. While outsiders role as motivator or facilitator or technical expert for natural resource management may not pose any threat to share of benefit to members of community, the market agent for natural resources, and one who claims stakeholder's right certainly do. Anyone who claims share of benefit is generally not welcomed in existing collective action arena.

In contrast, in many cases, outsiders are internalized through negotiation process. In Gujarat province of India, every village allows cattle owners from Katchh (a perennially drought prone region) to use the village pasture land and in return these cattle owners also take care of the cattle of the local people as well as the pasture land. In Rajaji National Park in the state of Uttaranchal (India) when local Gujjar tribes (traditional cattle owners) were allowed to tend their cows and buffaloes inside the national park also witnessed more effective monitoring of park. This happened as Gujjars out of gratitude prevented any illegal intrusion and pilferage and cattle dung also continues to enrich forestland.

However, for sustainable resource management such arrangement must look beyond the horizontal reciprocity. External intrusion embraced in the social capital framework (reciprocity, trust, institutionalization process, social network), may create more opportunities. What type of arrangement with external intrusion would help in building a new social capital and institutional arrangement is need to be addressed and explored.

Guaranteeing Entitlement for Individuals

Will social capital and better CPR management guarantee the incremental entitlement at each actor (individual)? Will all the actors have equal share in incremental benefit? – are the question always haunt both the individual actor and CPR facilitators. If improvement in natural endowment (resource pool) does not ensure incremental benefit at individual level, the collective action may face serious threat. It is therefore of paramount importance that distributive justice must be practiced. By distributive justice I refer a condition of equity in benefit sharing and also providing opportunities for economic welfare to each individual actor. To combat poverty in rural India, it is essential that each individual should have incremental entitlement to be operationalized both in short and long term. The success of CPR management thus refers not to health of resource but the additional entitlement of the actor as well.

Commons property resources (CPRs) theory

The CPRs concept ('commons'[1]) is as old as the natural resources, but its quantitative measurement is of recent origin. However, the studies on management practices of CPRs by and large were relied on the historical and ethnographic research methodologies in the past. In the middle of the twentieth century, the CPRs as a physical phenomenon started to be used repeatedly by scientists from other disciplines to close the interdisciplinary gap. As we have moved into the 21st century, more methodological choices have been made in support of the study of CPRs and its management practices.

In the 1990s the mainstream common property resources (CPR) theory (Berkes, 1989, Bromley, 1992, Ostrom, 1990, 1992) sought to examine how and when common property resources have been successfully managed by commoners without state intervention or privatization[2]. Property relations are seen to be crucial determinants of the manner by which people use and manage common property natural resources[3].

Natural resources no longer belonged to the communities, they belonged to the state. Communities were relegated to custodians of the environment, and had to follow state initiatives that were often very much against the traditional concepts of forests, land, and water. How did people and local communities justify or come to terms with such exploitation? What is the role of local communities, the role of leaders (widely defined) in shaping the discourse of exploitation and hence successfully challenging externally-imposed rules on their communities? The same people who practiced sound resource management at one point in time destroyed those same resources at a later date. Researchers who also seek to explain why collective action and commons management emerge, persist and decline at particular points of times and in particular places. These are questions that are frequently-asked these days in the development literature.

Like all public goods, it is difficult to say who is at fault when natural capital (nature's goods and services – Costanza et al., 1997) declines. Without rules, individuals tend to overuse and under-invest in it; they are tempted to take benefit without contributing anything – in effect free ride (Hardin, 1968). When such public goods and services are considered free and valued at zero, the market indicates that they can be made valuable by converting into something else. So the profit from converting forest into timber is counted on nation's balance sheet, but all lost services (wild foods, fodder grasses, climate regulation, biodiversity, medicinal herbs) tend not to be subtracted. Social institutions based on trust, reciprocity, and agreed norms and rules for behaviour, can mediate such kind of unfettered private action. New thinking and practices are required, particularly to develop forms of social organization that are structurally suited for natural resource management and protection at the local level. This means more than just reviving the old institutions and traditions. It calls for formation of new forms of organizations, associations and platforms for common action.

Much of the natural resources like forest, pasture, water management systems, and fishing zones are used as commons in India. Farming households have collaborated on water management, labour sharing and markets; pastoralist co-managed pastures; forest dependent communities collectively managing the forest; and fishing families managing aquatic resources jointly. Such collaborations have been institutionalized in many forms of local associations through clan or kin or village groups, traditional leadership, water user's association, tree growers' co-operatives, grazing societies, youth clubs, self-help groups, temple committee, etc. These common property resources (CPRs) currently contribute some US$ 5 billion a year to the incomes of poor rural households in India, or about 12% of household income of poor rural household (World Bank, 1998). This is about two and half times of total World Bank lending to India in fiscal year 1996.

Although constructive resource management rules and norms are embedded in many cultures and societies, from co-operative water management system of western and northern India; *Gouchar* (cattle grazing land) land management of Saurashtra; shifting cultivation system of north eastern India; to forest management of tribal groups, it has been rare for the importance of such local groups and institutions to be recognized in recent agricultural and rural development. Developmental policy and practice have tended to be preoccupied with changing the behaviour of individuals rather than of groups or communities. As a result, agriculture has had an increasingly destructive effect on environment (Huxley, 1960; Palmer, 1976; Ostrom, 1990; Kothari et. al., 1998). In some context, loss of institutions has provoked natural resource degradation. In India, the loss of management systems for CPRs has been a critical factor in the increased overexploitation, poor upkeep, and physical degradation of natural resources during the past half century. Jodha (1990) reported that only 10% of the studied villages retained traditional practice of regulated grazing in village pastureland causing serious fodder scarcity. Elsewhere, when collective irrigation management system was replaced by private ownership or operation system it resulted in substantial degradation of both surface and ground water resources (Pretty, 1995; Singh & Ballabh, 1997; Kothari et al., 1998). One study of 25 completed World Bank agriculture projects found that continued success was clearly associated with institutional building (Cernea, 1987). In this study it was found that twelve of the projects achieved long term sustainability, and in all these projects local institutions were strong. In the others, the rates of return declined markedly contrary to the expectations at the time of project completion. The outcomes were unsustainable where there had been no attention to institutional development and local participation.

This vital distinction makes the degradation of open access resources far more likely than that of common property. According to Stevenson, true open access resources are quite rare. More often, resource degradation result from the fact that state –owned property (often land that was formerly managed as part of a common property system) is exploited by local people who resent its privatization and act in accordance with the Turkish saying "one would have to be a despicable fool not to help oneself to state property" (quoted in Berkes and Taghi Farvar, 1989P10).

Shepherd makes a similar point, emphasizing the failure of many colonial and post-colonial governments to recognize group-based as well as individual property systems (Shepherd,1992 1993) Shepherd also argues , like Hardin, that population increase can be a major factor in the decline of common property resources management in the absence of state intervention(Shepherd, 1992c; 1993a). In the model illustrating indigenous and participatory forest management (see figure 1.1) Shepherd shows that common property resources management develops in 'stage two 'where "some resource scarcity is experienced," but start to decline in 'stage three' when "there are too many people or too many interests for the size of a resource" and the management cost being to outweigh the benefits" (Shepherd, 1993a pl).

This is where the similarity between Shepherd's and Hardin's model ends, as Shepherd is very critical both of Hardin's concept of 'individual rationality leading to mass irrationality' (Shepherd, 1992c p73) and extend to which Hardin's assumptions about commons have been retained by many development practitioners. Instead , Shepherd argues that if a suitable approach can be found, it may be possible to maintain certain 'stage three 'systems as functioning common property resource management systems or even to "roll them back towards stage two" (Shepherded, 1992a)

She also argues that given 'helpful state intervention' (Shepherded, 1993a; 1993b) in the form of participatory or joint resources (particularly forest) management. It may be possible to re-create common property resource management in certain situations. To assist development practitioners and state officials who are thinking of investigation participatory approaches, Shepherd has developed a second model which indicates where and in which situations common (autonomous or joint) resource management is most likely to be successful.

As Shepherd's second model shows, interest in and enthusiasm for common property resource management has not been confided to academic circles (Shephedd. 1992a; 1993a; 1993b). Development planners within government bodies, donor agencies and nongovernmental organizations (NGOs) have all come to see the potential of common property resource management for future participatory development initiatives (see, for example, Warren et la, 1995a;Warren and McKiernan ,1995; Slikkerveer and Dechering, 1995;Von Liebenstein, 1995;McNeely,1995; McCracken,1995; Altieri and Yurijevic, 1995; Hadley and Schreckenberg, 1995).Of particular interest are the reciprocal obligations (social capital) inherent within common property resource management systems that have potential to ensure greater livelihood security, equitable resource distribution, participation in the production system, resource conservation and ecological sustainability.

CPR Social Capital and Development

At the same time, radical environmental literature was taking encouraged the development of more critical research on the relationships between poverty and environmental degradation (Redclift, 1984; 1987; Eckholm, 1984; Blaikie, 1985; World Commission for Environment and Development, 1987; World Bank, 1992; Joeckes et al, 1994; Reardon and Vosti, 1995). Reardon and Vosti (1995), for example, draw a distinction between 'welfare poverty' (based on income or calorific intake) and 'investment poverty' arguing that the alleviation of the former will not necessarily help households to address environmental problems as they may still be too 'investment poor' to pay for resource improvements. Presumably by the same token, such households will also be too investment (and welfare) poor to refrain from activities that cause environmental degradation.

Particularly influential in the growth of interest in community-based resource management has been the criticism directed at Hardin's 'tragedy of the commons' model (Hardin, 1968) which showed that Hardin's so-called commons were not common property resources at all, but open access resources (Berkes, 1989; Berkes and Taghi Farvar, 1989; Singh, 1991a; Stevenson, 1991). The distinction between common property and open access resources is an extremely important one as community access to true commons is restricted, whereas that to open access resources is not. According to Stevenson 'common property is a form of resource management in which a well-delineated group of competing users participated in extraction or use of a jointly held, fugitive resource according to explicitly or implicitly understood rules about who may take how much of the resource' (Stevenson, 1991 p46). Open access resources, by contrast, are characterized by an 'absence of rights and duties' which 'means that the institution of property does not exist' (*ibid, p49*).

Some of the situations where common property resource management is thought most likely to be successful are where local communities both perceive a need to protest a resource from further exploitation and feel that the benefits of collusion are likely to exceed the costs of establishing such a system (Wade, 1986; Stevenson, 1991). There must also be a belief that the benefits to be realized from community management would exceed those that could be achieved by individual-level exploitation.

Other conditions that encourage the establishment of successful common property resource management systems include a scarcity of resources, an easily defined used group and a powerful or well respected local leader who is able both to mobilize villagers' support for common property resource management and to provide a means for ensuring that the system of rules and duties for resource exploitation are enforced (Wade, 1986). Management is made easier if both the resource and its users are well defined (Blaikie *et al*, 1986; Stevenson, 1991) and the system of limiting resource use (such as when access to the resource is permitted, how much of it can be taken and what maintenance duties are expected in return) is well understood by the community. Kinship linkages and socio-cultural and economic homogeneity within the group can be particularly helpful for minimizing the risk of conflict between members and encouraging cohesion and unity with the user group. If this can be achieved, the incentives for treating the common property resource as a type of extended private property and for keeping outsiders away are likely to be greater (Gadgil and Iyer, 1989; Singh, 1991a).

Certainly if further degradation of open access resources can be prevented through the recreation of common property resource management systems, much of the social upheaval associated with resource privatization could be prevented (Gibbs and Bromley, 1989). This is particularly true in areas where there is a strong traditional of common property management or where local communities can recall a time when community based resource management was widespread. Common property management may also make financial sense in that infrastructure costs such as fencing, labour, transport and building can be shared by the community (Stevenson, 1991).

Common property resources have received most attention as part of the new emphasis within rural development on the value of learning from local environmental knowledges and management strategies, encouraging the participation of local people in development projects and ensuring that such projects are acceptable to them. Some of the findings from this work have shown how commons in many developing countries are an important resource for poorer and landless community members who rely heavily upon them for fuel wood, fodder and, to some extent, food (Korton, 1986; Shiva, 1986; 1988; Singh, 1986; Bahaguna, 1991; Kumar, 1991; Sengupta, 1991; Singh, 1991a; 1991b).

Other work has emphasized how community-based systems of common property (particularly forest) management can ensure the sound management and equal access of community members to vital subsistence resources such as fuel wood, construction timber, animal fodder and irrigation water (Arnold and Campbell, 1986; Blaikie et al, 1986; Singh, 1986; Shiva, 1986; Wade, 1986; Gadgil and Iyer, 1989; Sengupta, 1991; Shepherd, 1992a; 1992b; 1993b). In response to this interest, a number of countries have tried to re-establish systems of common property resource (particularly forest) management as a means of arresting deforestation and meeting local fuel wood and fodder needs.

Figure 2
Resource (CPR Social Capital)-Income Linkage

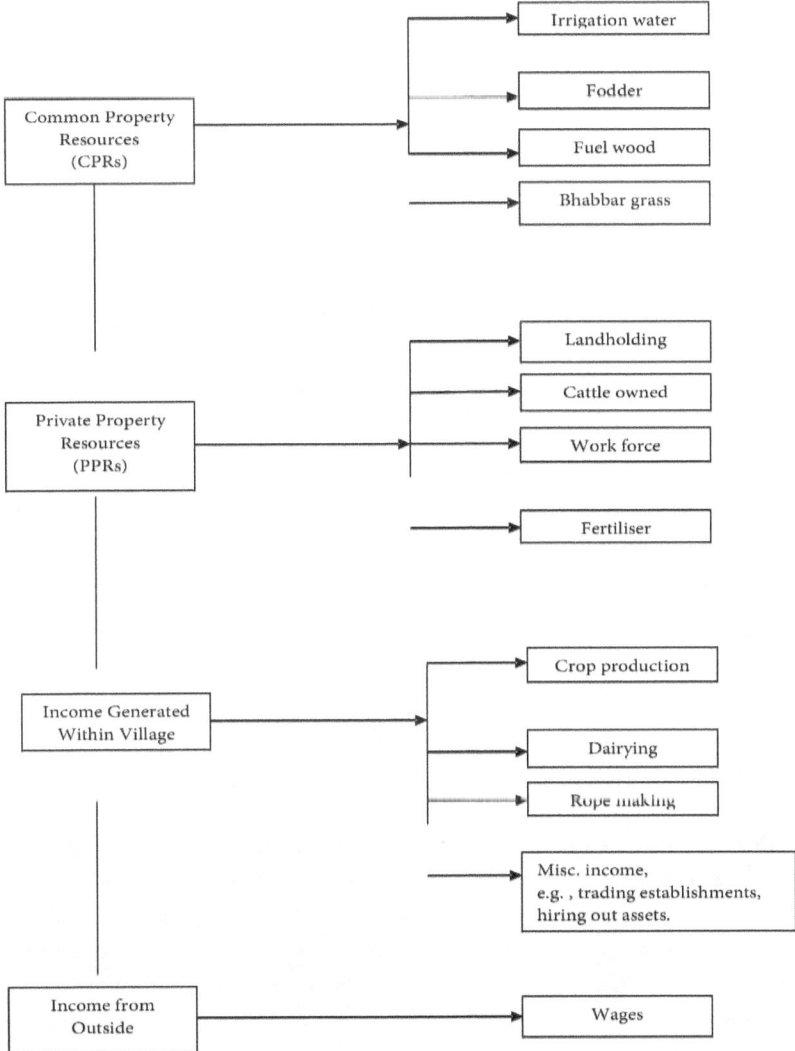

To conclude, common property resources have received most attention as part of the new emphasis within rural development on the value of learning from local environmental knowledge and management strategies, encouraging the participation of local people in development projects and ensuring that such projects are acceptable to them. Some of the findings from this work have shown how commons in many developing countries are an important resource for poorer and landless community members who rely heavily upon them for fuel wood, fodder and to some extent food (Korton, 1986; Shiva, 1986; 1988; Singh, 1986; Bahaguna, 1991; Kumar, 1991; Sengupta, 1991; Singh, 1991a; 1991b). With the exception of Mehrotra and Kishore's (1990), Kant *et al's* (1991), Katar Singh's (1994), N.S. Jodha's (1994), V. Shiva's (1998) works on CPR Management systems and silviculture knowledge, however, there have been relatively few Jharkhand studies (Jewitt,1998), Sinha and Suar (2003) and Shiva and Brand (2005) of forest management in tribal Jharkhand (India) that have tried both to reconstruct local forest management histories and to investigate the potential of participatory (or even autonomous) forest management to promote forest protection and regeneration. My own research has tried to close this gap somewhat by focusing on natural resource management through social capital in 25 *Adivasi-* dominated villages in the *Chotanagpur* and *Santhal Pargana* regions of Jharkhand (See Chapters 3 & 4).

Endnotes

[1] The commons, formerly known as the common property resources (CPRs), implies as a *'resource'*, as an *'institution'* and as a *'property regime'* that is commonly owned, managed and used by the community itself. Decisions about what crops to sow, how many cattle wide graze, which trees will be cut, which streams will irrigate which field at what time, are made jointly and democratically by the members of the community. Commoning is a way of life the roots of sustainability lie in it. Moreover, both commons and community are beyond the market and the state. They are governed by self-determined norms, and are self-managed.

[2] Common property resources management thinking is rooted in the debate sparked by Hardin's 'tragedy of the commons' thesis, which advocated either state intervention or private property to resolve the tragedy (see Hardin, 1968).

[3] But not the only determinants: the property rights school sees private property as the most appropriate way to make individuals 'internalize the externalities' generated through resource exploitation; 'efficiency considerations dominate the property rights school arguments' (Baland and Platteau, 1996: 36-7).

CHAPTER – 3

SIGN and Its Partners towards
CPRs and Social Capital

This Chapter builds upon the concept framed in Chapters 1 & 2, in particular its conceptualizations of social networking, Property Rights and CPRs. For in CPRs social capital regimes such as the research NGOs and villages, therein, and the control of access (the ability to mediate others' access) interlinks with organizational control of social capital access and usage, links with maintenance and system sustainability. In this chapter, we would like to explore the diverse and conflicting management practices made by voluntary organizations in 'CPRs social capital' works.

Voluntarism in India has passed through a number of phases. The Gandhian and other types of voluntary agencies that existed prior to Independence, on receiving government grants started working closely with and under the broad guidance of the government. They had lost the pioneering independent spirit that they had come to symbolize during the freedom struggle. In the second stage, there came a shift back to constructive work from 'progress' or 'development' or social networking (Social Capital). The next phase saw a new genre of activist groups come up, ready to struggle on behalf of the poor, landless, *Dalits* and other minority groups, against the state and dominant interests. There is a wide variety of such groups working in as different sectors as forestry, migrant labour, women, child labour, wasteland development, commons and so on.

The work done by some voluntary groups prior to independence provides historical links with the NGOs in the field today, and the following is a brief account of an early experiment in CPRs Social Capital regimes.

1. Gandhi's experiments in the 1920s and 1930s, undertaken at *Sevagram*, a village near Wardha (Maharashtra), had a strong moral tone.

2. Tagore's work introduced in 1922 at *Sriniketan* near *Shantiniketan* (West Bengal), is another such early experiment in social welfare.

3. The Rural Development Demonstration Centre introduced in 1921 at Marthandam (then a part of Travancore State, now in Tamil Nadu Kanyakumari District), had three important projects: the cooperative system, grassroots self-help and appropriate technology.

4. The Christian canal colonies, of which there were 83 (Protestant) peasant settlements throughout India, the major ones of which are along the canals of Punjab and Gujarat also undertook welfare work. The adult literacy classes were organized with the basic objective of teaching the villagers the means of reading the Bible. But modern institutions, like the cooperative credit societies to replace money lenders, and the demonstration farms where the peasants picked up, among other things, the latest agricultural techniques, were also introduced.

Depending on the nature of their activities, the NGOs have been classified as those involved in (i) relief and charity, (ii) development-oriented work, (iii) mobilization and organization, (iv) politics, and (v) political education. Another classification schema differentiates between them in ideological terms: (i) Gandhian or neo-Gandhian, (ii) Marxist groups, and (iii) Liberal groups. A further classification may be into (i) Gandhian/Sarvodaya, (ii) Marxist, (iii) Church-inspired/related, and (iv) Eclectic. (Borrow ideas from all the above mentioned models and are 'open' in that sense).

In ideology terms the NGOs can broadly be categorized as Gandhian, Marxist, Church-inspired and Eclectic. The Gandhian NGOs believe that the people of the village must solve the problems of the village by persuading the better off, the exploiting sections and by reminding them of their moral duties. The Marxist NGOs are primarily engaged in organizational work. They organize the people seeking to create an alternative system that is more egalitarian. For this purpose, they educate the people politically and facilitate local leadership to emerge.

The Church-inspired NGOs are of two types. Those that are run by former clergy and those that are run by the clergy under the direct auspices of religious institutions. Such NGOs, generally do not adopt a confrontational attitude and/or strategy. It is not necessary that they indulge in proselytization. Recently, their outlook has been more catholic than they are given credit for. They try to get around vested interests, if possible by co-opting them. They do not generally hinder government programmes. In fact, they supplement and complement government's development efforts, even though they may will be financially independent of the government. Their internal management is systematically organized.

Church-Centered Social Capital in Action

Of the various agencies responsible for social and cultural change among the tribals as well as other downtrodden communities of India, Christian missionaries may have the oldest claim. In fact, the missionaries set an example of high-spirited social service and reforms which was later followed by many others. For a number of centuries the Indian tribals lived in remote hills and forests almost uninfluenced by the mainstream of history and cut off from the Indian social and economic life.

When British policy of isolation resulted in large scale exploitation of the tribals by landlords, money lenders and contractors, it was the Christian missionaries who first went among them with various welfare schemes. They were also pioneers in the field of education. They opened the first hospitals in tribal areas and some of them even set ideal examples by caring for the lepers. When we wish to speak of an ideal social worker we say that he has a 'Missionary Spirit' (Elwin 1963:9,115).

In the beginning Christian missionaries confined their activities to purely evangelical work but they got little success. Later on it was realized that the only way to attract the tribals was to undertake the defense of their interests, especially in connection with the question of their rights regarding land tenure and landlord services. Hence the missionaries changed their approach and began to tell the people that they had come for the eternal welfare of their souls but were ready to help them in temporal affairs as well if they could trust them strictly to follow their advice.

It is good that the nine partner organizations of SIGN (the church-inspired NGOs) realized these and tried to evolve the poor tribal, *dalits* and marginalized population of the community in their own development so that their dependence on any authority - governmental or otherwise – is gradually reduced and they begin to strive for their own betterment with dignity. This has been tried to accomplish through different developmental as well as promotional programmes through social capital resources in rural and tribal Jharkhand of Eastern India. SIGN and its partner organizations believe that today what is paramount is not just the promotion of the 'private' or 'public sector but the need of building of the 'people's sector' which will be more effective in addressing the problem of hunger through CPRs Social Capital institutions.

This study, however, examines the role of 'social capital' and its functions in combating poverty and ensuring sustainable development. The SIGN (Social Initiatives for Growth and Networking) and its nine partner-organizations were selected from five different locations in Jharkhand of Eastern India for an in-depth study on the subject. Broadly speaking, the concept of social capital is relevant to-day because it deals with intangible social concerns in order to understand more complicated social processes and social relations within the larger and diverse socio-cultural structures. The study is also important to deal with the social norms and values that decide the livelihood opportunity and its sustainability as well as social cultural acceptability of any intervention initiated in a given community. CPRs social capital plays a crucial role in providing consumer goods and services to vulnerable sections of the tribal poor. CPRs such as village forests, grazing lands, rivulets and watershed drainages, help dry land farmers during crises periods.

Before discussing the role of NGOs in organizing practices and mobilizing social capital resources for community development of Jharkhand, it is essential to discuss, in brief, about the socio-economic characteristics of the area where the sample NGOs have actively been engaged for the cause of the poor tribal poor since decades.

About Jharkhand: The Operational Area of SIGN and its Partner Organizations

Jharkhand is a predominantly agricultural state where land comes first. The state is also an "Ethnological Museum" with 32 different tribes[1]. There are a number of competing demands on land, like agriculture, forestry, grasslands, urban and industrial (including mining) development, and social infrastructure. Obviously, land use will have to be related to soil quality and use and not land economics. Out of the total geographical area of 79,714 sq. kms, the net irrigated area constitutes 1.57 lac ha, which is only 8 per cent of the net sown area of the State. Moreover, there are 16 river basins in the state, and the ground water resource is 5482 million cubic meters. The average state of development of ground water in the state is approximately 20 per cent, which is less than the national average. The basin-wise per capita water availability, which is around 1859 cum3 per annum for the country as a whole, varies between 13,393 cum per annum for *Brahmaputra-Barak* basin to about 300 cum3 per annum for *Sabarmati* basin.

The Jharkhand geology consists of a mixed metamorphic and sedimentary rock structure which contains rich deposits of iron ore, manganese ore, mica, copper, coal and limestone. The existence of such a geographically concentrated supply of minerals has provided a basis for large scale heavy industrial development in the region since the late nineteenth century and has offered an alternative source of employment for a significant (though declining) number of local people. Indeed, the national importance of the region's mineral resources and industrial output has caused the Jharkhand to be known by many as the 'Ruhr of India' (Corbridge, 1986).

Lying within India's central tribal belt, the Jharkhand region has a significant, but not predominant *Adivasi* population. Over thirty two different Scheduled Tribes make up around 26 per cent of the region's population. Another 50 per cent or so is made up of various 'artisan castes' or *sadans*, many of which have developed a close reciprocal relationship (Social Capital) with the *Adivasis* and share a common cultural (and often religious) outlook (Nathan, 1988; Kelkar and Nathan, 1991).

The State is recognized as part of the 'Vth Schedule Areas' and *PESA*[2] in the Constitution of India. Under these the State of Jharkhand has 13 Scheduled Area Districts such as: Dumka, Godda, Deoghar, Sahabganj, Pakur, Ranchi, Singhbhum (East & West), Gumla, Simdega, Lohardaga, Palamu, and Garwa (with some districts having only partly Tribal Blocks). However, it is a matter of concern that almost all these districts are educationally backward and are poverty stricken. The literacy rate of Jharkhand is 66.4 per cent as compared to the national literacy rate of 73 per cent (2011). Of the 36.89 per cent below the poverty line people, Jharkhand has BPL figures of 54 per cent (Planning Commission July, 2013).

With a population of 85.44 lakhs Jharkhand state has the third largest scheduled tribe population in the country after Chhattisgarh (149.99 lakhs) and Orissa (95.32 lakhs). The scheduled tribes in Jharkhand state are mostly confined to the Chotanagpur Plateau and Santal Parganas plateaus.

The five most important tribes of Jharkhand state are the Santal, Oraon, Munda, Kharia and HOs. The Santals accounting for 23 lakhs population are concentrated in the Santal Parganas and neighbouring districts. The Oraons with a population of about 11 lakhs are found mostly in the districts of Ranchi and Palamau. The Mundas have an appropriate population of 10 lakhs and most of them inhabit Ranchi and Singhbhum districts. The HOs are confined to the Singhbhum district with a population of about 8 lakhs. These four main tribes constitute about 60 per cent and form a major portion of the tribal population of Jharkhand state. There are nine primitive tribes identified in the state, Hill Kharia, Mal Paharia, Sauria Paharia, Bujia, Korwa, Birijea, Birhor, Asur and Sabbar. Their population is approximately 1.68 lakhs. These tribes still live in the primitive socio-economic conditions. The level of technology is pre-agricultural and the level of literacy is extremely low. Their growth rate has continued to remain abnormally low compared to the rest of the population and there is an apprehension that if the present trend continues some of these primitive tribes may become extinct[3].

The areas inhabited by the tribals have generally difficult terrain. They are sparsely populated, hilly and poor in communication and infrastructure. The tribals of this area generally belong to the Proto-Australoid strain through traces of Mongoloid strain have been found in parts of Santal Parganas. They belong to thirty two different communities, each with a distinctive culture and ethos. The tribals differ widely among themselves in the level of socio-economic development. The number of people living entirely by hunting and food gathering as in the primitive times is very small. A few tribal communities still practice shifting cultivation but the majority of the tribals lives in villages and are subsistence cultivators. As most of the land is hilly it is difficult for them to produce any surplus. Many tribals are engaged in various mining and industrial activities as labourers. There are some artisan tribes who are engaged in rope-making, basket making, and cloth-weaving.

The tribals have had no written tradition. Yet, a different image of the Indian tribe is reflected in the tribal traditions, of which the vestiges are still available in many tribal societies. For instance, the term 'Kol' used for the Chhotanagpur tribals had originally a dignity attached to it. It is simply the corrupt form of the Munda word 'horo' or man, as the Mundas like some other tribals honorably called each other (Roy 1970:207). The tribals started resenting its use by the aliens, when it came to connote derogation to the tribals, as bad as 'dirty pig' (Grierson 1990:7). Further, the agriculturist tribals generally had a strong autochthonous feeling for the land they held, not as a matter of personal belonging but as community property. This is because, as the Mundas said of their reclaimed land: "we have snatched the field from the jaw of the tiger and the fang of the snake" (Hoffmann and Van Emleen 2:515). As original settlers many tribal groups had special privileges vis-vis others, who were allowed to settle among the tribals peacefully.

The culture and tradition of the tribals in Jharkhand state differ among themselves. Every tribe has its religious beliefs and rituals. Their rituals are closely linked with the agricultural cycle. They believe in Witchcraft. In recent years some of the tribals have included many gods and goddesses from other religions. A sizable population has adopted Christianity. The rest of the tribals practice 'tribal religion[4].'

Boiled rice is the staple food of the tribals but they do not produce enough to meet the requirements of the family for the entire year. In the lean seasons they mostly have a difficult time and live on coarse grains, *mahua* flowers, sweet potatoes, roots and leaves. '*Haria*' or rice beer prepared at home is almost an inseparable constituent of their celebrations. It is also used as an offering to the deities during worship.

Magnitude of abject poverty and backwardness among the *Adivasis*
The scheduled tribes of Jharkhand state could be divided into two categories: the landowning agriculturist HOs, Santals, immigrant Christian Mundas, Kharias and Oraons; and the small primitive communities who gave up shifting cultivations about six decades ago but are still in the process of settling down to agriculture. These smaller tribal groups are also employed as agricultural labour.

Table 10

Magnitude and abject poverty and backwardness among the social groups in the Jharkhand State of India

Social Group	Sectors			
	Primary	Secondary	Tertiary	Total
General	87.23	4.35	8.42	100.00
Scheduled Castes	95.30	1.19	3.51	100.00
Scheduled Tribes	89.28	3.15	7.57	100.00

Source: Primary Investigation, 2018.

The participation of scheduled castes and scheduled tribes in the primary sector is larger than that of other social groups, and in secondary and tertiary sectors conversely smaller. In the primary sector, most of them are engaged as agricultural labourers who have not been able to build up this assets or resources.

Agriculture is the main occupation of the tribal people. Agricultural operations are traditional due to lack of irrigation and other modern techniques of cultivation. Paddy, millet and pulses are the main crops. They also rear cattle and other livestock to supplement their diet. They also depend upon the forests and sell the various minor forest produces collected by them in the local market place called the 'haat'. Some people take to rope-making, weaving, basket-making and rearing of silk-worms to supplement their income. The 'haat' which is held once or twice on the fixed days of the week plays a very important role in the tribal economy. At the 'haat' the tribals sell their produce or collection and purchase articles of daily use, implements for agriculture and other household goods. The 'haat' is also a place for social gathering.

The institution of village *panchayat* has been a part of the traditional tribal village since a long time. The traditional village *panchayat* headed by the village head-man occupies an important place in the life of the tribals. The democratic character of the society in a tribal village is remarkable. A great deal of fellow feeling and brotherhood exists among the members in the tribal community. There is also the religious head-man who guides the religious aspects of the tribal life. These two headmen wield tremendous authority in the village.

The state government has introduced many protective laws and administrative measures since independence with a view to prevent exploitation of the tribals at the hands of the powerful sections of the population. The state government has identified 112 blocks in the entire districts of Ranchi, Gumla, Lohardaga, Singhbhum, Dumka, Sahebganj and parts of Godda and Palamau districts as areas of high tribal concentration in which special protective measures under the scheduled areas regulations have been enforced. The most important piece of legislation relates to ban on transfer of tribal land to non-tribals. There are special provisions in the Chotanagpur and Santals Parganas tenancy Acts, aimed at prevention of alienation of tribal land and for return of land to the tribal if such land has been transferred by fraudulent means. There are also special provisions to minimize the indebtedness of the scheduled tribes and to free them from the clutches of the unscrupulous moneylenders who have been troubling them for ages. Freedom of the bonded labourers, special provisions in the excise and forest policy of the state government are some of the other measures introduced in favour of the tribals.

The strategy for development of the scheduled tribes must take into account the special features of the tribal economy and culture. In the Twelfth Five Year Plan tribal development blocks were opened in the predominantly tribal areas of the state to bring about an all-round development through a community development approach.

But it was soon realized that the more advanced sections of the community took much greater advantage of these development schemes, resulting in making the gap wider between the tribals and non-tribals. The tribal development block approach proved to be ineffective in the absence of proper administrative set-up and protective aspects. A comprehensive view of the tribal problem was taken on the eve of the Twelfth Five Year Plan and a new strategy called the Tribal Sub-Plan approach was evolved.

The state of Jharkhand is known for its mineral resources, beautiful landscapes and Adivasi culture. It has 40 per cent of the mineral resources of the country, countless touristic places and 32 Adivasi ethnic groups with the population of 8.6 million who enjoy very close affinity with nature. Unfortunately, the huge deposits of mineral resources have turned out to be disastrous for nature and a curse for the Adivasis and the other marginalized communities in the state. The exploitation of mineral resources in the name of development has resulted in the exploitation of nature, the Adivasis and the poor. Presently the state is producing about 160 million tons of various minerals annually, worth Rs. 15,000 crore (approx. US $ 2.5 billion).[5] Ironically, the Adivasis living in the mineral belts are resource less and live in extreme poverty. The rivers like Swarnarekha, Damodar and Koina are carrying the wastes deposited by the steel and mining companies polluting water and the living creatures. The mining areas have become barren and many sites have been abandoned after excavation of coal, iron ore and bauxite. This is other side of modern development which is conveniently swept under the carpet.

After India's independence, Shree Jawaharlal Nehru, the first Prime Minister, with the lofty intention to address the issues of poverty, illiteracy and economic deficit, implemented the capitalist-socialist model of development in the country copying it from foreign countries. Thus, were built, the Heavy Engineering Corporation at Hatia, Ranchi, Bokaro Steel Plant at Bokaro and several dams in the region. In 1991 India accepted the liberal economic policy, paving the way for private entities in the mining sector. The present policy of 2005 Foreign Direct Investment has hugely increased investment by national and multinational corporations' in this sector. Consequently, more forests have been destroyed for mining activities, huge agricultural lands have been acquired for establishment of industries and Adivasis are left with no option but to leave their habitat, home and livelihood. Displacement has become the story of their life with hardly any rehabilitation. On the other hand, the benefits of these development projects have enhanced the wealth of a few and those who were forced to sacrifice everything for the sake of "growth" and "development" are struggling for their survival. The natural consequence is migration of these Adivasis in search of labour.

The youths are getting exasperated and are running away to cities. Unfortunately, many of them end up destroying their youthful life. In recent years, the Jharkhand has emerged as a vulnerable state for trafficking of women and children; for forced labour and slavery. Thousands of children from Jharkhand are traded and trafficked by placement agencies to domestic homes in Delhi and other cities in India. The children and women remain in slavery and bonded labour like conditions. Several cases of sexual slavery have also been reported from rescued victims from Jharkhand. The victims who are working as domestic help in various urban household across the country are often made to work in pathetic conditions. A rapid assessment of domestic workers in 8 districts (the most affected with problems of migration) was done by ATSEC Action against Trafficking and Sexual Exploitation of Children) Jharkhand and Research Plus Group, Ranchi. The findings of the study indicated that most of the trafficked victims are below 20 years and many of them are children. Many of them are in slavery like conditions and earn below minimum wages. The main destination for migration is Delhi.[6]

Jharkhand also has a long way to go in the health care of its inmates. Poverty and ignorance are rampant in the State keeping 36.96% under poverty line. Of the approximately 4 lakh children born in Jharkhand every year, 20,800 die before completing their first month, while approximately 29,600 children are unable to complete their first year.[7] Some of the major killers of infants and children are: complications before delivery-35%; complications during delivery-23%; tetanus-15%, pneumonia-11%; diarrhoea-2%. The children who do not survive are faced with their second challenge; getting adequate and proper nutrition to help them grow. In Jharkhand approximately 55% of the children below 5 years of age are malnourished. 45% of under 5 children dying can be attributed to malnourishment.[8] Jharkhand's present maternal mortality ratio (MMR) is 261 per 100,000 live births and the infant mortality rate is 39 per 1,000 live births.[9]

The green forests are disappearing. The rivers are getting heavily polluted. 141 rivers in the state have lost their natural flow and several districts have suffered from drought in last couple of years. The beautiful land of the Adivasis who lived in the lull of nature is gradually disappearing too. Protests are heard everywhere as lands are being taken away from them. In the words of Laudato Si[10] (LS) it is the violence in our hearts that has affected the soil, the water, the air and all forms of life. It is time for deeper introspection if our hearts feel the cry of Jharkhand and join hands together to make a difference.

The communities in the mining areas are facing severe health problems, water crisis, environmental crisis, lack of education, lack of health facilities. If that be the actual situation, mining is for what?

How ethical is to grab the natural resources from the communities and sell it in the market to meet the corporate greed? How long these natural resources would be sold? Can human beings sustain it without the natural resources?

"Today, however, we have to realize that a true ecological approach always becomes a social approach; it must integrate questions of justice in debates on the environment, so as to hear both the cry of the earth and the cry of the poor"(LS 49). "In fact, the deterioration of the environment and of society affects the most vulnerable people on the planet; both everyday experience and scientific research show that the gravest effects of all attacks on the environment are suffered by the poorest" (LS 48).

The wealth of the world is concentrated in the hands of a few and the gap between the rich and the poor is ever on the increase.

International and national policies are at place to eradicate hunger and alleviate poverty but because of human greed the earth is plundered in favour of the rich and powerful mindless of acts, laws and policies. If need be, even policies are modified to suit the greed of a few leaving the poor to bleed and cry. Their misery continues in manifold ways. Poverty is taking different forms. Global inequality is ever on the increase because of lopsided development policies. The increase in migration, trafficking, infant mortality, malnutrition, lack of safe drinking water for the poor, homelessness, hunger and misery raises questions against the very notion of today's development. Environmental degradation and social breakdown are interconnected affecting the poor the most.

"We are faced not with two separate crises, one environmental and the other social, but rather with one complex crisis which is both social and environmental. Strategies for a solution demand an integrated approach to combating poverty, resorting dignity to the excluded, and at the same time protecting nature" (LS 139).

In this chapter, the profile of SIGN and its nine partner-organizations is described. The actual physical, social, economic situation under which they have been operating is provided. A description of the organizations is given and the social economic and environmental efforts in the fields of CPRs social capital practices are described hereunder, one by one.

Introduction to Social Initiatives for Growth and Networking (sign), Ranchi

SIGN	Long Term Strategy
Founded	2009
Location	3rd Floor, Social Development Centre, Dr. Camil Bulcke Path, Ranchi (Jharkhand)
Structure	Social Forum of the Catholic Bishops Regional Council of Jharkhand and Andaman.
Staff	12 (Full time)
Area of Operation	Rural and Tribal Jharkhand
Coverage	674 villages and 15 Districts
Project	Implementing through nine partner-Organizations located in different Locations of Jharkhand.
Target Population	Marginalized and Indigent Tribal Groups
Size of Partner-groups:	Nine
Character:	Indian Church-inspired NGO
Director:	Rev. Fr. S. Christu Das

Vision, Mission and Goal

SIGN (Social Initiatives for Growth and Networking) is the official Body of the Catholic Bishops of Jharkhand and Andaman for social concern and human development. It anchors the effort of the eight social service societies of the diocese of Ranchi, Gumla, Jamshedpur, Simdega, Khunti, Daltonganj, Hazaribag and Dumka in promoting a just and humane society based on the gospel values of love, peace, equality and dignity to all. SIGN works with the diocesan institutions in collaboration with Government and likeminded organizations. It came into existence in 2009 with the social concern programmes like NRM, Agriculture, Governance and Inter-religious Harmony. Jharkhand and Andaman are immediate focus areas for operation[11].

A.   Physical

The area where SIGN works in Jharkhand is sub-mountain and land hills sub-tropical as well as mid-hills sub-humid. The area is semi-forested, with deforestation going on. Deforestation, and as a consequence soil-erosion is the major environmental problem in the area. Formerly the tribals made use of the forest in a more or less sustainable way, through collection of forest produce.

B.   Social

90 percent of the covered population of SIGN belongs to scheduled tribes, mainly Oraon, Munda, Kharias, Santhal, Ho, and Paharia. About 764 villages including 211 hamlets are covered, comprising about 360000 inhabitants. There is still not much migration. Some seasonal migration for day-labour takes place during the slack season.

The target group consists of, children, local youth, women and small marginal farmers. The project aims to reach the entire community through training and capacity building, teachers training, rallies, IMI, NRM; education support to children, health in fields vital for self-reliance, The NGO sector working on skill development programme is another target group of SIGN.

Women get more attention in the agricultural and employment generating activities through formatting of SHGs. In health and food processing they get special attention. The target group is organized in traditional Panchayats, with inherited leadership. (Social Capital).

C.   Economic

A main source of income of the population is rain fed paddy. Additionally the tribals grow a large variety of vegetables, pulses and fruits during the rainy season.

The physical condition of the area however does not provide income and food from agriculture for longer than 6 months. Additional income comes from day-labour and forest produce, and remittances.

Tribal families own 3-7 acres of land per family, about 1-2 acres of this is arable.

Modern high yielding rice varieties have almost completely taken over from the traditional varieties. Most of the traditional varieties have been wiped out, because of introduction of HYVs. Not many agro-chemicals are used. Women participate in farm work and are doing most, if not all, of the household activities.

The organization

Vision and Aims

The vision, mission, and goal embrace revitalization and regeneration of local knowledge, the study of cultural and intellectual traditions, and experimentation with indigenous solutions for problems faced by the tribal communities. This is done in the following fields: Kishan Clubs, Traditional medicine, Indigenous wisdom in agriculture, village technology, innovative schooling for rural children and forestry, modern ways of cultivation, etc.

SIGN's policy regarding women empowerment is positive. It tries to integrate women in their existing programmes, particularly through self-help groups of various assets creation activities.

Structure

SIGN is a social-action oriented organization, registered as a social concern and development in 2009. It was founded by the official body of the Catholic Bishops of Jharkhand. The Board of Governing is the highest body.

The campus where SIGN is located is in the premises of Social Development Centre (SDC), which itself is located at Dr. Camil Bulcke Path, Ranchi (Jharkhand). The SIGN is currently funded by grants, donations, and corpus and capital funds sources. It has good working relationships (Social Capital) with a big number of like-minded organizations in Jharkhand and all over India and abroad.

Activities

In brief the main activities of SIGN consist of the following:

1.   Social and Community Mobilization

SIGN with the collaboration of the UNICEF India, has been engaged in social and community mobilization programme in the five priority districts, namely-- Latehar, Palamu, Pakur, Sahibganj and West Singhbhum of Jharkhand since 2014. In fact, the community mobilization for improving child health programme was launched by SIGN with the support of UNICEF India, state government and community members themselves. The coverage through health system strengthening in five high priority districts of Jharkhand is seen in the following Table:

Table 11

District, Block, Partner and Village wise Community Mobilization for the Improving Child Health through Health System Strengthening in Five High Priority Districts of Jharkhand

S. No.	District	Block	SIGN Partners	No. of Panchayat	No. of villages covered
1	West Singhbhum	Jagnathpur	Catholic Charities (CC)	16	165
2	Palamu	Chainpur	Samaj Vikas Sansthan (SVS)	35	183
3	Latehar	Mahuadar		14	104
4	Pakur	Amrapara	Dumka Social & Educational Society (DSES)	10	122
5	Sahebganj	Barhait		22	190
Total				97	764

The implementation of the project has been possible with the local partners Catholic Charities, Jamshedpur for West Singhbhum, Samaj Vikas Sanstha, Chandwa for Latehar & Palamu and Dumka Social and Educational Society, Dumka for Pakur & Sahibganj particularly in the 5 blocks of Mahundarn, Chainpur, Amrapara, Barhait & Jagnathpur. The project focused on 764 villages i.e. 364 new villages and the 300 villages of the pilot phase under the social mobilization spectrum.

2. State Level Trainings and Capacity Building.

This is one of the important activities of SIGN. At the state level capacity building workshops were conducted in a cascading manner for 93 health workers coming from 43 health centres across the same districts. The contents of the trainings were IPC Module, Nutrition, Concept of VHND and its procedure, Routine Immunization, Prevention & Management of Diarrhoea & Pneumonia, etc. SIGN also has conducted many State level trainings on other themes like agriculture, natural resource management, tribal culture, heritage and rights, climate change and ecology etc.

3.   Trainings for Gram Sabha Groups and Villagers

Gram Sabha is the backbone of the village community. It is the main community based organization that gives legal identity to the villagers. Therefore, one of the main concerns was to give input on tribal rights and heritage to the members of the Gram Sabha. Organizing such programmes was not possible without the help of the diocesan directors. The villages where the diocesan directors are operative, those villages were the main focus for inputs though a breakthrough was made in the neighboring villages too because of the interest shown by some of the Gram Sabha members of the project villages. Opportunity was also used to set the concept of Gram Sabha within the governance system of the tribals, which was certainly democratic, participatory, and people centered.

The numbers in the training was not always encouraging though the level of participants was higher as they understood the concept more than others. Most of the members of the Gram Sabha are being used by the PRI institutions for their own advantage. Local governance is taking a back seat and people are losing their innate quality to be leaders of the community. The training programme called them forth to be more diligent in preserving and promoting local tribal leadership to the advantage of the tribal communities.

4.   Training for Self Help Groups and Women

The SHGs are a vital medium to spread important concepts of development. SIGN used this platform of the partner diocese to spread the good news of 'awakening the tribal soul'. Women leaders and SHG members participated in these trainings on tribal rights and heritage. They were very much disturbed by exiting tribal scenario and especially the fate of the youth, who are theirs sons and daughters. They realized that safeguarding the precious values of the tribal community is very important for a better tomorrow of the communities. They vouched to take up the matter in their meetings and work for the preservation and promotion of tribal values and heritage. Many of the women groups all across the dioceses took up this theme of the 'awakening the tribal soul' as the theme for the International Women's Day celebration on 8th March on consecutive years.

5.   Teachers Training

The idea behind providing such types of trainings on basic health and hygiene to the teachers of the area was to enlighten their knowledge so that they can easily become agents of change among the students and their parents during the course of time.

6.   Educational Support to Children

The support is given to 2167 children (mainly tribals) to develop an educational system that reflects indigenous cultural, social and scientific traditions. The system also supports the parents of the children in improved agricultural practices and livelihood options in order to make their agricultural efforts sustainable. The support is also extended to the children in the slums of Ranchi.

7.   Farmers Club and NRM

The intervention through integrated livelihood initiatives and NRM provides unique component of educating, capacitating and awakening farmers towards indigenous wisdom and knowledge of the tribal communities in the sector of agriculture and modern methods of cultivation. About 684 farmers coming from different parts of Jharkhand received 5 days intensive trainings conducted in 19 different batches at KVK, Hazaribag as well as in the partners' places for 1800 farmers. Trainings for farmers and Kisan Mitra are ongoing endeavours. The trained farmers in turn where mandated to train at least two farmers in their neighborhoods. Planting of fruits trees is promoted through provision of seedlings, training in grafting, etc. The well-known Dr. Prabhat Kumar, agricultural scientist of KVK, Hazaribag is developing local rice varieties that give higher yields and are better suited for this environment and SIGN is taking the effort to the field. This is still in a research stage.

Table 12

SIGN with its partners implemented the following in
39 villages of 19 panchayats, 10 blocks and 8 districts of Jharkhand

S.No.	Activities	2011-12	2012-13	2013-14	Total
1	Farm Field Bunding	1228403 cft	141530cft	126427 cft	1496360 cft
2	Nadep Compost Pits	621	00	00	6 21U (384cft)
3	Tree Plantation	11466	606	00	12072 TP
4	Farm Pond	08	01	00	09 Units
5	Loose Boulder Checks	00	85	48	133 Units
6	Renovation of WHs / Percolation Tank	00	08	10	18 Units
7	Construction of WHs / Percolation Tank	00	03	00	03 Units
8	Provision of Vermin, Wash, Azolla	00	61	00	61 Units
9	Provision of Soil Test	00	429	389	818 F
10	5% model of rain water harvesting system	00	00	18	18 Units
11	CCT & SCT	00	01	00	01 Acre
12	Renovation of Pond	00	01	01	01 Unit
13	Organic Farming Fencing	00	00	01	01 Unit
14	Renovation of Well	00	00	20	20 Units
15	Land Leveling	00	00	01	01 Unit
16	Provision of Seed Distribution	00	00	504 F	504 F
17	Construction of New Pond	00	01	00	01 Unit

Source: Annual Reports of SIGN, 2011-2014.

8. Adolescent Health

SIGN has been pioneering in supporting the health personnel of the faith based organizations engaged in health mission in the rural areas of Jharkhand. The support ranges from the publication of Standard Treatment Guidelines (2 editions); cascade trainings on the use of the STG; handholding help for resetting the health centres as per the requirement of the Clinical Establishment Act; organizing capacity building programme on various relevant health topics, especially adolescent heath etc. SIGN took it very seriously and through the interested partners formed 'Saheli Sangathans.' across Jharkhand, especially in the districts of Gumla, Latehar, Palamau and Dumka.

9. Creating Awareness through Rallies

Rallies are other features of the intervention to mobilize and create awareness among people. Rallies are collaborative effort of SIGN partners, Government departments, PRI members, communities, and schools to bring awareness in a larger way. 40 such rallies were organized with different themes on special health days. The rallies were organized with prior permission from civil surgeons and other district authorities. UNICEF and the government health departments supported the rallies by supplying playcards, banners and pamphlets on special health days. Government officials, PRI members and schools took initiatives to organize special rallies on the occasion of IDCF. Rallies were good tools in spreading awareness among the village communities especially on child health.

10. Awakening the Tribal Soul

The campaign "Awakening the Tribal Soul" across the state of Jharkhand is one of the major interventions of SIGN implemented through the support of the partner organizations. The main focus of the intervention was to recapture for the tribal folks their rich ancestral traditions, socio-cultural heritage based on equality, sharing, fraternity, democratic governance, natural connectedness to nature etc. along with their rights and entitlements. SIGN conducted more than 1395 workshops covering

207464 plus people. Preservation and promotion of the cultural nuances and rich tribal ethos was the focus of mission, 'Awakening Tribal Soul'. SIGN also published 3 booklets in Hindi to support the intervention: 1. The Fifth schedule, 2. Tribal Heritage and Rights, 3. The Important Adivasi Heroes of Jharkhand. 4. Powers of the Gram Sabha as per PESA Act. The movement to awaken the tribal soul has received a positive response.

Effects

a.   Social effects

As stated above that SIGN is a people oriented social concern and human development training and research organization. Its effects have to be assessed in terms of the quality of knowledge based on programmes developed and designed by SIGN for the target group and transfer of the same to the partner organizations and other NGOs working in the same setting. Programme activities don't aim at and actually don't lead to a big impact on local organizational structures and power relations in the village. However, SIGN has a conscious policy of working with NGOs, local organizations and groups who focus their work on such structural change. Thus SIGN indirectly contributes to the social process in areas in which it has expertise. The contributions are following:

1.   Alternative approach to primary health care based on exploration of local herbal resources and local knowledge of people.

2.   Method for building viable cooperatives for food, technology based on forest resources applicable for all tribal areas.

3.   The intervention SCM through health system has made a definite impact in ensuring sustainable health care for the rural poor by creating social capital through the involvement of Teachers, Village Volunteers, SHG Leaders and members, PRI members, traditional leaders, Religious leaders, school children and community members who received different levels of training on child and maternal health. They have gained knowledge and

have learnt to play leadership roles in the community ensure a smooth functioning of VHND.

4. Tribal awakening and socio-cultural leadership

Through these programmes self-reliance and self-confidence of the tribal community is strengthened, while the need for external medical help and finances to pay for this is kept on a low level.

b. Economic effects

The forming of Farmer's Clubs for various village technologies is considered a valuable way to organize the tribal population into productive units. The same applies for the farmers' approach to cultivation and choosing livelihood options.

These undertaking are now virtually self-supporting. With these projects SIGN has proven to be able to set-up viable economic units that can sustain their functioning making use of locally available techniques and inputs.

The linkage of the Farmer's Clubs unit with the promotion of vegetables and fruit-trees in home gardens and orchards creates income, employment and is a contribution to a self-reliant economy. At this time of development no clear indication as to the potential long term economic effect in term of employment creation and income generation are available, more work remains to be done if the effect is to be measurable beyond the pilot project stage. The vegetables and traditional paddy cultivation might face difficulties in marketing its products, the scale of production is not yet so big to face immediate difficulties but more market-research and a restriction to well marketable products and technologies is advisable.

Of particular interest is the efforts made by SIGN to develop local rice varieties that can give comparable yield to that of HYVs. Its big advantage is the fact that it is developed in such a way that propagation through cloning and hybridization can be done by the farmers themselves, making them less dependent on external inputs and proving them with productive species, adapted to local circumstances. As this is still in an experimental stage, little can be said about the realized economic impact.

Trying to get an overall picture of the social and economic effects of SIGN' work one should realize that its social and economic effects become mainly visible in an indirect way. Through the strengthening and further development of indigenous and locally appropriate practices, the social and economic position of the tribal population in the study villages is made stronger in relation to forces that try to exploit the tribal's labour, assets and natural resources. Also the tribals are in a better position to make use of modern techniques coming from outside their community on their own term, making a fair comparison and/or combination of local and external or "modern" techniques and resources. It is noted that SIGN, although strongly promoting indigenous, locally available resources, certainly has no hostile attitude towards external "modern" practices. SIGN is conscious of the importance of choice of technology and its implication for those who control it.

c.   Environmental effects

The development of traditional medicine appears to incorporate a revaluation of the existing natural flora, thereby raising people's awareness about the importance of the natural environment, making a direct link between human health and the need for environment protection.

The introduction of modern methods of cultivation, although still on a modest scale, combined with the development of farmers' club units may lead to a sustained use of forest (fruit trees) resources, thereby protecting the existing natural forest and at the same time promoting the plantation of additional fruit bearing trees. It may be clear that a sound and healthy forest is of utmost importance to the tribal population to provide an economic base for development and at the same time prevent soil erosion. The long-term environmental effects of SIGN' activities may be such that a further erosion of natural and intellectual resources is prevented, promoting further revitalization of the tribal-community.

STORIES OF CHANGE

1. Volunteerism graduates Pramila

Pramila Baskey from Village Dobdiha, Panchayat Baramasia, District Sahibganj served as a Village Volunteer within the framework of the project, "'Social & Community Mobilization for Improving Child Health through Health System Strengthening". She joined the team of volunteers in 2015 and was relentlessly serving the cause of the women in the village. She participated in two trainings organized in Barhait block of Sahibganj district by the project team. She excelled in learning all about RI, diarrhoea, pneumonia management, promotion of balance diet and the other components of the project. She took it on herself the responsibility of educating the women of the village on the importance of immunization, the various services available in the VHND, colostrums & exclusive breast feeding, institutional delivery, nutrition etc. She went door to door, meeting women and striking a conversation with them on these subjects of importance. She also extended her help to Sewika Shanti Murmu and ANM Sunita Gupta on VHND days as there was no Sahiya in the village. She would remain at VHND centre till its closure for the day. The villagers, the front line workers and BTT did recognise her enthusiasm and dedication and requested her to be the Sahiya of the village. She happily agreed to be the Sahiya and continued to serve the community. Officially, the Gram Sabha during its meeting held in the village on 5th November 2016 decided to appoint her as the Sahiya and all formalities were completed in the presence of the frontline workers and BTT. Pramily Baskey is an inspiring example of volunteerism in the service of the other. A school drops out after class 4 graduated to be a Sahiya because of her passionate commitment to the cause of the women without counting the cost.

2. Action speaks louder than words

Mr. Mahendra Oraon, aging 50 and above hails from village Masmno of Mandar Block in Ranchi District. He is a marginal farmer and like the other farmers of the area was cultivating vegetables by way of traditional methods during *rabi* and *kharif* seasons. Unfortunately, the products did not fetch proper price in the competitive market because of the quality of the vegetables. The investment sometimes exceeded the profit taking into account all the inputs including free labour. He was rather disappointed with the efforts.

He had an opportunity to undergo training on quality agriculture and other livelihood options organized by SIGN. He understood the problems in not getting quality products even after hard labour and clarified the concepts on soil test, seed processing, pest management etc. After the training he began with the cultivation of French beans in a small plot applying the learning. He was surprised at the yield as well its quality. He got better price for his products in the market. This motivated him to start cultivating cauliflower in his field. Again to his astonishment and of the villagers each cauliflower almost weighed 1.5 kg and looked very healthy. His product dictated the market and he earned good money. His hard work continues but the story is always not rosy because of the lack of irrigation facilities and the erratic rains. He has set an example for the villagers that hard work coupled with clarified knowledge brings success. He set an example by doing, not just speaking. Action speaks louder than words.

3. Gram Sabha can make a big difference

The village Baromasia in Hiranpur Panchayat, P.S Barhait, Dist–Sahibganj, of Jharkhand State has 158 families with a population of 483

persons. SIGN had launched a program on child health connecting the pregnant and the lactating mothers with the VHND conducted in the villages on a stipulated date by government facilities. The finding by the project staff on a door to door visit in the villages showed that there were 20 dropout and 15 left out children from regular vaccination. On inquiry, it was found that the appointed ANM was not coming to the village for months. People could not understand the reason for her continued absence, nor were they bothered by her absence as they did not have much idea about the importance of ante-natal, post-natal checkups, immunization, colostrums feeding, exclusive breast feeding etc. The project staffs felt that before approaching the ANM to find out the reasons for her absence the village community should be educated on these subjects. Therefore, they made a request to the village Gram Sabha on 14th January 2015 for a Gram Sabha meeting and was finalized to hold the meeting on 21st January 2015. The concerns around child health were discussed from the perspective of one thousand days continuum care. The Gram Sabha was convinced about the importance of child health and decided to approach the ANM to request her for regular VHND in their village. Meanwhile the ANM who heard about the meeting realized that before the Gram Sabha members reach her house she should visit the village and clarify the issue. Her problem was the tough terrain and transportation. Her reasoning was accepted but with the promise of the Gram Sabha to extend all required support, the ANM was very regular for the VHND. All the drop outs and left outs got the vaccination and everything got regularized. Gram Sabha can make a big difference even in mission ANM.

4.   Right communication brings about transformation

Amrita Kumari, the 02 years old daughter of Krishna Choudhry and Sandhya Devi from Village & Panchayat Rabda, Rabda 3 VHND site, Block Chainpur, District Palamu was born at home and was given no vaccination. It was her first pregnancy and delivery and she was hesitant to go for checkups during pregnancy. Her in-laws were also not aware of the need of ante-natal checkups and the need of vaccination. A Rally was organized in this village on International Breast Feeding Day, 28.08.2016 and again after three months a Nukad Natak was staged on 24.11.2016 explaining the importance of immunization, the services available in the VHND and the other related topics. Amrita's parents also witnessed both the programs. Interestingly, the programs had their impact on the couple and on 7.01.2017 VHND day they brought their daughter Amrita to VHND site setting aside all the myths. They met ANM Meera Kumari and told her they have brought their daughter for immunization. ANM was very happy as she too was aware about the negative attitude of the couple. The rallies and the Nukas Nataks became effective tools of communication and the ANM was impressed by the increased number of children in her VHND Centre.

5.   Neighbours' envy and an inspiration

Mr. Dimister Minj and wife Esther have 5 children. They are from Barisa-

Nakti village in Asni Panchayat of Gumla District, Jharkhand. Dimister, a marginal farmer was engaged in the cultivation of his land in the most conventional way. The family had a hand to mouth existence. He received an opportunity to participate in 5

days residential training program organized by SIGN, Ranchi in Holy Cross Krishi Vigyan Kendra, Hazaribag. The training was an eye opener in his life as a farmer.

Mr. Dimister came back home as an enlightened person. He was willing to take risk and apply the learning in the field. He gave up random cultivation of vegetables but adapted to market demand, explored irrigation possibilities, took up soil treatment, seed treatment, selection of good seeds, use of organic manure with minimum chemical fertilizer etc. as per the guidelines. Many of the other farmers were skeptical of his exploration but the determined Demister continued with his efforts.

His determination and the application of the learning gave more life to the soil and the outcome was seen in the produce. He scaled up his efforts and engaged in multiple agricultural activities earning within a year an income of Rs. 150,000.00 after all the expenses and labour inputs. He became the neighbour envy and inspiration.

6.   Self Help from Self Help Group

Pratima Devi Singh of Rangigocha village in Anandpur block of East Singhbhum district is a member of Adarsh Jagriti Mahila Samiti of which Meena Devi is the president. Devendra Singh, the husband of Pratima Devi is an awakened person too. Both of them have been participating  in many of the workshops conducted by SIGN in partnership with Catholic Charities, Jamshedpur on Natural Resource Management, Self Help, Livelihood Options, Rights, Entitlements etc. The impact was that supported by her husband Pratima Devi Singh applied for a loan for Self-Employment under the Prime Minister Self Employment Scheme.

She received Rs. 300,000.00 with a subsidy of 35% and the loan to be returned within 5 years with 13% interest. She has already bought from Balasore, Odisha, 6 machines for making leaf plates and leaf bowls with a generator and a stabilizer.

The production has already started and they are getting order from neighbouring markets. However, Pratima or Devendra has to undergo training in Ranchi for furthering their skill and to be certified to be in the business which they are planning to undertake shortly. The leaves for both plates and the bowls come from forests because of which almost 100 people can earn their daily bread and 10 people can get job directly under them. They have believed fiercely and the machines will do the rest.

7. Determination gives wings to life

Mrs. Sumi Soren of Kalapani village from Dumka District of Jharkhand state faced lot of problems due to economic uncertainties. She lived in a small hut. She worked as a daily wage labourer and managed to make a small saving with the SHG in her village. The members were very sympathetic towards her and gave her a loan to engage in agricultural activities in her own field. The members also directed her to undergo training in KVK Hazaribag organized by SIGN, Ranchi. She readily  acknowledged the offer and was a proactive student in the KVK for 5 days. She equipped herself with fresh knowledge and skills. She already was endowed with sufficient attitude towards life. She is a competent person now and dared to apply all her learning in her field. The fields yielded good crop and Sumi could fetch an income from the local market. She learnt the art of making a life for herself without going out as a daily labourer. She refunded the loan and has become an active member of the SHG. She managed to pull down the dilapidated hut and make a better house for the family. Her determination has given wings to her life.

8.   Basanti Devi becomes Basant (spring) for Mahilas (Women)

Basanti Devi, from Bahranpur of Gurhet Panchayat, Sadar Hazaribag block, District Hazaribag is a member of Jagriti Mahila Mandal that

has 12 members. The group was linked to Jharcraft since 2009 through the FCC sisters working in collaboration with Jan Vikas, the Hazaribag partner of SIGN. They are mainly engaged in embroidery. Jharcraft purchases their products. Each woman using their free time at home is able to make an earning of Rs. 1000 to 1500. Basanti Devi because of her smartness in embroidery and hard work became a trainer. She has already given training to 5 batches of women earning Rs. 4000.00 per training. Her neat and beautiful handiwork on

embroidery has earned her many awards including a national award for the exquisite embroidery on a saree depicting the natural beauty of Jharkhand. The 'Daynik Jagaran', a daily carried an article on her on 21.02.2013 under women's empowerment section announcing the national award. She is holding the same in her hands in the picture. She also received certificates for her good work on 26.03.2010; 05.12.2012; 28.01.2013, one of which is held by her. Thus she has become the inspirational spring for the women in the neighbourhood and project area

9.   Farm bunding made quality difference in their lives

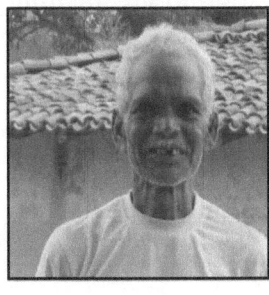

Mr. Julius Kullu of Obira Mahato Toli in the project area of Gumla partner was all smiles when he said that he has benefitted much because of the farm bunding carried out in 3 acres of his land. 'Erosion is reduced much and water stays in the new fields' he said. He managed to cultivate upland paddy which gave yield 5 times more than early days (160 kgs of paddy before and this year (800 kgs now). He also cultivated ground nuts and got 200 kgs. He cultivated tomato, spending Rs. 300.00 on seeds and manure. He received a profit of Rs. 2000.00 after family use and a generous sharing with neighbours while Mr. Bijay Kullu managed to get a profit of Rs. 5500.00 on tomato spending just the same amount of money on seeds (5gram) and manure.

The farmers have joined together in the village and they make their own nursery of tomato saplings. They feel very content and happy today though when farm bunding work had started in the village they were not sure of its future benefits.

10.   United with a purpose

Mr. Theophil Tigga hails from village Brambey, panchayet Brambey, block Mandar, district Ranchi. He began his income generation activity running a small hotel but then took to agriculture. He cultivated paddy as well as pea in his agricultural land. He also tried his hands in cultivating some vegetables. The work was more causal until he took training in 2015 organized by SIGN thorough Catholic Charities, Ranchi. The perspective changed and he became more earnest with his involvement. He used the knowledge gained in the training and

field responded to him. He went more for organic manure. Recently he cultivated cabbage, capsicum, cucumber, beans and green chilly in his land on a large scale.

The training scaled up his activity and from 50-60 dismal he cultivates now in 2 acres of land. His effort also got the attention of the government and he was given equipment for drip in 2016. He could budget water for irrigation using the facilities. He followed all the skills and the techniques while adhering to organic farming. The market opened up for his produces and he could demand a price in the market. Inspired by him 6 other farmers of the village also managed to get drip irrigation facilities. The initiative had a great influence on many farmers and gradually 22 farmers under his leadership are cultivating vegetables, paddy and other crops as per the learning gained during the training. They formed into a Kisan Group and have become a strong force in the village. They managed to bring electricity to the village and are using electric motor for lifting water for irrigation. He has become a natural leader in the village for all the sections of the people. Agriculture has changed his life and the life of the village. He has established that the impossible is possible when united with a purpose.

DUMKA SOCIAL AND EDUCATIONAL SOCIETY, DUMKA

Dumka Social and Educational Society, Dumka	
Founded	1981
Location	DSES office is located at the campus of SDC, Dumka Santhal Pargana, Jharkhand
Structure	The Social Forum of the Diocese of Dumka
Staff	9
Area of Operation	Dumka, Sahibganj, Pakur, Jamtara Districts of Jharkhand
Coverage	300 villages
Project	Formal; DSES is the implementing Agency
Target Population	Marginalized and Indigent Tribal Community
Partner-groups	Of SIGN
Character	Indian Church-inspired NGO
Director	Rev. Fr. Sonatan Kisku

Aims and Objectives of DSES

Initially, DSES was engaged in different kinds of activities geared to the uplift of tribal poors through formal and non-formal education, balwadis for the children, sponsorship, vocational training, natural resource management, watersheds, mother and child health care, alternative health care, community health work, malaria and kala-azar control programmes, education for the prevention of HIV/AIDS, self-help groups, women's empowerment, micro-finance activities, socio-economic development, cultural promotion, emergency relief service and such. After 2006, DSES started taking some new programmes apart from the above activities such as food self-reliance and livelihood resilience through agriculture practices, NRM by formation of Farmer's club; SRI methods of cultivation, etc.

Situation

a.   Physical

Dumka Social Educational Society (DSES), Dumka is a NGO active in Pakur, Sahebganj, Jamtara and Dumka Districts of Santhal Parganas Division of Jharkhand. The physical situation of the area is characterized by a monsoon climate giving an average rainfall of 1050mm/year. Most of the original forest has been removed. At the time of independence in 1947, 66% of this division was covered with forest. Now only eight percent is left, unevenly distributed. In the Blocks where DSES is most active, forest cover varies from 6 percent to 9 per cent.

Rainfed paddy is the main cultivation. 50% of lowlands are under paddy, pulses and maize. The other 50 percent lays fallow and is used for grazing.

Soil-erosion caused by rapid deforestation, removal of stones, and improper cultivation is a major environment constraint. Also, drought and erratic rainfall make agriculture risky and little productive.

b.   Social

80-85 percent of the people belong to scheduled tribes in the operational area of DSES, Dumka. Seasonal migration takes place to coal field and places where agriculture labour can be found. Young people are said to migrate more permanently to towns.

The project's target group consists of marginal farmers and landless families. In some programmes special or exclusive attention for women is given.

c.   Economic

The main source of income is rain fed agriculture (paddy). Other sources are: quarrying, mining, rearing of animals and collection of forest produce. 70 percent of the populations are small and marginal farmers, owning not enough land to feed their families. Modern farming, using HYV's and chemical inputs, is not commonly practiced. Government and commercial enterprises promote the use of HYVs. However they are often not made available in time. This has brought some farmers into serious problems.

Activities

DSES undertakes an extensive set of activities:

a.   Organization of women, SHGs

DSES spearheaded in the formation of Self Help Groups in this area forming more than 1100 plus groups in 602 villages. Each group had its own name and independent identity. The groups took up saving, inter-loaning, bank-linkage, micro-credit activities, livelihood collective actions while taking literacy classes under the pioneering effort of DSES called 'STAG (Skill Targeted Academic Growth). Enlightened couples from each village were trained on Crisis Management and Conflict Resolution adapted to the context and they in turn settled most of the domestic fights. The women also played decisive roles in the promotion of education through the number of Balwadies initiated by DSES and the prevention of malaria. The Mahila Committees put effective pressure on local government for education and health facilities, provision of drinking water and road construction. A saving and loan fund has been established and totally managed by the respective Mahila Committees.

b.   Total Eradication of Kala-azar

Dumka Social and Educational Society (DSES), Dumka having received a report about the 13 Kala-azar caused deaths within 4 months in Burudih, a village in Dumka District in 2005 and another report of 47 deaths in 2 consecutive years in Kalyanpur village, Shikarpara block, Dumka district began a massive program to address this issue. It signed a tripartite Memorandum of Understanding in 2006 with the Jharkhand Health Society (JHS), Ranchi, and Catholic Relief Service (CRS), Ranchi and roped in Dr. Amitabha Nandy, a research expert in the subject from CENTROMAP, West Bengal to be the technical consultant and resource person and identified 14 Hospitals in the district of Dumka, Pakur, Sahibganj and Godda to network in the effort to eradicate Kala-azar from these districts which are the Kala-azar endemic districts of Jharkhand. DSES conducted search camps, advocacy meetings with all its community-based organizations, especially the Self Help Groups to identify the Kala-azar affected persons, worked in very close proximity with the government health facilities and the 14 hospital-network under the very able guidance of Dr. Amitabha Nandy with the aim to eradicate Kala-azar from Jharkhand following the method of institutional treatment and care. Within the period of 2006 - 2011. DSES managed to get 3981 patients treated and fully cured admitting them in the selected 14 hospital networks under the tripartite agreement and 3336 patients referred from the search camps to the Hospital. Today, Kala-azar is almost non-existent in Jharkhand thanks to this major effort conducted under the proven assumption that human is the only known reservoir of the infection and the treatment of maximum number of patients would open up the possibility of containing the disease and even eradicating the same.

c.   Natural Resource Management

DSES initiated activities through the SHGs and the Farmers clubs for the right management of the natural resources locally available by capacitating them in water budgeting, quality agriculture, organic farming, pest management, social fencing etc. The farmers put into practice the concept of social fencing by guided pasturing of cattle during vegetable cultivation; budgeting water for cultivation and other village needs, broom making, leaf plate making when leaves are plenty on the trees, organic farming etc. One of the major interventions was using the backyard of the house for nutrition garden, or kitchen garden to promote green intake during meals. The programs had their effects captured in many reports of the projects and could be also seen in many of the villages.

Effects

a.   Social Effects

As many of the activities of DSES are specially targeted at women, the effect on women may be particularly interesting. The SHG programme is directly improving the economics and social condition of 465 women in these selected villages, especially landless, since they are the specific target group for this programme. The danger of overburdening the women exists but DSES seems to be well aware of this and landless women have little work in agriculture, as they do not have their own fields.

The 'Self Help Group' among women of DSES has the possibility of gradually increasing the participation of women-beneficiaries in decision making. It increases their claim making power regarding government as some examples have shown in Chapter – 4. In the long run they will gain a better bargaining power within the family and community.

The training of women in various economic and social activities will have concrete effects on the beneficiaries as DSES' women extension workers are working among women beneficiaries.

The children education centers are likely to improve the relation between the extension workers, village volunteers and the target population (Social Capital). There is also the possibility of awareness rising about the ill-effects of deforestation, harmful land use and use of available natural resources.

The combined effects of various environment oriented activities like Afforestation, ecological agriculture and horticulture could work as a collective action (Social Capital) to improve their resources. It is noteworthy to maintain that DSES aims at development, based on the needs and the capabilities of the target group. The speed with which new activities are taken up or extended is therefore very much dependent on the outcomes of genuine target-group participation. This at the same time guarantees – as far as possible – that the result of DSES's action will be lasting.

b.   Economic Effects

The economic effects of income generating activities of DSES are tangible. Increased employment opportunities for the target population, better wages and prevention of migration of women to urban centers.

The credit position of women is improved as women can contribute to and draw upon a common fund for emergency needs. This will perhaps not affect the total economy of the village, but it will contribute to the improvement of the family economy since most of women's income will be used for the improvement of the family. At the same time, it enhances community feeling and self-management.

Introduction of Ecological or Low External Input Agriculture will in the long run help the local farmers. Presently, the farmers get insufficient income from their land to support their family. One of the aims of the Kisan Club programme is to improve the yield of the farmers. It has already been observed that one technique (using green manure) has resulted in increase in yield; a better land use planning to improve the soil, water harvesting and other ecological farming methods will increase the output per unit area. This also will reduce the external inputs substantially, like costly irrigation, chemical inputs, etc., thus helping the farmers financially. The introduction of fruit trees and poultry will also increase the income of the farmers.

Furthermore there is the possibility of creating agro-based cottage industries (e. g. Seri-culture) which will generate employment and income.

c. Environmental effect

Income generating activities generally do not aim at improving the environment or preventing environmental degradation. The extension and training programme in ecological agriculture and the introduction of agro-forestry have long term effects on the environment. This specific project (Farmer's club) has started only recently the mission was not able to give a definite assessment of its environmental effects.

Changing over to an ecological farming system is possible in the region for the following reasons:

1. As there is little irrigation presently and farming is mostly rainfed, modern agriculture has not damaged the environment and affected the cropping pattern as much as in other areas. People of the area still practice some of the ecologically sound techniques as was done traditionally.

2. Deforestation appears to be a major factor in the environmental degradation of the area, causing soil erosion, depletion of plant diversity and causing water scarcity. There is a scope for influencing and arresting this trend as DSES had taken steps in the right direction by introducing Afforestation and ecological agriculture.

3. As forest and agriculture are both ecologically linked and economically supportive to the people, the twin efforts will lead to better and sustainable resource management at village level. Specifically it will lead to a search for techniques of water conservation, soil protection, creating diversified plant assets

and integrating different aspects of the environment for the benefit of the people.

GRAM UTTHAN KENDRA, GUMLA

Gram Utthan Kendra (GUK), Gumla	
Founded:	1992
Location:	Gumla Diocese Premises Dist. Gumla (Jharkhand)
Structure:	Governing Body of the Catholic Bishop of Gumla
Staff:	17 field staff
Area of Operation	All blocks of Gumla and three blocks of Simdega in Jharkhand
Coverage	418 villages through 23 Wisdom Councils
Project	Implementing agency
Target Population	Marginalized and Indigent Tribal Groups
Character	Indian Church-inspired NGO
Director	Rev. Fr. Mark De Brouwer S. J.

Gram Utthan Kendra (GUK), Gumla

SITUATION

a.   Physical

The area is undulating and in some parts hilly, nearby the river plain. There are little irrigation facilities. The water of this irrigation scheme is allocated to other parts of the region.

b.   Social

Women have equally hard work in agriculture as men, and are responsible for household work, collection of fuelwood and drinking water. The role of women in community decision making is meager, through the Wisdom Council's discuss common issues in joint meetings of men and women.

c.   Economic

Agriculture is the main source of income. Most of it is rainfed. Some farms have irrigation, using perculated water flowing through cannals and rivers. Main crops are paddy, maize, pulses, oil seeds, and other cash crops. Cash crops are increasing over the last 10 years.

20% of the population is landless, 50% of the landholders own less than 2.5 acres, 20% between 2.5 and 5 acres. Off-farms employment, stone cutting, vegetables and fruit selling. Seasonal migration takes place.

ORGANIZATION

VISION AND AIMS

Gram Utthan Kendra was registered as a Diocesan office at Gumla in 1994 with the following aims and objectives:

1. Conscientisation of target groups of the area towards participatory development;

2. Facilitating skill development training of the development youths;

3. Providing irrigational facilities to the marginal farmers.

The establishment of village Wisdom Councils therefore is central in GUK's policy. A good organizational structure and a better use of the existing agricultural potential through land reclamation form the basis on which the development of the area should take place. Social, economic and equal participation of women and men is considered an important aspect of development. Women's issues are also addressed through Wisdom Councils. GUK's agricultural policy takes the existing farming practices as a starting point. As stated earlier these farmers in the area are familiar with hybrid seeds and chemical inputs since long ago. In case of land reclamation GUK provides these inputs in the form of loans. Reduction of external inputs and increased use of organic manure is taken up later in training programmes. In GUK's view the first crops from reclaimed land should give positive results and confidence to the farmers. Experiments with organic manure etc. should therefore be taken up at a later stage only.

STRUCTURE

There is a director and staff consisting of 15 paid staff members and 12 (8 male, 4 female) village animators. The 70 village animators get a small remuneration for their work and are responsible for training and giving assistance to Wisdom Councils and in literacy training.

ACTIVITIES

GUK's activities are spread over in 418 villages with 3824 beneficiaries. The main activities of GUK consist of the following:

a. 1050 irrigation projects were completed since 1994. Each irrigation project enables seven families to gain cash income through vegetable cultivation just after the paddy harvest is completed.

b. 108 new irrigation wells were constructed during 2016-2017.

c. 106 young people were trained in different trades as per local demands on a higher income. The trades were carpentry, bamboo furniture manufacturing, tailoring, two wheeler mechanics, and electronic electricians.

d. Accessing welfare schemes: total 1316 beneficiaries benefited from different schemes provided by JTDs, Pradan, Krishi sewa Kendra, ATMA, and government of Jharkhand during 2016-2017. The schemes and the beneficiaries benefited through were construction and renovation of 315 ponds; Construction of 349 goat sheds; 312 chicken sheds; 7 pig sheds, 23 for weed-laborers 131 for seeds; 40 for fertilizer; constitution of toilets (15220; new houses (927); wells (168).

e.   Training activities: Training is given to village-animators and farmers. Subjects are: poverty and its cause, cultivation methods and organic manuring, formation of farmer's clubs etc. 107 agriculture seminars with 4359 participants were organized by GUK from 1994 to 2018.

Procedure for performing responsibilities

1.   Four step were adopted Under conscientisation of target group strategy:

    a.   Character formation seminars

    b.   Agriculture Seminars

    c.   Local evaluation by Wisdom Councils

    d.   Report to GUK Supervisors' Meeting.

2.   The selection of villages for the cause rested on their willingness and capability to form unity and production groups. GUK could select 4 such groups. The number of trainees was near the planned number of 69 participants till date. The subjects were: Self-analysis, Environment analysis, group influencing, Goal setting, Time management, and general goal of life.

3.   The sustained attention and the demand for more were surprising. It shows a real thirst for wisdom and knowledge. The results show increased production of paddy (SRI method) and especially the adoption of cash crop in all irrigable parcels. The increase in production of vegetables is phenomenal. The marketing is done in local bazaar where the demand is always to buy.

4.   Regular fortnightly meetings were held at 23 wisdom councils. The council meetings regroup the council committees and their supervisors. They planned the seminar dates on the villagers' demand. They summoned the desired instructors on the fixed dates. This independent manner showed their progress in taking responsibility for council events. Minutes of each meeting were recorded and a copy forwarded to GUK for further reporting.

5. The main training centre for skill development of dropout youths is at IRI Bariatu – Institute for Rural industrialization. From 1977 to 2016, 12000 youths were trained in different trades with the object to be independent entrepreneurs in their own rural environment.

6. The best system turned out to be local sources run by councils. This reduced expenses (Social Capital) as trainees are trained in their own neighboring or in their own village. 5 councils organized 6 months training for tailors mainly girl trainees. 50 were trained. Some have tailoring groups and other transport their machines to the local bazaars and earn income there.

7. Sources of water are mainly large wells, since the water in paddy fields where monsoon rain flows above or underground since ages. Some three weirs were built specially in Petitoli, where water and enthusiasm both (CPRs and social capital) are in abundance. Some villages managed to divert rain water during the rainy season from the hillsides. These irrigation are all immediately successful for 7 to 50 families, an example is given below.

EFFECT

SOCIAL EFFECT

The developmental activities have succeeded in the establishment of 23 Wisdom Councils in the villages in which GUK is active. The functioning of the council has certainly strengthened the bargaining power of the community vis-à-vis governmental institutions. Examples of positive results can be found in the tapping of government subsidies, implementation of housing

programmes and drinking water projects, etc. Equally significant is the confident approach to Government schemes and the cooperation (social capital) with any other local NGOs. The results were impressive due to the active participation of the Wisdom Councils.

In the villages councils have settled disputes and have taken action on atrocities against women. Successful pressure has been put to increase local wages. An indicator for the internal strength of the council is the regular saving habits and the proper records of meetings and SHGs loans. As women and men are organized in order to use council as a platform to express their needs and to discuss common issues among themselves.

Communication and negotiation between men and women of the area is in an advance stage. Although regular joint meetings are held, the men's point of view remains dominant. Regarding the sharing of costs and benefits from the activities undertaken, women have something to gain and something to suffer. Women however will no doubt have to do more work on the fields reclaimed for their families, reducing their abilities to earn an independent income from day-labour, forest produce, etc.

An interesting effect of the organizational work of GUK is the establishment of a Wisdom Council. This council has taken up important common issues. The Council has become an influential institutions or resource (social capital) in the area. It can take-up pressure roles, a function that GUK would not be able to perform.

ECONOMIC EFFECTS

The main economic effect of GUK's programme comes from land-reclamation activities. Land-reclamation increases the self-sufficiency of small and marginal farmers have to supplement their meager farm income with insecure day labour or resort to seasonal migration. GUK's training programmes try to reduce risks and to secure a reasonable crop. Small scale irrigation facilities and contour-bunding are used on the reclaimed lands. The other economic activities are taken up: cattle-rearing and wage earning. This indicates also a concern for the landless and mitigates the unequal benefits from the wages.

GUK's training and extension activities in the field of agriculture aim at maximizing the use of vermincomposed by promoting the use of organic manure. Apart from its ecological effects, the shift to organic manure reduces the dependency on external inputs. Consequently, the need for external credit and the risk of continuous indebtedness in case of crop-failures is reduced.

GUK has worked out the following analysis to show the difference between traditional farming of paddy and the system of maize and pulses. If only maize is grown, the farmer's net income may run at a loss of Rs 210 per acre if the farmer uses inter-cropping (maize/pulses) the net results may go up to Rs 2000. – Per acre.

ENVIRONMENTAL EFFECT

The use of HYVs, fertilizers is common in the area. GUK takes up this issue in training sessions for village-animators and farmers. It tries to introduce a 'moderate modern technology' using dung or vermicompost as manure. The yields in the first year went down but have gradually equaled and eventually even surpassed the earlier figures.

Training and demonstration of intercropping patterns may have lead to risk reduction and better control over pests and diseases. The author could not quantify however to what extent this has reduced the application of agro-chemicals. The increased market-orientation of agriculture in the area and consequently the cultivation of cash-crops may lead to a seriously outflow of nutrients, endangering the sustainability of farming in this region.

CHANGES

INDIVIDUAL AREA

1. Farmers' families have realized through character formation seminars that they have multiple resources at hand, which

necessitate a proper use of their time. A change appears to be that examples of well gardening are imitated. This paramount in "keeping people busy" and out of mischief.

2. Priority of pride is taken by the cooperation with other NGO's like PRADHAN, JTDS, SIGN, SANJIVANI, etc. Council leaders have acquired the self-confident to intelligently cooperate with whatever is offered to them by these NGO's and getting immediate benefits. This is very valid also for Government projects from NABARD, ATMA Fishery department, Land leveling office. Whole groups go regularly to Ranchi for fishery training. This has become an ongoing programme. On the long run, it is stable leadership that counts. (Social Capital).

3. GUK achieved a permanent system of rural organization. Individual goodwill has grown into a network of rural leadership in the form of social capital.

   This network creates trainers: character trainers and agricultural trainers. They are capable of conducting seminars that change tribal villages from different impoverished tribals to self-confident leaders of their community.

   Training centers were created in the councils for skill training of village drop-outs.

   Examples of irrigation schemes were created that can be imitated in every tribal village.

   Model night schools are now organized and financially self-supporting. This model is spreading to neighboring council areas.

The author concludes that regarding the social aspects, GUK has been quite successful in establishing an impressive numbers of wisdom councils in the area. This council forms a good basis for further action in the various fields. With the combination of more ecologically sound farming techniques and the use vermincomposed, GUK has increased the economic potential of lands belonging to marginal farmers. Regarding environmental issues, a sound approach is adhered to; through it may be advisable to devote more time to the pre-appraisal and monitoring of possible environmental effects of land-reclamation and watershed management.

VIKAS KENDRA, SIMDEGA

Vikas Kendra, Simdega	
Founded	1993
Location	Vikas Kendra, Simdega P.O. Gotra-835223 (Jharkhand)
Structure	Governing Body of the Catholic Diocese of Simdega
Staff	5
Area of Operation	Simdega District
Coverage	13 villages at present
Target Population	Women and children, Youth Marginal farmers, Rural Artisans
Character	Indian Church-inspired NGO
Director	Rev. Fr. Kishore Lakra

VISION

Vikas Kendra, Simdega, visualizes a just, well-educated and empowered society based on the human and Christian values (love, justice, peace, harmony, equality and dignity)

MISSION

To build up an awakened, well organized and disciplined society that safeguards the human and constitutional rights and interests of all the classes of the people of this area specially the women and children, youth, tribals, dalits and backwards with the collaboration of the church organizations, institutions and likeminded Govt. and Non-Govt. organizations.

GOAL

To build up a just and humane society.

Situation

a.   Physical

Vikas Kendra, Simdega (VKS) is a NGO active in Simdega, District of Jharkhand. The physical situation of the area is characterized by a monsoon climate. Most of the original forest has been removed. At the time of independence in 1947, 46% of this region was covered with forest. Now only two percent is left, unevenly distributed. In the Blocks where VKS is most active forest cover varies from 4 percent to 6 percent. Rain fed paddy is the main cultivation.

"Project on Natural Resources Management": The geographical condition of the diocese of Simdega is highly undulating. There is no option left besides doing single cropping due to acute dependency on monsoon and lack of irrigation facilities. Major portion of rainwater flows away. To bring some relief in such situation there is a need of soil and water conservation measures. Vikas Kendra has taken up a project supported by Caritas India and SIGN Ranchi for developing Self Governance through Right Based Approach in NRM in Jharkhand. It is being implemented in Bolba block of Simdega District. Goal of this project is promoting diversified sustainable livelihood by developing self-reliance and self-governance in NRM through right based approach in Malsara and nearby villages Bolba Block.

b.   Social

80-85 percent of the people belong to scheduled tribes in the operational area of VKS. Seasonal migration takes place to coal field and places where agriculture labour can be found. Young people are said to migrate more permanently to towns in Secondary Sector i.e., construction. The project's target group consists of marginal farmers and landless families. In some programmes special or exclusive attention for women is given.

c.   Economic

The main source of income is rain fed agriculture (paddy). Other sources are: rearing of animals and collection of forest produce. 80 percent of the populations are small and marginal farmers, owning not enough land to feed their families.

Activities

VKS undertakes a few sets of activities:

a.   Organization of women, SHGs

Vikas Kendra worked in many villages in the past years and built its activities around Self Help Groups among women and they all have been graduated having their linkage with bank and other government initiatives. The effort of Vikas Kendra has created this linkage. Now there are few groups with Vikas Kendra though it is not concentrating much in this area as most of the groups are linked with the government run programs especially on livelihood and micro-credit activities.

b.   Natural resource Management

Vikas Kendra too was very actively involved in Natural Resource Management in the rural villages of Simdega District especially in Malsara area. They supported the farmers on water conservation measures, forest protection, farm bunding, land leveling etc. The farmers were very much supported by these interventions. They were also capacitated in many areas like pest management, organic farming, SRI, SWI, vegetable cultivation, kitchen garden etc. Many farmers are trained and the number would go beyond 500. Today these farmers are organizing themselves into farmers clubs.

Simdega also initiated many programs on tribal rights and entitlements to equip the tribal population all about the provisions in the Constitution of India and in the law of the country which are in their favour focusing too on the rich heritage of the tribal people.

Effects

a.   Social

As many of the activities of VKS are targeted at women, the effect on women may be particularly interesting. The SHG program is directly improving the economics and social condition of 165 women, especially landless, since they are the specific target group for this programme. The '*Mahila sabha*' concept of VKS has the possibility of gradually increasing the participation of women-beneficiaries in decision making.

The training of women in various economic and social activities will have concrete effects on the beneficiaries as VKS' women extension workers are working among women beneficiaries. The children education centers are likely to improve the relation between the extension workers, village volunteers and the target population (Social Capital). There is also the possibility of awareness rising about the ill-effects of deforestation, harmful land use and use of available natural resources.

b.   Economic Effects

Introduction of Ecological or Low External Input Agriculture will in the long run help the forest dwellers and local farmers. Presently, the farmers get insufficient income from their land to support their family. One of the aims of the Kisan Club programme is to improve the yield of the farmers. Furthermore there is the possibility of creating agro-based cottage industries (e. g. Seri-culture) which will generate employment and income of the family under VKS coverage.

c.   Environmental effect

It is true that the extension and training programme in ecological agriculture and the introduction of forestry have long term effects on the environment. This specific project (Farmer's club) has started only recently the author was not able to give a definite assessment of its environmental effects.

During the survey author observed that the deforestation appears to be a major factor in the environmental degradation of the area, causing soil erosion, depletion of plant diversity and causing water scarcity. There is a scope for influencing and arresting this trend. As forest and agriculture are both ecologically linked and economically supportive to the people, the twin efforts will lead to better and sustainable resource management at village level.

HOFFMAN SOCIAL SERVICE SOCIETY, KHUNTI

Hoffman Social Service Society, Khunti	
Founded	1994
Location	At P.O. Khunti Dist. Khunti
Structure	Governing Body of Khunti Diocese, Jharkhand
Staff	7
Area of Operation	Murhu, Torpa, Karra, Arki and Khunti Blocks
Coverage	46 villages
Target Population	Marginalized and Indigent Tribal Groups
Character	Indian Church-inspired NGO
Director	Rev. Fr. Xavier Topno

Vision

To build a disciplined, organized and developed community based on Gospel values-love, justice, peace, service and cooperation.

Mission

To ensure social justice, integrated and substantial development of all strata. Especially the poor, marginalized, tribal and DALIT (a lower caste) of Khunti Catholic Diocese through collective efforts of various organizations, departments, religious organizations, government and non-government institutions.

Goal

Strengthening the Civil Society to enhance their standard of living by proper management of natural resources and through active involvement in making the system at village level work for the people in Jharkhand.

Situation

A.   Physical

Hoffman Social service Society (HSSS), Khunti is located at Kunjla, 4 kms from Khunti, the district headquarter. Physical area is characterized by a monsoon climate covered with forest. In the block where HSSS is operation, the forest coverage is 8-12 percent. Soil-erosion caused by rapid deforestation, removal of stones, and improper cultivation is a major environmental constraint.

B.   Social

- Munda tribes are found in the operational area.
- The project's target group consists of marginal farmers and landless families.

C.   Economic

60 percent of the populations are small and marginal farmers, owning not enough land to feed their own families. Modern farming, using HYV's and chemical inputs, vermin composting are being practiced in Rabi, Garma and Kharif crops.

Activities

a.   Training of SHGs for income generating activities.

b.   Training in livelihood promotion.

c.   Training in livestock management.

d. Training in Lac cultivation

e. Extension cum training in ecological cultivation

The HSSS has been engaged in Natural Resource Management activities in many villages of its operational area capacitating the village folks in reclaiming wasteland, land-leveling activities, bunding, check-dams and renovation of ponds. The farmers are being organized into Kisan Clubs and they are given training on various aspects of quality agriculture. More than 475 farmers already trained in SRI, SWI, organic farming, preparation of organic manure etc.

f. Health education is another major area where HSSS is working in 25 villages in Khunti District through Self Help Groups especially in malaria control efforts through preventive and promotive methods. The women are given training on health and hygiene, cleanliness and herbal practices. Kitchen Garden is another major component in the intervention for balance diet.

g. Training in entitlement

h. Training in social audit and family budgeting.

Effects

A.   Social Effect

As many of the activities as stated above are target oriented. These effect on women, children and on diverse field of social life. The SHG programme is directly improving the economy. The children education centers are likely to improve the relation between the extension workers, village volunteers and the target population (Social Capital). There is also the possibility of awareness rising about the ill-effects of deforestation, harmful land use and use of available natural resources. The combined effects of various environment oriented activities like Afforestation, ecological agriculture and horticulture could work as a collective action (Social Capital) to improve their resources.

B.   Economic Effect

The economic effects of income generating activities of HSSS are both tangible and intangible, increased employment opportunities for the target population, better wages and prevention of migration of women to urban centers, etc. the credit position of women is improved as women can contribute now to draw upon a   SHG's fund during crisis period. Agriculture, so far used to be only for self-sustenance, is now viewed as one of the main income generating activities. Presently, the farmers get insufficient income from their land to support their family. One of the aims of Kisan Club programme is to improve the yield of the farmers.

C.   Environmental effect

The extension and training programmes in ecological agriculture and forestry have long term effects on the environment. This specific project (Farmer's Club) had started only recently the objectives of HSSS were not able to give a definite assessment of its environmental effects.

JAN VIKAS KENDRA, HAZARIBAG

Jan Vikas Kendra (JVK), Hazaribag	
Founded	2006
Location	Jan Vikas Kendra P.O. & Dist. Hazaribag (Jharkhand)
Structure	Governing Body of JVK, Hazaribag
Staff	27
Area of Operation	Hazaribag, Kodarma, Ramgarh, Chatra, Bokaro Districts
Coverage	288 villages: 5 Districts
Project	Implementing Agency at the Grass Roots.
Target Population	Marginalized and Indigent Tribal Groups
Character	Indian Church-inspired NGO
Director	Rev. Fr. Tomy A.J.

Vision, Mission and Goal

Jan Vikas Kendra Hazirabag (JVK) is a NGO working on human trafficking and other related issues for the welfare of ST/SC women. And develop practical but scientific mode of rehabilitation for them. To establish a network to combat Human Trafficking and develop scientific and realistic mode of rehabilitation centre for trafficked children and women. The JVK has been engaged in different kinds of activities related with CPRs Social Capital geared to the uplift of the poor through balwadis for the children, sponsorship, vocational training, natural resources management, watersheds, mother and child health care, alternative health care, community health work, self-help groups, women's empowerment, micro-finance activities, Socio-Economic Development, cultural promotion, emergency relief services and such. After 2006, JVK started taking some new programmes apart from the above activities such as food self-reliance and livelihood resilience through agriculture practices, NRM by formation of farmer's club, SRI methods of cultivation, and to combat trafficking of children and sexual abuse.

Situation

a.   Physical

JVK is an active NGO in Hazaribag Division of Jharkhand. The service area of JVK has spread in more than 100 villages of Bokaro, Ramgarh, Chatra, Koderma and Hazaribag district.

b.   Social

Seasonal migration takes place to coal field at Bokaro and Ramgarh, Micafield at Koderma and other places where agricultural laborers are found. Young people are said to migrate more permanently to Kolkota and Asham.

c.   Economic

The main source of income is agriculture. Other sources are: rearing of animals and collection of forest produce. 70 percent of the populations are small and marginal farmers, owning not enough land to feed their families.

3.   Activities

1. Better livelihood option through agriculture.

2. Construction of check dam and water harvesting tanks.

3. Training of famers on SRI, SWI.

4. Training on domestic product preparation through SHGs.

5. Legal training for village committees.

6. Campaign against human trafficking through street plays.

7. Skill training for the trafficked victims.

Awareness programme for people in the village

Various trainings, workshops, rally and street plays regarding trafficking have brought awareness in the people and there is considerable improvement and understanding in the people and in the society as a whole.

Legal training for village vigilance committee at District level

The members of vigilance committee appreciated the initiative taken by Jan Vikas Kendra on this issue of rescue and rehabilitation of the trafficked victims. Various short movies and power point presentations were shown to the members to strengthen them and to have clear understanding of the topic towards child labour and rights to education, etc.

Campaign against Human Trafficking through street plays

The street play team was very active and they used the local language of the people to make them understand about the issue on trafficking, migration, fake marriage, importance of education, ill effects of alcohol, etc.

Skill Training for the Trafficked Victims

During our visit to the villages and having good rapport with the people we have realized that due to poverty and other reasons many children drop out of from the school and for their survival they get involved in the house of the rich people or in any hotels for work. JVK has conducted skill development training for 35 victims who were rescued from trafficking during the reference year.

Effects

A.   Social

As many of the activities of JVK are specially attempted against human trafficking and rehabitation of women and children in Jharkhand, the effect on women may be particularly interesting. JVK had constructed two check dames in the operational area. Besides the same number of water harvesting tanks were constructed. The training of women in various economic and social activities have concrete effects on the beneficiaries.

The children education centers are likely to improve the relation between the extension workers, village volunteers and the target population (Social Capital). There is also the possibility of awareness rising about the ill-effects of deforestation, harmful land use and use of available natural resources.

The combined effects of various environment oriented activities like Afforestation, ecological agriculture and horticulture could work as a collective action (Social Capital) to improve their resources. It is noteworthy to maintain that JVK aims at development, based on the needs and the capabilities of the target group.

B.   Economic Effects

The economic effects of income generating activities of JVK are tangible. Increased employment opportunities for the target population, better wages and prevention of migration of women to urban centers are helpful for them.

The credit position of women is improved as women can contribute to and draw upon a common fund for emergency needs. This will perhaps not affect the total economy of the village, but it will contribute to the improvement of the family economy since most of women's income will be used for the improvement of the family. At the same time, it enhances community feeling and self-management.

Introduction of SRI and SWI methods for cultivating the crops will in the long run help the local farmers. Presently, the farmers get insufficient income from their land to support their family. One of the aims of the Kisan Club programme is to improve the yield of the farmers. It has already been observed that one technique (using green manure) has resulted in increase in yield; a better land use planning to improve the soil, water harvesting and other ecological farming methods will increase the output per unit area. This has reduced the external inputs substantially, like costly irrigation, chemical inputs etc. thus helping the farmers financially by reducing transaction costs (Social Capital), the introduction of fruit trees and poultry have also increased the income of the farmers.

SNEHADEEP, HOLY CROSS, HAZARIBAG

Snehadeep, Holy Cross, Hazaribag	
Founded	2005
Location	Holy Cross Institute, Holy Cross Road Hazaribag-825301 (Jharkhand)
Structure	Governing Body of HCCCC, Hazaribag
Staff	11 (Male-5; Female-6)
Area of Operation	Hazaribag, Giridih, Kodarma
Coverage	35 villages: 3 Districts
Target Population	25000 (Poor, Vulnerable & Marginalized
Character	Indian Church-inspired NGO
Director	Sr. Britto H.C.

Genesis, Origin and Growth

Snehadeep Holy Cross is a unit of Holy Cross Institute, which is registered under Society Registration Act 1860 on 2005. Snehadeep was the first health center in eastern India desiccated to HIV and AIDS patients. Initially the services were started at Sitagarh in 2005 with a small health center for the HIV/AIDS patients later due to increased inflow of the patients a need was felt for a full-fledged hospital which turned shape as a Snehadeep Holy Cross Community Hospital.

Vision

We envisage a healthy society where people especially the poor and marginalized live in harmony with creator, self, with one another and with the environment.

Mission

- Improving the life of PLHIVs.
- Collective effort and support in providing health services.
- Developing responsible management, competent, and client – centered personnel and in providing appropriate technology to maximize its benefits to stakeholders.

Objectives

- To show compassion for all, serve preferentially the poor, the vulnerable and marginalized.
- To empower health care needs and access health care rights.
- To promote health care and prevention of diseases in communities.
- To facilitate spiritual assistance

Activities

- SHG groups
- Children's club

- Mushroom cultivation

- Skill development training programme

- Vocational training

Snehadeep Holy Cross, Hazaribag (SHCH)

SHCH was established as Snehadeep – Care Centre on 14th February, 2005 to give Services to people living with HIV and AIDS, with its vision of improving the life of PLHIV and AIDS, Sitagarha, Hazaribag. Formally it was started in Holy Cross Convent, where we got two rooms, one dining room, one Kitchen room, 10 beds for patients. It was a humble beginning where we could accommodate only 12 patients and with 2 doctors, 2 counselor, 3 nurses, 5 health workers and 6 outreach workers. The number of the patients increased in number we had no other choice than constructing a hospital where we admit and take care of them. In the middle of March, 2009 we shifted to Tarwa. It was the first centre in Jharkhand State.

SHCH started facility for orphan and partially orphaned children living with HIV/AIDS. It is an attempt to comprehensively address the multiple issues of HIV infected children so as to prepare them for productive and constructive lives by providing them with protection from stigma and discrimination in the absence of their near and dear ones. In a nurturing environment, children are provided with educational and recreational opportunities, adequate nutrition, health care and psychosocial support.

Major achievements are as follows

- This is the first Community Care Centre for PLHIV in Jharkhand state started in 2005.

- Collaboration with state govt. AIDS Control Society in 2006.

- Establishment of HIV/AIDS Awareness wing in 2006.

- Formation of Jharkhand State Network for PLHIV with the help of Jharkhand Sate AIDS Control Society.

- Initiated the formation of District level and Block level networks for PLHIV.

- Establishment of 11 Drop in Centre in 4 districts.

- Formation of legal Aid Cell.

- Getting two times "A" grade rank from National Aids control organization (NACO).

- Residential School for Children living with HIV/Aids.

- 3600 new PLHIV has been registered in the centre and getting treatment.

Challenges Today

We are running the Community Care Centre (CCC) under the National AIDS Control Programme (NACP-II) since 2006. Under this programme we are providing care, support and treatment services for people living with HIV/AIDS of Jharkhand State. Till 31st March 2013 total 3600 PLHIV directly benefited through this programme. Under the National AIDS Control Programme (NACP-IV) there is no provision for medical treatment for the people living with HIV/AIDS from 1st April 2013. As we know that stigma and discrimination associated with HIV/AIDS are the greatest barriers preventing infected people from getting adequate care, support and treatment and thus alleviating the impact and spread of HIV/AIDS. Through several years of working experience with PLHIV we have realized that the most the PLHIV don't want to avail care and treatment services from public health service delivery points because of the following reasons:

- There is still stigma & discrimination exists in the Medical Sector.

- No confidentiality is kept in a common ward.

- A very sick HIV positive woman is in the waiting room with her children. Because her in laws threw her out of the house and she has no place to go.

CATHOLIC CHARITIES SOCIAL SERVICE SOCIETY, RANCHI

CCSSS, Ranchi	
Founded	1982
Location	Post Box No. 05, Dr. Camil Bulcke Path, Ranchi-834001 (Jharkhand)
Structure	Official organ of the Archdiocese of Ranchi
Staff	Project Staff- 6; Supporting Staff-11 (Male: 7; Female: 4)
Area of Operation	Ranchi and Lohardaga District
Coverage	150 villages
Project	Formal; Implementing Agency
Target Population	Marginalized and India Tribal Groups
Character	Indian Church-inspired NGO
Director	Rev. Fr. Anil Kujur

Vision

To establish a just and humane society especially through empowerment of the disadvantaged in particular of women and children.

Mission

To serve the unprivileged tribal, dalits and the marginalized sections of the region.

Objectives

- To perform works of charity for the benefit of those in need and in particular to bring to victims of natural or other disasters, such as drought, famines, floods, fire, epidemics, riots, wars etc.

- To engage in an promote social service and community development, without distinction of caste and creed through self-help methods, establishing a just order, creating a spirit of national pride and civic sense, leading to integral development of men and to a true and complete humanism.

Broadly speaking, Catholic Charities Ranchi has been engaged in various activities such as (i) "Swadhikar" which is Right based project, (ii) Food Self Reliance and Livelihood Resilience through Agriculture Practices, integrated livelihood initiatives and Natural Resources Management by Capacitating farmers, (iii) Awareness creation towards Promotion of Livelihood (iv) Community Based Natural Resources Management and Integrated Livelihood Promotion, (v) Providing Employable Skill training for Migrating and Trafficked Tribal school dropout Youths. Catholic Charities had been trying to empower unprivileged Tribals and marginalized farmers of the region particularly women and children.

Problems in the Past

Agricultural was the only source of livelihood option for the people. Once the paddy cultivation got over people used to move out from the villages in search of job to the cities. People used to go to the brick kilns in search of labour and sometimes even stay for months to ear an income. Families migrating in search of job left the education and health of their children in tatters.

Situation after the intervention of Catholic Charities

Catholic Charities supported the people for making check dams and other irrigation facilities as irrigation was one of the major issues. The intervention became a great success and people began to have water almost throughout the year for cultivation. Therefore, they took to vegetable cultivation having received training on the same. They started vegetable cultivation like tomato, potato, pea, gram, wheat, cucumber, brinjal, pumpkin etc. Agricultural products are sold in the

nearby market Bero, Pisca Nagri and Lapung and thus marketing the vegetable is not a major issue. 16 farmers do vegetable cultivation throughout the year. The irrigation for the vegetables is carried out with the help of diesel water pumps and electric pumps. The difference in the economical and livelihood activities has put a hold on migrations and farmers stay at home and cultivate in their land. They are able to take care of the education of their children too.

Construction of Check Dams with Collective Action

Three check dams were constructed by Catholic Charities with the help of villagers in the year 2006. The three check dams were named as Masia

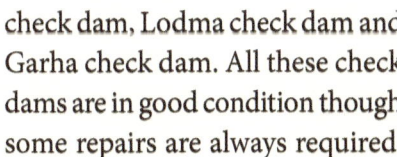

check dam, Lodma check dam and Garha check dam. All these check dams are in good condition though some repairs are always required.

Protection of Community Forest and Grazing Lands

People started getting their basic needs through agricultural goods and pet animals. The community has good cooperation with one another as a result the community forest is managed and protected well. The community detailed on different aspects the condition of the people before intervention of the Catholic Charities Ranchi. Villagers did not cultivate throughout the year nor do grazing of cattle. There were number of people migrated to meet their basic requirements. Children's education was hampered. People were addicted to alcohol with poor health condition. So it could be said that the community was not in peace and harmony.

Catholic Charities also took up renovation of ponds and construction of loose bolder check dams and such activities which have supported the farmers in different ways to increase their livelihood. Many of the farmers are now in Kisan Club working together for their wellbeing.

SAMAJ VIKAS SANSTHA, CHANDWA, LATEHAR

Samaj Vikas Sanstha, Chandwa, Latehar	
Founded	1998
Location:	Samaj Vikas **Sanstha**, P.O.Chandwa Dist. Latehar-829203 (Jharkhand)
Structure	Governing Body consisting of 7 members, Chair Person – The Bishop of Daltonganj Catholic Diocese
Staff	12 (Full time)
Area of Operation	Rural and Tribal Jharkhand
Coverage	3 Districts: 249 villages
Project	Formal
Target Population	Marginalized and Indigent Tribal Groups
Size of Partner-groups	Nine
Character	Indian Church-inspired NGO
Director	Rev. Fr. Alphonse Bakhla

Samaj Vikas Sanstha (SVS), Chandwa Latehar

1.   Situation

A.   Physical

The operational area of SVS is the Palamau region consisting of the three districts of Latehar, Palamau and Garhwa. This region has a monsoon climate (June-October) with an average rainfall of 600-700 mm/year. Variation in rainfall is very high, with occasional sudden heavy rains and long dry spells during the rainy season itself. Severe droughts are common, with a drought occurring approximately every 3 years. The area has an altitude of 500-1000 m, with 22% hilly terrain. The soils are relatively deep and fertile. Severe droughts and erratic rainfall are considered to be the main environmental constraint in the area. Soil erosion and degrading fertility of the soils structurally affect the potential for productive agriculture.

B.   Social

Most of the people in the area are small and marginal farmers (65%); 26% possesses no land; 50% of the landholders have less than 5 acres of land. Seasonal migration to places like Kolkata, Delhi, Mumbai and to states like, Kerala, Karnataka, and Haryana are a common practice. 68 percent of the population belongs to tribal communities. SVS reaches out at the moment to 249 villages. Landless and marginal farmers are the target group. Official Panchayats exist but are of little relevance to the existing problems.

C.   Economics

The main source of income is rain fed agriculture. A relatively wide range of crops is grown: paddy wheat, pulses and fruit trees, allowing two crops a year. Modern, High Yielding varieties (HYV's) are commonly used. Both men and women have active tasks in agricultural work; apart from this women carry a heavy workload in the household.

2.   The Organization

Vision and aims

Strengthening the civil society to enhance their standard of living by proper Natural Resources Management and through active involvement in making the system at village work for the people in Latehar district in particular and Jharkhand, in general.

It is SVS's conviction that the bad agricultural situation, the poor economic assets, bad infrastructure and negligence from government's side has kept most of the villages in the area deprived from any form of economic or social development. Instead, social structures fall apart (migration), the environment deteriorates and poverty is widespread. SVS's objective is "to make the people realize themselves, through actual demonstration that they can look after their basic economic needs, through collective efforts."

It wants to teach people how to reduce their dependence on the monsoons, and how to enhance their agricultural production through introduction of better methods and better inputs. Pressure should be put on government to take up issues related to the rural poor. In SVS's analysis, political or class-related issues are made explicit. But SVS does not promote of approve of confrontationist attitude with the government, but only tries to connect the people directly to the various welfare steps introduced by the government. Their approach is basically one of area development: To promote economic development and social justice in the area through demonstration and assistance.

With regard to agriculture, SVS's tries to enhance this economic position of the farmers by giving them better access to the required inputs, credit facilities and setting up water-catchment and water-management schemes. Farmer's organizations (Farmers Club) are established to implement these activities and to take over more responsibilities gradually.

Women are given special attention in the regular programmes, through special women's activities. Some institutions were also found to be existing such as Mahila Mandals (Self Help Groups), destitute women's home, supplementary income scheme and training for income generation, free legal aid and family counseling. Furthermore seminars for women activists and rallies are organized.

Structure

SVS is a Christian-inspired NGO, founded originally in 1969 with the name Catholic Charities. It was founded in response to the severe drought that hit the Palamau region in late 1960s. It was mainly involved in relief work. Later it started working with food for work programme supported by CRS (Catholic Relief Service) and went on to create cultivable paddy and agriculture fields along with water bodies. Later in 1993, the organization was formally registered with the name, Samaj Vikas Sanstha, under the Societies Registration Act. The organization has a General Body and a Governing Body that meets twice during the year. The Director assumes the main responsibility for both the day-to-day running of the organization as well as its policy directions with the approval of the Governing Body.

The organizational set-up is basically structured along its main programmes: Rural development, Health programme, Women development. It must be noted that some of the "Higher" positions are occupied by women. Staff members generally have quite high levels of education.

3.   Activities

SVS had started working in villages like - Sons, Bullu and Kita in Sassan Panchayat, in the villages of Chetag Panchayat, in villages like Saidup, Mayapur, Aksi, Musurmu and others for many years. In Sons, and Kita villages, SVS had been working on and off from 1998. In these villages, forest committee was formed and SHGs for women folk were organized during the year. Besides community-based organization were formed for collective action and for collective farming during the period number of activities like land leveling, creation of water bodies, training programmes, etc. were taken up.

The main activities of SVS are the following:

Target group participation takes place through work on the construction of dams, wells and plantations (for which food or wages are paid) and a financial contribution of 10-20% to the costs of purchased investments (mainly pumps). To date 230 community wells and 136 check dams were built in the area. A demonstration plot of former barren wasteland demonstrates the potentialities of good water-management, irrigation techniques and erosion control.

a. Skill Training: Training programme for Driving and mechanics, Nursing Assistant, electric motor winding, carpentry and masonry have been conducted. This programme provides training in technical and life skills, and makes the candidates fit for life and fit for job, leading to credible source of livelihoods.

b. Women's programme: This programme aims at enabling women to have a meaningful co-existence and respectable life in a male dominated society. It gives refuge to destitute women, provides free legal aid, gives vocational training and tries to rehabilitate destitute women, socially, psychologically and economically.

c. Children's programme: In 37 villages Balawadis (kindergarten) are established with community participation. Such study centres in villages enable children to study and receive guidance in their studies. Furthermore there are 30 playground and recreation centres. Cultural and games tournaments are conducted every year.

d. Primary Health care: This programme provides health education, basic curative and preventive health care through mobile clinics, and training of mid wives. Family planning is promoted and eye operation camps (cataract) are carried out. Herbal plantation is done in some villages for eradication of iron deficiencies and vitamin A. 25 village women from different villages are trained as mid-wives, who assist deliveries.

Effects

A.   Social effects

The most important achievement in the social field is the establishment of 'Farmers' Clubs' consisting of marginal farmers in each of the villages of SVS's project area. This organization is the springboard for most of the activities designed to improve the economic and social well-being of the villagers. The organization's committee plays an important and decisive role in the selection of the beneficiaries for the various projects introduced by SVS. It maintains intensive contacts with the village-level workers and looks after timely repayment of loans. A special forum has been created by SVS to pressurize government departments for starting development programmes in the hitherto neglected small villages and hamlets situated in the hilly terrain.

B.   Economic effects

As 90% of the area in which SVS works is drought-prone, the water-related activities such as community wells, lift irrigation and check dams have been a good choice to enhance the economic situation of the farmers.

These activities have boosted the rural micro-economies in several ways: Provision of temporary labour (work on well, dam); waste-land cultivation, ability to produce a second crop and prevention of seasonal migration are some of them.

Many of these activities made earlier investment from the government, productive and beneficial to small farmers. e.g. (dams built under EGS).

While trying to improve productivity in agriculture through improved methods, SVS has also insisted upon minimum use of chemical feritilizers and has encouraged farmers to use organic farming methods to ensure sustainability of soil fertility. The provision of chemical farm-inputs may have given a rise in productivity though it is doubtful whether this can be maintained in the long run.

C.   Environmental effects

SVS has made a significant contribution to stem environmental degradation in the project area, by prevention of soil-erosion through improved rainwater conservation measures including surface run-off control. The prevention of soil-erosion has facilitated agricultural based economic development through lift irrigation systems installed on community wells as well as replenishment of groundwater resources.

The large-scale provision of fertilizer may however endanger the fertility of the soil in the long run. This already has the risk of exporting too much organic matter from the area. The high level of fertilizer use may further deplete soils with essential nutrients and endanger its texture and structure.

SVS introduces environmentally friendly techniques in the area such as alley-cropping, use of tank silt, organic manure and soil-conservation. This however seems to be a somewhat fragmented approach. A more comprehensive view on sustainable land-use could be developed. The team has witnessed a growing interest from SVS's side into this matter.

SVS's demonstration plot on farmer waste-land and the experimental Afforestation programme, have promising implications for a sustainable area development, as already many villages have shown keen interest.

In the social field SVS has established an effective participatory structure for its activities. It has achieved a lot also for destitute women. Economically SVS has significantly enhanced the situation of many marginal farmers. Both the economic and the environmental sustainability of these agricultural activities need more attention. SVS is advised to further elaborate a comprehensive view on the environmental implications of agriculture in this area. Training and consultation will be necessary.

CATHOLIC CHARITIES, JAMSHEDPUR

Catholic Charities, Jamshedpur	
Founded	1970
Location	Patel Bagan, Sundarnagar Jamshedpur Jharkhand
Structure	Governing Body of the Catholic Bishops of Jamshedpur
Staff	21 including field Staff
Area of Operation	East and West Singhbhum, Saraikela, Kharsawan Jharkhand
Coverage	131 villages: 3 Districts
Project	Implementing agency
Target Population	Marginalized and Indigent Tribal Groups
Character	Indian Church-inspired NGO
Director	Fr. Alwin C.V
Director	Rev. Fr. C. R. Prabhu

Vision Mission and Objective

Vision: A just and Humane Society based on the Gospel values of equality, love and peace.

Mission: To uphold the human dignity of the oppressed and marginalized through a process of empowerment.

The Catholic Charities, Jamshedpur (CCJ) works towards evolving and developing a just and human society where each person is accepted and respected as a human being, and treated with dignity, values of equality, fraternity and freedom are nurtured and nourished, and atmosphere of peace and harmony is maintained and where people live in dignity, collectively shaping their own dignity.

Development here is understood not as accumulating more or having more but of people being more, just concerned, cooperative, healthy, educated, more sharing and caring, self-planned and self-reliant, thus being more human.

Goal

To bring about the KINGDOM of GOD in the society we live in and the people we work with. It means working towards building up of a JUST SOCEITY.

OBJECTIVES

- To promote first and foremost the development of human being irrespective of caste and creed, giving special attention to the under privileged and poor section of the society, specially the tribals, dalits and the marginalized.

- To give people faith in themselves, hope to improve their condition, understanding of their duty and responsibility towards others, especially towards their own village community and their broaders neighborhood (district, state and country)

- To help the communities to realize that they alone can bring a lasting change in their own conditions and to motivate them to do so

- To develop and train those human talents and resources which are latent in every community, always aiming at in the integral development of the human person, which includes peace, justice, freedom, brotherhood, self and mutual respect.

- To sponsor and promote, socio-economic development activities especially those which encourage self-help hard-work and thrift, develop skills, know-how and competence leading to increased production and better the economic status of the rural communities, priority being given to those projects which benefit people directly over those which go to strengthen institution, without excluding them however, create a spirit of national pride and civic sense, leading then to integral development of persons and to a true and complete humanism

- Undertake rehabilitation, relief and welfare work, for the benefit of those in need, particularly victims of natural and other calamities such as drought, floods, famines, epidemics, war etc., whether in the territory of the society or outside of it, as the situation demands.

Programmes

Soil and Water Conservation

In this context, CCJ aims to enhance the productivity of crops by developing soil fertility and water restoration for irrigation purpose.  Its strategy emphasizes on 'Ridge to Valley approach' for land and water development. Over the years, CCJ has gained vast experience of developing micro watershed in areas like Tonto & Chakradharpur in West Singhbhum district and Kuchai & Chandil in Seraikela-Kharsawan. This strategy has generated awareness among community for conservation of their own resources by mobilizing the community for cost sharing either in cash or kind.

Agriculture

Catholic Charities worked with small and marginalized families struggling for food security for entire year. Despite of having cultivable land, they lacked guidance and support for interventions to convert their land from semi productive to better productive land.

Paddy is the main crop cultivated by the farmers in the working area. The efforts taken by CCJ in motivating families to learn sustainable way of cultivation has changed the scenario. Capacity Building programs, Technical training with demonstrations of cash crop cultivation, mixed cropping, promotion of organic manure and networking with agriculture departments at Block and District level have increased the statistical data for families who turned out their production for 6-9 months to 12 months. CCJ helped the farmers to prepare resource planning and seasonal calendar to diversify the crop production. Now families take up vegetable cultivation, pulses cultivation, cultivation of oil seed and nutritional garden. Technical training inputs were also given to the women involved in field. There are more than 150 Self Help Groups that have adopted cultivation in group.

The micro water programmes have turned out 30% of barren land into cultivable land. CC also has helped the famers to raise finances from government and other institution. Organic farming in the area motivated SHG women to adopt selling of organic manure as an enterprise.

Women Empowerment

The organizational strength of 609 Self Help Groups are visible in the area and others are also learning from the efforts of women. With the passage of time mother-in-law and daughter-in-law are members of same groups. This reflected the attitude of understanding and openness among women. The organization always highlighted extraordinary success by ordinary women to encourage others. The continuous process of capacity building changed the simple women to courageous women who now raise their voice for the welfare of vulnerable people

Women Cooperative

The seed of Self-Help Groups has grown into 12 Cooperatives. In hard to reach area like Manoharpur, Tonto, Chakradharpur, women walked 7-8 kms to attend cluster level meeting of SHGs. The joy for progressing unitedly is visible in the efforts made by women in the area. 7385 women taking part in various development activities in family and society is indeed an accomplishment. They emerged as successful volunteers who are helping the needy.

3 SHG cooperatives namely Nav Chirag Mahila Bachat Evam Sakh Swalambi Sahkari Samity, Manoharpur and Jharna Mahila Bachat Evam Sakh Swalambi Sahkari Samity, Chakradharpur, West Singhbhum are registered as credit and Sarswati Sakh Swalabi Sahkari Samity, Chakuliya, East Singhbhum is registered as small enterprise development organ.

The members of Cooperative are getting easy credit for the purposes like education, business, livestock rearing and collective farming. 65% women are involved in Income Generating Activities. They are earning Rs. 5000 to Rs. 12,000 which is an additional income in the family. These women are directly becoming part of social and economic changes in the communities.

Governance

The constitutional body at village level has its own significance. It provides electoral platforms where people can meet and discuss their common problems, and consequently, understand the needs and aspirations of the community.

Panchayati Raj Extension in Scheduled Area Act (PESA) came into existence in Jharkhand in the year 2010. The organization has played a vital role in establishing Coordination between Traditional Gram Sabha Leaders and elected Panchayat Level Leaders under PESA Act.

Capacity building programs, workshops and booklets helped in generating awareness among leaders, elected members and villagers about their roles and responsibilities in Gram Sabha. The Gram Sabha meetings which were conducted only for the sake of sanctioning schemes under 'Top to Bottom Approach' is changed to 'Bottom Up' approach. Planning was done by the villagers during Gram Sabha meetings, approved by the executive committees which further submitted to the Block Office through Panchayat Samity members.

This practice has created confidence among villagers about tapping of schemes on time. The State Government of Jharkhand initiated 'Yojna Banoa Abhiyan' as preparing planning in Gram Sabha which was successful in the project area due to awareness of men, women and youth about process of preparing plan.

Health
The organization uses its resources mainly Health Care Centers existing in rural areas for spreading awareness on health care measures. The Nurses in the centers have taken responsibility to reach out every single family in connection with achieving the motto- HEALTH FIRST.

Mother and Child Health Care
The organization always promoting health awareness classes during SHG meetings where women gathered for meeting. Focus was given on strengthening of Village Health Nutrition Day by mobilizing women and children with Adolescent to avail health services. The counseling of pregnant mother and family members with health care trainings transformed into positive action.

Adolescent Health
The organization believes in holistic development of the society. It has designed interventions together with Adolescents to address issues like sexual and reproductive rights, child marriage, out of school adolescent, malnutrition and anemia, menstrual hygiene and consequences of substance use.   6508 households having 4466 Adolescent Girls and 4243 Adolescent boys are part program.

Malaria Control Program
Reduction and control of incidents of Malaria has been always one of the main concerns of Catholic Charities Jamshedpur, for it is working in the malaria prone area. It has generated awareness to on Human- Vector control for minimizing transmission of malaria, access to the appropriate malaria diagnostic, treatment and referral services in their villages. The intervention includes regular health education activities, street play and trainings which involved health personals, link workers and villagers. Linkages with Government Department have been established to tap medicine and malaria kit time to time.

Environment Conservation

Catholic Charities Jamshedpur has done tremendous work in Deojhari

village of Jamdih Panchayat of West Singhbhum District of Jharkhand State. It focused on activities such as Watershed, Agriculture, Health, Education and Environment. Initial days were challengeable due to lack of knowledge. The people were

trained and discussed about their problems in meeting. They formed groups such as Farmers Club, Women's Club etc. for the well-functioning of the intervention. Mr. Gardi Sinku, Mr. Naresh Sinku, and Budhram Sinku went to Darewadi Village of

Maharashtra state for excursion led by supervisor in 2007.

It was a great experience. On return they called a meeting and shared their experience. Darewadi village was surrounded by thick forest. The people over there cut the trees for their own purposes. Later on they began to face many problems- drinking water, agriculture and so on. They realized their problems and began solve it by themselves. They worked together for water harvesting, CCT, SCT, and Gully Plug Tree Plantation. It was their initiative to protect natural resources.

This motivated Gardi and others. They formed Jungle Rakchha Samiti for the protection of forest. We had meeting with members decided to protect 200 acres of forest area. Everyday two members of Jungle Rakchha Samiti are on duty in the forest. People are inspired by this and they are planting different trees in their own land. We help each other in building house, agriculture. We are able to do all works on time. Thus, we can save money and time.

Kissan Samity made land fertile for 28 small land holder farmers

When most of the farmers are struggling for irrigation in summer, Sora Gara Kissan Samity (20 members), in Tuiya village has set an extraordinary example by introducing water conservation method in its area.

Shyam lal Jamdua, a Supervisor being motivated by earthen check dam constructed in Sirkapi and Ichakuti villages with the support of SIGN in the area decided to do

something for the farmers who were struggling very hard to protect their summer paddy during peak dry weather due to lack of irrigation facility in Tuiya village. He started convincing 10-12 farmers about the benefit of earthen check dam.

Different opinions and even negative words did not crush his dream rather he became more determined to check the flow of water in the rivulet. He took the farmers to the earthen nala site for learning. The convinced members of Kissan Samity finally decided to construct on their own. The initiative was taken by members namely Somai Jamuda, Gonda Jamuda, Pongle Jamuda, Suru Jamuda and others for

planning and construction. All the members of Kissan Samity with the help of Shayam lal, put efforts in constructing the loose boulder check.

This intervention has enabled 28 farmers to cultivate summer paddy in the area where only 10-12 farmers were engaged earlier. Presently, farmers without any difficulty are getting better yield. They have also allowed landless farmers if any are willing to cultivate the nearby fields of theirs.

Voluntarism

12 Women SHG Cooperatives are functioning in the blocks namely (Chakuliya and Jugsalai cum Golmuri) in East Singhbhum, 5 blocks (Tonto, Jagnathpur, Manoharpur, Chaibasa and Chakradharpur) in West Singhbhum and 2 blocks (Kuchai and Kharsawan) in Seraikela-Kharsawan district initiated by Catholic Charities.

The Board of Directors of the Cooperatives take care all the concerned activities like regular meetings, book keeping, decision making, loan allocation etc. Leadership capabilities emerged among the women. 287 women from these groups have been elected as 'ward members' (representing a village area). The elected representatives include ordinary members as well as group leaders. 287 elected women representatives are active in the panchayat, attending meetings regularly, carrying out responsibilities etc. As a result social security schemes like Janani Suraksha Youjna (Maternity benefits schemes), old age pension, Widow Pension and Disability Pension are made easily accessible to the target women. Leadership has given rise to volunteerism.

Social harmony

Rural society is split by the hierarchical caste system that has traditionally discriminated against those at the bottom – the Scheduled Castes – as well as those outside it, for example the Scheduled Tribes. Divisions are found also among the higher caste categories.

The fact that the majority of SHGs are single-caste groups is based on the principle of 'affinity groups' and neighbourhood proximity (members living nearby can more easily get together, and village neighbourhoods are usually caste based). Catholic Charities, Jamshedpur, which has an inclusive development approach, has managed to bring these groups together rising above caste, or creed, or other considerations. It takes lot of time and demands much patience but the fruits are very sweet. People learn to sit together, discuss together and plan together things that are important for the development of their village. There is some degree of interaction across castes, including SCs and different sub-castes. It breaks down prejudices and pre-conceived ideas.

The result is social harmony and fellow feeling. This is seen across all the 12 Women SHG Cooperatives. Cooperatives seem uniquely placed to support their members on issues of social justice affecting women. 167 SHGs, (with some groups mobilising together on single issues) had taken up issues such as domestic violence, prevention of child marriage, and support for widows to remarry.

Collective action

The Cooperatives at Manoharpur, Ichagrah and Toklo work together with SHGs at their respective places in addressing issues that affect not only their own members, but also others in the larger community. These involved, improving community services like education, health care, village road), trying to stop alcohol sale and consumption (31%) etc. They also took initiative to spread awareness by participating in campaigns like pulse polio, literacy and immunization. The most common single type of action taken up by SHGs is the attempt to close down local liquor outlets. Alcoholism and the accompanying problems of domestic violence, the drain on household finances, impaired health care issues, which have been taken up regularly by women groups. Dealing with these issues is a major struggle, which pits women not only against a behavioural syndrome, but also against institutional and business elements, which have a stake in continuing to sell alcohol and make money out of it. However, the SHG women groups have been strong in their mission.

The mobilisation of women through village or cluster networks, or cooperative, was a significant feature of effective community action. These actions infuse confidence to take up any violation of rights and entitlements, etc. Women in the SHGs have learnt the art of working for common good.

Thus, Catholic Charities Jamshedpur has taken up an important role in the reconstruction and development of women-*Adivasis* and *Dalits* in general, and *Birhors*, *Sabhors* and *Paharias,* in particular. Whatever service it renders for these unprivileged and marginalized groups in its operational area is the net addition to total development of the East and West Singhbhum districts of Jharkhand and Purulia district of West Bengal. Viewed from this point of view, efforts of Jan Catholic Charities assume great social, economic and cultural significance in the context of alleviating hunger and poverty of the area where it works.

Concluding Remarks

I started in this chapter that both the government of Jharkhand and the Christian-inspired organizations are providing a set of potential solutions to some of the most severe problems facing Jharkhand today. These solutions are models of organized, long term viable villages, and all their constituent programmes. At this time the models are a few as compared to Jharkhand's population. Yet, the destructive effects of the centralized consumerist society are mounting and people all over India are losing faith in the system's ability to right itself, or even to hold together to the end of the country. Tension are mounting perhaps the evidence of healthy villages in contrast to the experience of the system's failures will move more people to direct their lives towards building alternatives.

The SIGN and other partner development organizations located in Jharkhand State of this study are all citizens of India who have chosen to work among the powerless to alleviate poverty and to build a new social order. Poverty in Jharkhand is a painful puzzle: the poor are uneducated, atomized, and own few economic inputs. Economic opportunities do exist, but some more initiatives are required to seek them out, a combination of education and self-confidence to establish them, and some capital to get started and tide one through initial mistakes. The government wants economic growth, but finds it more productive to assist those who are moderately well off. The schemes the government does direct to the most poor are channelled through inefficient and often corrupt bureaucracies, so their effectiveness is limited. There are both similarities and differences in the strategies of the projects we have discussed. All ten organizations make some effort to help the villagers gain access to government programmes meant for them.

Private entrepreneurs place a strong emphasis on helping villagers get government programmes, fighting corruption and encouraging government officers to implement their schemes as fully as possible. They have trained and educated the people in such a manner that they have the most participatory and self-sufficient people's organizations. SIGN for an example, was able to find enough technically skilled staff and advisors and to teach villagers the practical skills for managing the agricultural and NRM works, but that are not unusual. What is special is that SIGN set very high standards for its programmes and built them into action. Its work demonstrates that villagers do need to take on new values attitudes in order to run economic programmes efficiently and with priority to the poorest.

However, to view village development as individuals helping individuals is inadequate. The poor are poor because they are powerless, and since they are powerless they are generally oppressed; used or ignored. They are poor as a result of the socio-economic system, and it is run by the powerful for the powerful. Most of them well off people in the service area are fully occupied advancing their own interest and in the process perpetuate the system that supports them. The Christian inspired organization considers their work to be building the villagers' power so they can claim their due from the system.

At first these development organizations set themselves up as advocates the villagers' rights, particularly the CPR's rights. Over time they try to help villagers reach a point where they can protect their own rights and advance their own interest within the system. Education is a prerequisite, and legal aid helps, but the villagers' main source of power is their numbers organized through single village and area wide committees. At Gram Utthan Kendra (Gumla) and Samaj Vikas Sanstha (Chandwa), the villages were able to stop most local injustice and petty corruption just by getting organized (collective efforts). They are able to influence government structures at least up to the district level through mass marches and by making common demands. Each project the village committees, wisdom council, farmers' clubs are able to use the power of numbers strengthen their position in relation to outside economic institutions.

The author concludes that the social effects of SIGN' activities will lead to a sustained use of indigenous resource and knowledge, leading to a stronger position of the tribals in the local area. Economically the programme has positive effects for those who directly participate in the income- generating activities. The wider application will depend on the transfer of indigenous wisdom and silvicultural knowledge with appropriate technology to other social action groups dwelling in the same geographical settings.

However, the author is of the opinion that the social effects of SIGN seem to be sustainable. The economic effects so far are not widespread, but significant for those able to participate in income generating activities through livelihood promotion programmes, NRM and training. The social effects of SIGN, DSES, GUK, JVK, SVS, Catholic Charities, and Jamshedpur will lead to a sustained use of indigenous resources and knowledge (CPRs Social Capital. The long-term environmental effects of these organizations' activities may be such that a further erosion of natural resources is prevented, promoting further revitalization of the tribal community. Moreover, in the social field Snehadeep Holy Cross, Hazaribag has established an alternative participatory structure for its activities. It has achieved a lot also for destitute, deprived and stigmatized sections of the Society. Regarding Vikas Kendra, Simdega,

HSSS, Khunti, and CCSSS, Ranchi, organizations, a sound approach is adhered to, though it may be advisable to devote some more time to the programme implementation.

It is important to note that the weak linkages of both the farm forestry and CPR's with the agricultural sector were noticed. Farmers under the 'farmer club' go in for improved breeds of cattle. It will reduce the pressure on CPRs and increase the income of the farmers. It is important to ensure the involvement of local people, especially the females, in the management of those resources. The village communities, partner - organizations of SIGN and development agencies should work coherently in a participatory mode in planning, development, management and benefit- sharing of 'CPRs Social Capital' to avert the proverbial 'Tragedy of Commons' (CPRs Social Capital).

Endnotes

[1] Tribe is essentially a politico-administrative category. In the 1931 census an attempt was made by the colonial administration to list the 'primitive tribe'. Shortly thereafter, the Government of India Act of 1935 registered them as 'backward tribes'. After Independence, special provisions for the administration of these peoples were mode under which they were listed in separate schedules of the constitution, this creating the term 'scheduled tribes'.

[2] 'The Fifth Schedule' of the Constitution provides an administration and control of 'Scheduled Areas and Scheduled Tribes' and gives powers to the Governors to make regulations for the peace and good governance of the scheduled areas. The Provisions of the Panchayats (Extension to the Scheduled Areas) Act, 1996, popularly known as PESA Act is meant to enable tribalsociety to assume control over their own destiny to preserve and conserve their traditional rights over natural resources ('Commons').

[3] Areeparampil, M. 1995. *Tribals of Jharkhand: Victims of Development* (*A Story of Industries, Mines and Didpossesion of Indigenous Peoples*). New Delhi: Indian Social Institute, pp. 35-36.

[4] Pinto, C.B. 1968. "The Church and Social Welfare in Truth Shall Prevail," in L.P. Vidyarthi (ed). *Applied Anthropology in India: Principles, Problems and Case Studies*. Allahabad: Kitab Mahal, p. 125. Quoted by D.K. Panigrahi in *Social Change*, 23 (nos. 2&3 June-Sept.) 1993, pp. 90-96.

[5] Dungdung Gladson.2015. *Mission Saranda: A War for Natural Resources in India*. Ranchi: Deshaj Prakashan. pp.45-46

[6] "Childhood on Fire" ATSEC Jharkhand-2010, Report by Bharatiya Kisan Sangh Ranchi (ATSEC Jharkhand).

[7] (SRS-2013).

[8] (lancet Medical Journal, 2013).

[9] (SRS,2009).

[10] "Earth: Our Common Home" in Laudato Si (Ten relevant themes for reflection and action, published by an effort of Social Initiative for Growth and Networking (SIGN), Ranchi.

[11] Annual report of SIGN, 2017-18.

CHAPTER – 4

Social Capital in
Micro Settings Villages of Tribal Jharkhand

There are some of the major conceptual and analytical issues to which we have discussed in the previous chapters. However, any research on 'CPRs social capital management' is incomplete without an empirical counter-part, at least by way of illustration or as a case study. By bringing empirically – based substance to the previous chapter's macro level- context its test the representations made in the reviewed literature on Tribal Jharkhand and its CPR social capital scenario, while examining the relevance of various actors, programmes, policy initiatives, legislations, and other processes to the case of the research hamlets' households and their CPR management and silvicultural knowledge resources. In this chapter, the discussion centres upon the 'CPR social capital' fields of the 25 research villages selected from the mountainous regions of tribal Jharkhand in the Eastern India.

Two agro-climatic zones, viz.; sub-mountains and low hills sub-tropical zone (zone – I), as well as mid-hills sub-humid zone (zone –II) of Jharkhand State were selected for the comprehensive study. These two zones account for 80 percent of cultivable land harbor around 85 percent of the total human population and livestock. The multistage stratified random sampling technique has been used (see chapter I section III).

Ranchi, Hazaribag, Chatra, Latehar, West Singhbhum and Gumla, Khunti and Simdega districts from zone – I, and, Dumka, Sahibganj, and Pakur districts from zone-II were selected. Angara block from Ranchi district; Simaria block from Chatra district; Ichak, Sadar block Hazaribag from Hazaribag district; Barwadih block from Latehar district; Anandpur block from West Singhbhum district; Palkot, Basia, Gumla, Bishunpur blocks from Gumla district; Torpa block from Khunti district, and Bolba and Simdega blocks from Simdega district and all of Zone-I were selected randomly. Likewise; Shikaripara, Dumka block from Dumka district; Talihjari, Pathna block from Sahibganj district; Pakuria block from Pakur district from Zone-II were selected randomly. Total 25 revenue villages from all selected districts and blocks were selected at random. In all 444 sample households belonging to marginal and small categories were selected from all the sample villages. The practices towards social capital in these sample villages are discussed in detail through the personal observation and field study method. As a matter of fact that the case studies have enormous potential to facilitate deeper and wider understanding of the dynamics knowledge and ideas for reshaping policies, programmes and procedures in the context of social capital in general and social development thinking in particular. Selection of villages for the objective study is given in Table 13.

Table 13

Evolutionary Features of 25 Sample Villages/Hamlets of Jharkhand State of Eastern India

Name of the District	Name of the Village	Total geographical Area (in ha)	Forest Area (in ha)	No. of Households	Population	Sample Households	Population Character	Structure of a Governance	Constitutional[1] and Operational Rules Framed by	Date of Initiation of the Programmes by the Organizations
1. Dumka	Sitasal	317	NO	66	310	7	Homogeneous	GBMC	Villagers	25-7-2001
	Darbarpur	325	16	144	642	14	Heterogeneous	GB	Villagers	13-6-2001
	Bishubandh	77	NO	66	328	07	Homogeneous	GB	Manjhii Hadam	31-10-2005
	Khayerbani	91	NO	98	414	10	Homogeneous	GB	Villagers	31-10-2005
2. Sahibganj	Gangtia	156	NO	135	555	14	Homogeneous	GB	Villagers	21-10-2005
	Tilbitha	58.08	NO	32	146	3	Homogeneous	GB	Villagers	8-9-2005
3. Pakur	Rajabari	273	NO	172	787	17	Heterogeneous	GB	Villagers	10-4-2015
	Murgadanga	73	NO	68	304	7	Homogeneous	GB	Villagers	15-5-2015
4. Gumla	Kulabira	1511.72	NO	556	2895	56	Homogeneous	GB	NO	16-7-2010
	Sarubera	2900	13	366	1774	37	Homogeneous	GB	NO	7-7-2013
	Chatakpur	200.18	NO	65	352	7	Homogeneous	SHG	NO	7-7-2013
	Jorgotoli	1366	NO	95	475	10	Homogeneous	SHG	NO	5-2-2011
	Mamarla	468	NO	260	1288	26	Homogeneous	SHG	NO	6-1-2009

	Village									Date
5. Simdega	Malsara	2322	16	489	2689	49	Homogeneous	SHG	NO	7-1-2013
	Belgarh	412	ND	86	418	9	Homogeneous	SHG	NO	7-1-2013
6. Khunti	Latauli	1697.87	16	218	1228	22	Homogeneous	ED	NO	2-2-2008
	Hario	655	8	35	175	4	Homogeneous	ED	NO	3-2-2011
7. Chatra	Angara	890.42	36	84	445	8	Homogeneous	ED	NO	2-1-2013
	Sos	966	13	75	544	8	Homogeneous	ED	NO	2-1-2013
8. Hazaribag	Dahwa	133	15	35	163	4	Homogeneous	SHG	NO	2-1-2013
	Kalan	298	ND	370	1951	37	Homogeneous	ND	NO	2-1-2011
9. Ranchi	Banpur	852.11	16	305	1578	31	Heterogeneous	ED	Villagers	1-6-2016
10. Latehar	Saidup	864	15	394	2147	39	Homogeneous	ED	Villagers	13-2-2014
11. West Singhbhum	Rungikocha *	444	13	141	688	14	Heterogeneous	ED	Villagers	16-3-2013
	Koenjali	100.11	10	36	173	4	Homogeneous	ED	Villagers	12-2-2014
Total				4391	22469	444				

Source: Field Research (2018): Focus Group Discussions.

Rungikocha is a part of Goilkera official name. There are 126 other villages which come under Goilkera branch office.

The above Table 13 gives a brief idea about the total number of villages, households under study by village and by hamlet. It was from these 25 villages/hamlets that the data was collected. The data collection was done at two levels; one was at the village/hamlet level and other at the household level. Hence the questionnaire was also prepared at two levels. One was at the village level, which provides an idea about the village's demography, cultural and religious characteristics, CPRs social capital practices, etc. The method used for village/hamlet data collection was rapid appraisal, key informant and group discussion. This data was only used to create village profile and sampling design. A systematic random sampling was used to collect household's data. Since most of the villages/hamlets are homogeneous as the number of households increased less proportion of households were sampled. Using the above design the total of 444 (10.11 per cent) households were sampled. In some of the hamlets, we discarded a few questionnaires due to inconsistency of data. These inconsistencies were very minimal and error was identified only at the last stage of analysis.

Table 14

CPRs Social Capital in Sitasal Village

District: Dumka	Block – Shikaripara	
Total Geographical Area (In ha)	317	
Total Forest Area (In ha)	Nil	
Total CPRs Land (In ha)	14.33	(community pastures, wastelands, common dumping, and threshing grounds, watershed drainages, village ponds, rivers and their banks)
Number of households	66	
Total population	310	
Adults (above 14 year)	Male : 103	Female : 93

Children (0-14 year)	Boy : 61	Girl : 53
Caste/Tribe – Wise Distribution:		
Name of the Caste/Tribe	**Number of households**	**Population**
Scheduled Tribe (Santhal)	66	310
Scheduled Caste	Nil	Nil
Total number of literates		
Adults (above 14 year)	Male : 60	Female : 40
Children (6-14 year)	34	26
Livestock population: (%)	Bovine 60.74	Ovine 39.26
Physical products through CPRs		
• Food and fiber items	Jackfruit, Mango, Papaya	
• Fodder	Grazing land available	
• Fuel and timber	Not available	
• Water	Wells and Hands pumps, small Tank	
• Manure	Fertilizers	
CPRs Contributions		
• Employment creation	No	
• Income generation	through SHGs (Nine SHGs are at work)	
• Asset accumulation	very little	
• Sustenance of village Community	based on agriculture and labour	
• Grazing of animals	common lands	
• Protect new plantation	no	
• Reduce weed infestation	not reported	

Social Capital Core Factors at work in the village: (collective action through the formation of SHG)

Source: Primary Survey 2018.

Sitasal is a tribal village. All are Santhals. The total geographical area of the village is 317 hectares (ha). The total cultivable land in the village is 126.30 ha i.e 40 per cent of the total geographical area. The village is connected with a pucca road. The nearest post office for the village is in Gamra. The village has a balwadi.

The people of the village have, on an average, one ha of Land. There is a need for more livelihood support programmes for the betterment of the people in this village. There is a need to give importance to activities related to health and income generation in the village, although SHG is very active in this village. The name of SHG is 'Chai Champa Swayam Samuh'. The members are engaged in different activities for asset creation. Dumka Social and Educational Development Society (DSES), Dumka started working in this village from 25.07.2001. Now the village is self-independent. It has two PDS shops which serve the villages of their immediate needs.

Empowering women was one of the most important key areas of DSES work. The empowerment of women in turn would help them cater to the needs and aspirations of their families, provide better education to their children, have a say in their family matters and thus inculcate in them a feeling of substance. Emphases were given on the formation of SHG groups and provide training on the concept of SHG and encouragement to undertake income generation activities. This makes them conscious for their social, economic & political rights.

The geology of the village does not reveal anything striking except the ordinary gangetic alluvium. There is no mineral of importance. The settlements are compact and large in terms of area. 94.02 per cent of the total workforce is engaged in the primary sector, and of which 91.54 per cent is in cultivation. Employment is the secondary and tertiary sectors accounts for two per cent and 3.98 per cent respectively. There has been no significant change in the occupational structure between 2011 to 2017. The main source of drinking water is handpump.

During the study it was found that SHG groups of Sitasal are involved in various activities like vegetable cultivation, PDS, Piggery, Poultry farming, goatery etc. Except two families, no cases of landlessness are found in the village. These two families have come from elsewhere and settled down here. Due to irregular rainfall and scarcity of irrigational water, agriculture is practiced for only six months and for the rest of the year villagers have to depend on wage labour for which they are being paid wages @ Rs 260/- per day. This way, the villagers get food security for six months only. The village has no forest, but the villagers have their own ownership trees in front of their houses which generate incomes and supplement to the families.

Earlier the DSES had provided agricultural training to the villagers. As a result the agricultural yield has now improved – 4-6 quintals per acre. The villagers have now started practicing *rabi* crops. By investing Rs 20,000/- per ha on vegetable farming they earn an income of Rs 60,000/- per ha from vegetable cultivation like cauliflower, cabbage, tomato, etc. Currently, there is no intervention of DSES in this village but still villagers have trust on DSES and its staff members.

Table 15

CPRs Social Capital in Darbarpur Village

District: Dumka	Block – Dumka	
Total Geographical Area (In ha)	325	
Total Forest Area (In ha)	16	
Total CPRs Land (In ha)	19.11	(Community pastures, wastelands, common dumping, and threshing grounds, watershed drainages, village ponds, river and their banks)
Number of households	144	

Total population	642	
Adults (above 14 year)	Male : 270	Female : 236
Children (0-14 year)	Boy : 72	Girl : 64
Caste/Tribe – Wise Distribution		
Name of the Caste/Tribe	**Number of households**	**Population**
Scheduled Tribe Santhal, Paharia (Sarna)	134	587
Scheduled Caste	Nil	Nil
OBC - Lohara	10	55
Total number of literates	Male : 60	Female : 40
Adults (above 14 year)	Male : 135	Female : 71
Children (6-14 year)	143	13
Livestock population: (%)	Bovine 60	Ovine 40
Physical products through CPRs		
• Food and fiber items	(Amla, Fruits leaves, Ber, Jackfruit, Jamun, Mahua, Kend, Mango, Piyar, Tassar)	
• Fodder	(Common land)	
• Fuel and timber	(available)	
• Water	(wells, Tanks and Ponds)	
• Manure	(vermicompost)	
• Others	(Medicinal plants)	
CPRs Contribution:	through SHGs (Nine SHGs are at work)	
Employment	25 persons	
Income generation	25 persons through forest products	
Asset accumulation	not very impressive	
Sustenance of village Community	Ten families through forest wood collection and selling	

Grazing of animals	common lands	
Protect new plantation	not in practice	
Reduce weed infestation	not recorded	

Social Capital Core Factors at work in the village :(Leadership and social ties,)

Source: Primary Survey 2018.

Darbarpur village is located in Dumka Tehsil of Dumka district in Jharkhand. It is situated 33km away from Dumka.

Darbarpur village is a hilly area. The total geographical area of village is 325 hectares. Only 16 ha i.e.5 percent of total land is under forest. Darbarpur has a total population of 642 peoples. There are about 144 houses in Darbarpur village. Dumka is nearest town to Darbarpur, about 40 Km. away from Dumka district headquarters.

Most of the households in the village belong to the scheduled tribes (134 households). As stated above that the village has a total geographical area of 325 ha, of which 165.77 ha are the total cultivable land. However, only 137.88 ha are being used for cultivation. The village is connected with a pucca road. The nearest post office for the village is in Gamra at a distance of 10 kilometers and the nearest market for the village is in Dumka at a distance of 40 kilometers from the village. The village has an *Aanganvadi* and a primary school. The Primary Health Centre for the village is in Dumka. All but 131 households in the village have electricity connection. There are 3 public wells, 5 private and 16 public hand-pumps, 2 public ponds in the village.

The village is situated in a spares forest area and is spread into several localities. First of all the SHG was formed by the acting effort of the villagers (women) and DSES staff. Initially, 20 members joined the SHG. The group was provided with a leaf plate making machine. The group started working very well with the making and marketing of *Dona*. After some months the machine broke down. Due to lack of coordination between the groups and lack of able leadership, the groups started disintegrating. However, at the time of data collection, a few groups were active in their trades. Like Sitasal village, this village is also working independently. The existing problems reported by the villagers were poor infrastructure facilities like bad or no roads, poor or no health services, unemployment and poverty. When enquired about the changes taking place in quality of life of the villagers, the beneficiaries submitted that DSES had started working in the village very well during 1996, but now they visit us very rarely and the village has always been neglected. In all, it may be said that DSES intervention has brought about very little change in the quality of life of the villagers. But still villagers have full faith on the guidelines provided by the DSES from time to time.

Table 16

CPRs Social Capital in Bishubandh Village

District: Dumka	Block – Dumka	
Total Geographical Area (In ha)	77	
Total Forest Area (In ha)	Nil	
Total CPRs Land (In ha)	3.11	(Community pastures, wastelands, common dumping, and threshing grounds, watershed drainages, village ponds, river and their banks)
Number of households	66	
Total population	328	
Adults (above 14 year)	Male : 108 Female : 102	Female : 236
Children (0-14 year)	Boy : 64	Girl : 54
Caste/Tribe – Wise Distribution		

Name of the Caste/Tribe	Number of households Population	Population
Scheduled Tribe (Santhal)	64	319
Scheduled Caste	Nil	Nil
Muslim	2	9
Total number of literates:	Male : 60	Female : 40
Adults (above 14 year)	Male : 67	Female : 45
Children (0-14 year)	53	22
Livestock population: (%)	Bovine 78	Ovine 28
Physical products through CPRs		
• Food and fiber items	(Jackfruit, Mango Jamun)	
• Fodder	(waste land)	
• Fuel and timber	(ownership trees)	
• Water	(wells and hand pumps)	
• Manure	(fertilizer)	
CPRs Contribution		
Employment	No	
Income generation	through labor, cultivation and piggery	
Asset accumulation	No	
Sustenance of village Community	No	
Grazing of animals	on common lands	
Grazing of animals	common lands	
Protect new plantation	not in practice	
Reduce weed infestation	not recorded	

Social Capital Core Factors at work in the village: (social networking)
Source: Primary Survey 2018.

Note: The village is still managed by 'Manjhi Hadam' (a traditional tribal leader).

Bishubandh village is located in Dumka Tehsil of Dumka district in Jharkhand. It is situated 11 km away from Dumka, which is both district & sub-district headquarters of Bishubandh village. The total geographical area of village is 77 hectares. Bisubandh has a total population of 328 peoples. There are about 66 houses in Bishubandh village. Dumka is nearest town to Bisubandh.

Most of the households in the village belong to the scheduled tribe, with 64 households out of 66 belonging to the scheduled tribes. The total geographical area of the village is 77 ha out of which 37 ha are cultivable land. The village has a SHG named 'Champa Baha Group'. The village has a primary school of 5th standard, but has no health centre. The village is without having forest coverage but has a good number of bamboo trees and fruit-trees of its possession.

Though it is lowest it is better than some of the other villages in this region for study. However, there is a need to improve the economic condition of the people in these villages as the income index is not up to the mark. There is a need to give more importance to activities related to education and income generation in the village.

Table 17
CPRs Social Capital in Khayerbani Village

District: Dumka		Block – Dumka
Total Geographical Area (In ha)	91	
Total Forest Area (In ha)	No	
Total CPRs Land (In ha)	3.11	(Community pastures, wastelands, common dumping, and threshing grounds, watershed drainages, village ponds, river and their banks)
Number of households	98	
Total population	414	

Adults (above 14 year)	Male : 143	Female : 138
Children (0-14 year)	Boy : 70	Girl : 63
Caste/Tribe – Wise Distribution		
Name of the Caste/Tribe	**Number of households Population**	**Population**
Scheduled Tribe (Santhal)	98	414
Scheduled Caste	Nil	Nil
Total number of literates:	2	9
Adults (above 14 year)	Male : 93	Female : 63
Children (6-14 year)	58	33
Livestock population: (%)	Bovine 77	Ovine 23
Physical products through CPRs		
• Food and fiber items	Jackfruit, Mahua, mango,	
• Fodder	common land	
• Fuel and timber	firewood	
• Water	wells, Hand pumps	
• Manure	Composed	
CPRs Contribution		
Employment	through SHGs and wage laborers	
Income generation	through SHGs and cultivation	
Asset accumulation	through piggery and goatery	
Sustenance of village Community	no	
Sustenance of village Community	No	
Grazing of animals	on common lands	
Grazing of animals	common lands	
Protect new plantation	not in practice	
Reduce weed infestation	not recorded	

Social Capital Core Fact in the village: Leadership and Social Ties
Source: Primary Survey 2018.

Khayerbani village is located in Dumka Tehsil of Dumka district in Jharkhand, India. It is situated 15km away from Dumka, which is both district & sub-district headquarters of Khayerbani village. Rampur is the gram panchayat of Khayerbani village. The total geographical area of village is 91 hectares. Khayerbani has a total population of 414 peoples. There are 98 houses in Khayerbani village. Dumka is nearest town to Khayerbani.

Khayerbani is a revenue village. Khayerbani is a village dominated by the Santhal community. The village is connected by pucca road. It has five SHG groups. It has a Primary school. The Primary Health Centre for the village is in Kuruva at a distance of 12 kilometers from the village.

As stated above that the village has five SHG groups of different names. All are active in mobilizing women and generating income for them. However, amongst them '*Champa Baha* Self Group' is very popular for maintaining sanitation of the village under '*Swachh Bharat Abhiyan*' campaign.

Table 18
CPRs Social Capital in Gangtia Village

District: Sahebganj		Block – Rajmahal
Total Geographical Area (In ha)	156	
Total Forest Area (In ha)	No	
Total CPRs Land (In ha)	2.33	(Community pastures, wastelands, common dumping, and threshing grounds, watershed drainages, village ponds, river and their banks)
Number of households	131	
Total population	555	
Adults (above 14 year)	Male : 213	Female : 200

Children (0-14 year)	Boy : 79	Girl : 63
Caste/Tribe – Wise Distribution		
Name of the Caste/Tribe	**Number of households**	**Population**
Scheduled Tribe (Santhal)	81	363
Scheduled Caste (Lohara)	04	18
Muslim	50	174
Total number of literates		
Adults (above 14 year)	Male : 163	Female : 103
Children (6-14 year)	82	65
Livestock population: (%)	Bovine 50	Ovine 50
Physical products through CPRs		
• Food and fiber items	fruits leaves and fruits flowers	
• Fodder	Nil	
• Fuel and timber	sisham, jackfruits	
• Water	wells and tank	
• Manure	fertilizers and pesticides	
CPRs Contribution		
Employment	seasonal	
Income generation	agriculture forestry and labor	
Asset accumulation	through government schemes like fishery	
Protect new plantation	not active	

Social Capital Core Factors at work in the village: collective action

Source: Primary Survey 2018.

Gangtia is a small village in Rajmahal block in Sahibganj district of Jharkhand State. It comes under Bhaat Bhanga Santhali panchayat. It is located at a distance of 29km from the district headquarters. This place is at the border of Sahibganj and Maldah districts. Local language is

Hindi. Total population of the village is 555 and number of houses are 135. Female population is 47.38 per cent. Village literacy rate is 74 per cent and the Female literacy rate is 47.38 per cent only.

Gangtia is a village comprising of 6 hamlets, namely Tiridtola, Sadaktola, Manjhalitola, Karmbatola, Dhodkutola and Bherandatola. The nearest post office for the village is in Kalanchak at a distance of 5 kilometers. The nearest market for the village is in Littipada at distance of 20 kilometers, on an average, from all the hamlets. There are 2 Aanganvadis and 2 primary schools. The primary health centre for the village is in Taljari at a distance of 5 kilometers from all the hamlets of the village. All households in the village have electricity connection. There are 14 public wells and 21 public hand-pumps in the village.

People depend on agriculture. There is a need for more economic programmes that will help to improve the economic condition of the villagers by giving them work opportunity. There is a need to give more importance on activities related to betterment of health and income generation programmes too.

Table 19

CPRs Social Capital in Tilbitha Village

District: Sahibganj	Block – Pathna	
Total Geographical Area (In ha)	58.08	
Total Forest Area (In ha)	No	
Total CPRs Land (In ha)	2.33	(Community pastures, wastelands, common dumping, and threshing grounds, watershed drainages, village ponds, river and their banks)
Number of households	32	
Total population	146	

Adults (above 14 year)	Male : 45	Female : 41
Children (0-14 year)	Boy : 30	Girl : 30
Caste/Tribe – Wise Distribution		
Name of the Caste/Tribe	**Number of households**	**Population**
Scheduled Tribe (Sarna)	32	146
Scheduled Caste	Nil	Nil
Total number of literates		
Adults (above 14 year)	Male : 31	Female : 22
Children (6-14 year)	25	13
Livestock population: (%)	Bovine 77	Ovine 23
Physical products through CPRs		
• Food and fibre items	Domer, mango, mahua	
• Fodder	waste land	
• Fuel and timber	Nil	
• Water- wells hand pumps		
CPRs Contribution		
Employment	Nil	
Income generation	Through SHGs	
Asset accumulation	goatery	
Sustenance of village Community	not observed	
Grazing of animals	on common lands	

Social Capital Core Factors at work in the village: social ties

Source: Primary Survey 2018.

Tilbitha village is located in Pathna Tehsil of Sahibganj district in Jharkhand. It is situated 20 km away from sub-district headquarters Pathna and 90km away from district headquarters.

The total geographical area of village is 58.08 hectares. Tilbitha has a total population of 146 peoples. There are about 32 households in Tilbita village. Pathna is nearest town to Tilbhita.

Initially, women of the village formed a SHG named 'Muskan' in 2011 and started managing it themselves. Currently, three such SHGs are at work in the village. Each group has 13 members. These groups are doing well with the present savings of Rs. 52/- per member per month. The members of the group meet twice in a month i.e. on 2nd and 17th day of each month for self-introspection.The group has its own savings account in the *'Vananchal Gramin Bank, Bishanpur.'* The total savings of all the three groups till date (04.10.2018) were of Rs.35, 637/-. For the development of the poor families, SHGs started a piggery work. The piggery shed was constructed by the SHGs themselves. The training for piggery was provided by DSES at Dumka. The entire Self Help Group was taken to the Birsa Agriculture University, Ranchi for a day to get training and exposure on piggery. During the field work in October, 2018, the author observed that the pigs are reared professionally by the SHG members. The members were making a good profit out of this newly embraced profession.

Table 20

CPRs Social Capital in Rajabari Village

District: Pakur	Block – Pakuria	
Total Geographical Area (In ha)	273	
Total Forest Area (In ha)	No	
Total CPRs Land (In ha)	2.33	(Community pastures, wastelands, common dumping, and threshing grounds, watershed drainages, village ponds, river and their banks)
Number of households	172	
Total population	787	
Adults (above 14 year)	Male : 273	Female : 223
Children (0-14 year)	Boy : 160	Girl : 131
Caste/Tribe – Wise Distribution		

Name of the Caste/Tribe	Number of households	Population
Scheduled Tribe (Christian)	170	776
Scheduled Caste (Lohara)	2	11
Total number of literates		
Adults (above 14 year)	Male : 108	Female : 67
Children (6-14 year)	79	39
Livestock population: (%)	Bovine 77	Ovine 23
Physical products through CPRs		
• Food and fibre items	Domer, mango mahua	
• Fodder	waste land	
• Fuel and timber	Nil	
• Water	wells hand pumps	
CPRs Contribution		
Employment	Nil	
Income generation	Through SHGs	
Asset accumulation	goatery	
Sustenance of village Community	not observed	
Grazing of animals	on common lands	

Social Capital Core Factors at work in the village: Mutual trust, reputation, reciprocity, leadership, social networking, social ties, collective action.

Source: Primary Survey 2018.

Rajbari is a village placed in Pakuria Block of Pakur district. The village is situated in rural part of Pakur district of Jharkhand. The village has 172 households.

According to own Census 2018, Rajbari's population is 787 persons out of this, 433 are males whereas the females count 354. This village has 291 kids in the age bracket of 0-14 years. Out of this 160 are boys and 131 are girls.

Literacy rate in Rajbari village is 37.60 per cent. Only 243 persons out of 787 are educated.

As stated above that Rajabari is a Tribal *(Santhal)* village comprising of 172 households and it falls under Basantpur *gram panchayat.* Occupation-wise, the villagers can be divided in to three categories 1. stone crasher employees 2. self-employed (workers), and 3. cultivators. There are around 40 stone crasher employees in this village. According to Mr Yogesh Soren, worker of DSES Dumka said that we are just maintaining our relationship with the inhabitants. We are bearing a lot but we are following the proverb- *"for getting something we need to loose something".* DSES has been providing assistance to the village since 2008. The villagers were doing well during the period. Currently, there are eight SHGs at work in the village. Although the village has no forest as such but every households have their own social forestry, kitchen garden and bamboo trees. Farmers of the area do cultivation through SRI method as provided by SIGN through farmer's clubs.

This is because most of the people in the village do not have land. There is a need for more livelihood support programmes in these villages to improve the economic condition of the people. Particularly, there is a need to give more importance on income generating activities in the village.

Table 21

CPRs Social Capital in Murgadanga Village

District: Pakur		Block – Hiranpur
Total Geographical Area (In ha)	73	
Total Forest Area (In ha)	Nil	
Total CPRs Land (In ha)	2.33	(Community pastures, wastelands, common dumping, and threshing grounds, watershed drainages, village ponds, river and their banks)
Number of households	68	

Total population	304	
Adults (above 14 year)	Male :100	Female : 92
Children (0-14 year)	Boy : 70	Girl : 42
Caste/Tribe – Wise Distribution		
Name of the Caste/Tribe	**Number of households**	**Population**
Scheduled Tribe (Sarna)	67	300
(Christian)	1	4
Scheduled Caste	Nil	Nil
Total number of literates	Male : 108	Female : 67
Adults (above 14 year)	Male : 31	Female : 23
Children (6-14 year)	21	10
Livestock population: (%)	Bovine 77	Ovine 23
Physical products through CPRs		
• Food and fibre items	Domer, mango, mahua	
• Fodder	waste land	
• Fuel and timber	Nil	
• Water	wells hand pumps	
CPRs Contribution	Through SHGs	
Employment	Nil	
Income generation	Through SHGs	
Asset accumulation	goatery	
Sustenance of village Community	not observed	
Grazing of animals	on common lands	

Social Capital Core Factors at work in the village: collective action

Source: Primary Survey 2018.

Murgadanga village is located in Hiranpur Tehsil of Pakur district in Jharkhand. It is situated 12 km away from the sub-district headquarters and 15km away from Pakur. The total geographical area of village is 73 ha. Murgadanga has a total population of 304 persons. There are about 68 houses in the village. Hiranpur is nearest town to Murgadanga.

Murgadanga is comprising of 3 hamlets, namely Chetantola, Talatola, and Latartola. Chetantola is dominated by the scheduled tribes (Santhal) with most of the households (41) belonging to them. The nearest post office for the village is in Gobarghusi at a distance of 5 kilometers on an average from all the hamlets of the village.

The village has six SHGs of different names. Livelihood promotion project is also going on in this village but has a lot of problems regarding maintaining accounts and cash balance. The village is poor in all respect. The reason for this is that the dependency of the people on agriculture is very large. There is a need for more programmes that will help in improving the economic condition of the villagers. The life expectancy index i.e. 0.369 is the lowest; it falls in the low category. This is because of high child mortality between the years 2017-2018. There is a need to give more importance to activities related to betterment of health and income generation in the village.

Table 22

CPRs Social Capital in Kulabira Village

District: Gumla	Block – Gumla	
Total Geographical Area (In ha)	1511.72	
Total Forest Area (In ha)	Nil	
Total CPRs Land (In ha)	2.11	(Community pastures, wastelands, common dumping, and threshing grounds, watershed drainages, village ponds, river and their banks)
	68	
Number of households	556	
Total population	2895	Female : 92
Adults (above 14 year)	Male : 1139	Female : 1111
Children (0-14 year)	Boy : 335	Girl : 310

Caste/Tribe – Wise Distribution		
Name of the Caste/Tribe	**Number of households**	**Population**
Scheduled Tribe (Sarna)	316	1560
Scheduled Caste	240	1335
Total number of literates	Male : 108	Female : 67
Adults (above 14 year)	Male : 389	Female : 311
Children (6-14 year)	215	195
Livestock population: (%)	Bovine 77	Ovine 23
Physical products through CPRs		
• Food and fibre items	Domer, mango, mahua	
• Fodder	waste land	
• Fuel and timber	although there is no forest in and around the village, but personal ownership trees like mango, sisham, bamboos are available around the village.	
• Water	wells hand pumps	
CPRs Contribution		
Employment	Nil	
Income generation	Through SHGs	
Asset accumulation	goatery	
Sustenance of village Community	not observed	
Grazing of animals	on common lands	

Social Capital Core Factors at work in the village: leadership

Source: Primary Survey 2018.

Kulabira village is located in Gumla Tehsil of Gumla district in Jharkhand. It is situated 18km away from Gumla. The total geographical area of village is 1511.72 hectares. Kulabira has a total population of 2895 peoples. There are about 556 houses in the village. Gumla is nearest town to Kulabira.

The village is dominated by the scheduled tribe with about 60 per cent of the households belonging to them (316). The total geographical area of the village is 1511.72 ha of which 7855.10 ha are only for cultivation. However, only 637.53 ha are being used for cultivation.

The village is divided into four *tolas*-1. Panderia, 2. Lathatoli, 3. Pahartoli and 4. Kulabira itself. The village has no forest of its own. But it has several trees of mahua, mango, bamboo, etc. either at the individual ownership pattern or at the community possession and ownership right. All the *tolas* were organized under the female leadership of Shanti Devi. She has her own tailoring centre at work in the village. The village has *Mahila Mandal* for the female folk and Farmer's Club for the male-members. For the first time, Gram Uthan Kendra (GUK), Gumla entered this village in 1994. During this phase, GUK was engaged in providing night school, construction of wells, dams and *dohars*. The villagers started participating in the monthly meeting of GUK at Gumla and started taking active part in the decision making process. It provided services to the villagers till 2013 and then moved out from the scene. During the study, the author visited this village twice and found that the villagers have been engaged in rope making and basket making activities. A typical community-based lift irrigation system which was promoted by GUK in order to lifting water from dams up to terraced agricultural fields located around the village. A pump house was constructed near the water source to protect the pump. The project irrigates 8-12 hectares of land owned by 17-25 farmers. The entire project is implemented with the full participation (social capital) of both men and women in site selection, design, installation, maintenance and water distribution (sharing benefit model). It has also been observed during the field visit that villagers have formed a SHG by different names to organize the community, imbibe savings habit and to save themselves from financial exploitation. Further, it is said that "traditionally these people are all first generation farmers and hardly have any experience in vegetable cultivation, and that their lift irrigation project has stopped the outside migration to the large extent."

Table 23

CPRs Social Capital in Sarubera Village

District: Gumla	Block – Palkot	
Total Geographical Area (In ha)	2900	
Total Forest Area (In ha)	25.65	
Total CPRs Land (In ha)	31.33	(Community pastures, wastelands, common dumping, and threshing grounds, watershed drainages, village ponds, river and their banks)
Number of households	366	
Total population	1774	
Adults (above 14 year)	Male : 655	Female : 511
Children (0-14 year)	Boy : 308	Girl : 300
Caste/Tribe – Wise Distribution		
Name of the Caste/Tribe	Number of households	Population
Scheduled Tribe (Christian)		
Scheduled Caste	366	1774
Total number of literates	240	1335
Adults (above 14 year)	Male : 217	Female : 177
Children (6-14 year)	165	135
Livestock population: (%)	Bovine 77	Ovine 23
Physical products through CPRs		
• Food and fibre items	Domer, mango, mahua	
• Fodder	waste land	
• Fuel and timber	Nil	

• Water	wells hand pumps	
CPRs Contribution		
Employment	Nil	
Income generation	Through SHGs	
Asset accumulation	goatery	
Sustenance of village Community	25 % based on CPR's	
Grazing of animals	on common lands	

Social Capital Core Factors at work in the village: social ties

Source: Primary Survey 2018.

Sarubera is a tribal village with all the 366 households belonging to the scheduled tribes. The total geographical area of the village is 2900 ha of which 1105.07 ha is the total cultivable land but only 615.56 ha are cultivated. The village is connected with a pucca road. The village has an *Aanganvadi* centre and a primary school. The kids usually go to the *Aanganvadi* centre and to the primary school for getting education. The village has a *Mahila Vikas Mandal*, which looks after the functioning of the SHGs and other livelihood projects. The participation rate of the village is 68 per cent.

Today there is a *Van Suraksha Samiti* at work in the Sarubera village. The primary responsibility of the *Samiti* is to take care of the village forest (social forestry) and to give protection to the *Sal, chirongee and Kendu* trees which are commonly found in the forest areas. However, non-timber forest products like Sal's leaves, Sal's fruits, fuel wood, mushroom, and Sal tooth sticks are being collected from the village forest by the villagers for their domestic use as well as for mobilizing resources in terms of earnings.

However, there is a need for more livelihood support programme to improve the economic condition of the people living in the settlements.

Table 24

CPRs Social Capital in Chatakpur Village

District: Gumla	Block – Gumla	
Total Geographical Area (In ha)	200.18	
Total Forest Area (In ha)	No	
Total CPRs Land (In ha)	2.33	(Community pastures, wastelands, common dumping, and threshing grounds, watershed drainages, village ponds, river and their banks)
Number of households	65	
Total population	352	
Adults (above 14 year)	Male : 107	Female : 100
Children (0-14 year)	Boy : 76	Girl : 69
Caste/Tribe – Wise Distribution		
Name of the Caste/Tribe	Number of households	Population
Scheduled Tribe	65	352
Scheduled Caste	Nil	Nil
Total number of literates:		
Adults (above 14 year)	Male : 55	Female : 45
Children (6-14 year)	35	22
Livestock population: (%)	Bovine 77	Ovine 23
Physical products through CPRs		
Food and fibre items	Domer, mango, mahua	
Fodder	waste land	
Fuel and timber	Nil	
Water	wells hand pumps	
CPRs Contribution		
Employment	Nil	

Income generation	Through SHGs	
Asset accumulation	goatery	
Sustenance of village Community	technically the village has no forest, so contribution of CPR's on commun ity life is minimal.	
Grazing of animals - on common lands	on common lands	

Social Capital Core Factors at work in the village: reciprocity and exchange

Source: Primary Survey 2018.

Chatakpur village is located in Gumla Tehsil of Gumla district in Jharkhand. It is situated 10 km away from Gumla. Chatakpur has a total population of 352 persons. Gumla is nearest town to Chatakpur. The village has its own organization structure to be termed as a 'Wisdom Council', which meets with the villagers twice in a month.

Chatakpur is a tribal village with all the 65 households belonging to the scheduled tribes. The total geographical area of the village is 200.18 ha of which 75.56 ha are under cultivation. The village is connected with a pucca road. The nearest post office of the village is at Gumla. The nearest market is also at Gumla, 30 kilometers away from the village. The children of the village usually visit to nearby school for primary schooling. The Gram Uthan Kendra has been very active in the village since 1965.

Table 25

CPRs Social Capital in Jorgotoli Village

District: Jorgotoli	Block – Basia	
Total Geographical Area (In ha)	1366	
Total Forest Area (In ha)	No	
Total CPRs Land (In ha)	2.34	(Community pastures, wastelands, common dumping, and threshing grounds, watershed drainages, village ponds, river and their banks)
Number of households	95	
Total population	475	
Adults (above 14 year)	Male : 121	Female : 115
Children (0-14 year)	Boy : 131	Girl : 108
Caste/Tribe – Wise Distribution		
Name of the Caste/Tribe	Number of households	Population
Scheduled Tribe (Christian)	95	475
Scheduled Caste	Nil	
Total number of literates:		
Adults (above 14 year):	Male : 195	Female : 155
Children (6-14 year)	165	88
Livestock population: (%)	Bovine 77	Ovine 23
Physical products through CPRs		
Food and fibre items	Domer, mango, mahua	
Fodder	waste land	
Fuel and timber	Nil	
Water	wells hand pumps	
CPRs Contribution		
Employment	Nil	

Income generation	Through SHGs	
Asset accumulation	goatery	
Sustenance of village Community	not observed	
Grazing of animals	on common lands	

Social Capital Core Factors at work in the village: leadership, social networking

Source: Primary Survey 2018.

Jorgotoli is a revenue village comprising of three hamlets, namely Kadamtoli, Aharatoli and Simratoli. All the households in the village belong to the scheduled tribes. The total geographical area of the village is 200 ha. No forest area is found around the village. However, only 88 ha of land are being used for cultivation. There are 9 public and 1 private wells, 17 public hand-pumps and 6 public ponds found in the village. Most of the villagers are engaged in vegetable cultivation and lac cultivation as cash crops.

As stated above that Jorgotoli is a tribal village. All villagers have lands. In order to mobilise the women labor force, the wisdom council of the village started motivating the women to form a SHG to engage themselves in some economic activities and make themselves independent and empowered. Accordingly, the group members started taking up lac processing activities right from cocoon rearing to cocoon producing. The group started with a monthly meeting and a monthly deposit of Rs 20 per head. The meetings were conducted regularly on 10th and 25th day of every month. Gradually, with the passage of time the monthly saving per head increased to Rs 50 per head. The group has also opened a Saving Bank Accounts. The SHG members were given training on mushroom cultivation by the Jharkhand State Development Society. Now the group has a strong aspiration (social capital) for taking up some new self- employment like bee- keeping, rope making, basket making, etc for their continuity and self-reliance.

.

Table 26

CPRs Social Capital in Mamarla Village

District: Gumla	Block – Basia	
Total Geographical Area (In ha)	468	
Total Forest Area (In ha)	No	
Total CPRs Land (In ha)	2.22	(Community pastures, wastelands, common dumping, and threshing grounds, watershed drainages, village ponds, river and their banks)
Number of households	260	
Total population	1288	
Adults (above 14 year)	Male : 437	Female : 403
Children (0-14 year)	Boy : 288	Girl : 160
Caste/Tribe – Wise Distribution:		
Name of the Caste/Tribe	**Number of households**	**Population**
Scheduled Tribe (Santhal)	1288	260
Scheduled Caste	Nil	
Total number of literates		
Adults (above 14 year)	Male : 155	Female : 145
Children (6-14 year)	175	113
Livestock population: (%)	Bovine 77	Ovine 23
Physical products through CPRs		
• Food and fiber items	Domer, mango, mahua	
• Fodder	waste land	
• Fuel and timber	Nil	
• Water	Wells hand pumps	

CPRs Contributions		
• Employment creation	Nil	
• Income generation	Through SHGs	
• Asset accumulation	goatery	
• Sustenance of village Community	not observed	
• Grazing of animals	on common lands	

Social Capital Core Factors at work in the village: social ties and collective action

Source: Primary Survey 2018.

The agricultural cum training centre at Mamarla village was established on 23.05.2003 by the Gram Uthan Kendra, Gumla with a view to provide agricultural education and training, and to strengthen the organizational structure of the community of the area. Keeping this background in view, the GUK started organizing seminars/workshops/trainings on the subject related with agricultural education at the centre premises, of Mamarla village. From 1994, the GUK had started providing irrigational pumps, seeds, vermicomposts, bunding with water way, carpentry and blacksmithy trainings, mushroom trainings, pisciculture, mixed cropping and poultry farming trainings to the beneficiaries concerned.

The Wisdom Council of Mamarla was very active during the initial phase, but the work graph of the centre was started declining after 2013 due to various reasons, the most important among them are lacking of follow up strategy. However, the role of GUK is praiseworthy in organizing villagers for their good cause and promoting them through different economic activities for their livelihood. For an example, Miss. Anima Lakra, a young and energetic opinion building leader of the village had some two acres of land of her own. She somehow managed to get 11 piglets to open a piggery farm. Over the years she is doing well in her enterprise. The piglets gave birth to seven pigs out of four died and remaining three were sold in Rs. 10,000/-.

Table 27

CPRs Social Capital in Malsara Village

District: Simdega		Block – Bolba
Total Geographical Area (In ha)	2322	
Total Forest Area (In ha)	16	
Total CPRs Land (In ha)	7.5	(Community pastures, wastelands, common dumping, and threshing grounds, watershed drainages, village ponds, river and their banks)
Number of households	489	
Total population	2689	
Adults (above 14 year)	Male : 1003	Female : 956
Children (0-14 year)	Boy : 405	Girl : 325
Caste/Tribe – Wise Distribution		
Name of the Caste/Tribe	**Number of households**	**Population**
Scheduled Tribe (Sarna)	389	2066
Scheduled Caste (Lohara)	53	362
OBC	47	261
Total number of literates		113
Adults (above 14 year)	Male : 633	Female : 504
Children (6-14 year)	456	311
Livestock population: (%)	Bovine 65	Ovine 36
Physical products through CPRs		
• Food and fiber items	amla, ber, dumar, footkal, jackfruit, Blackberry, kend, piyar, sal	

• Fodder	common lands, private lands and protected forest	
• Fuel and timber	Asan, Acasia, Dahu, eucalyptus	
• Water	2 Tanks Tube-well	
• Manure	composed and fertilizers	
CPRs Contributions		
Employment	through forest 13 through water 3 and through land 13	
Income generation	through SHGs land, water and forest	
Asset accumulation	through hotty-culture, piggery and goatery	
Sustenance of village Community	moving towards but not sustained	
Grazing of animals	available about 5 ha.	
Protect new plantation	done through SHGs 3331 plants	

Social Capital Core Factors at work in the village: social ties, collective action

Source: Primary Survey 2018.

Malsara village is located in Bolba Tehsil of Simdega district. It is situated at 53km away from district headquarters- Simdega. The total geographical area of village is 2322 hectares. Malsara has a total population of 2689 persons. Simdega is the nearest town to Malsara. About 489 households are residing in this village.

Malsara is a village dominated by the tribal community; most of the households in the village belong to the scheduled tribes. The village is connected by a pucca road. The village has a primary school. The primary health centre for the village is at a distance of 18 kilometers from the village. All but 6 households in the village have electricity connection. There are 6 private wells, 6 public hand-pumps and 1 private pond in the village.

Malsara village has 16 hectres of dense forest surrounded by towering trees. Most households collect forest foods, fuel woods during the agricultural slack season- between November and May when their work loads are lower and the wood in the forest is fairly dry and easy to carry and sale. It has been reported that 55 percent of the sample households regularly collect various forest fruits and flowers. The most popular of these were Dahua, Kend and many others. Some of the most common forms of off-farm employment in the village include paid employment, small and petty trades, agricultural labour, casual labour, cash cropping and the sale of non-agricultural produce, etc. Although CPRs are very rich, due to lack of effective institutional set-up at the ground level, the tangible and intangible results were not apparent to the satisfactory extent.

Table 28

CPRs Social Capital in Belgarh Village

District: Simdega		Block – Simdega
Total Geographical Area (In ha)	412	
Total Forest Area (In ha)	Nil	
Total CPRs Land (In ha)	2.31	(Community pastures, wastelands, common dumping, and threshing grounds, watershed drainages, village ponds, river and their banks)
Number of households	86	

Total population	418	
Adults (above 14 year)	Male : 142	Female : 139
Children (0-14 year)	Boy : 78	Girl : 69
Caste/Tribe – Wise Distribution		
Name of the Caste/Tribe	**Number of households**	**Population**
Scheduled Tribe (Christian)	86	418
Scheduled Caste	Nil	Nil
Total number of literates:		
Adults (above 14 year	Male : 118	Female : 76
Children (6-14 year)	76	55
Livestock population: (%)	Bovine 77	Ovine 23
Physical products through CPRs		
• Food and fibre items	Domer, mango, mahua	
• Fodder	waste land	
• Fuel and timber	Nil	
• Water	wells hand pumps	
CPRs Contribution		
Employment	Nil	
Income generation	Through SHGs	
Asset accumulation	goatery	
Sustenance of village Community	not observed	
Grazing of animals	on common lands	

Social Capital Core Factors at work in the village: reciprocity and social ties

Source: Primary Survey 2018.

Belgarh village is located in Simdega *Tehsil* of Simdega district in Jharkhand. Simdega is the district & sub-district headquarters of Belgarh village. The total geographical area of village is 412 hectares. Belgarh has a total population of 418 peoples. There are about 86 houses in Belgarh village. Simdega is nearest town to Belgarh. Belgarh is a village having 2 hamlets namely, Grijan and Belgarh.

There are no landless families in this village. During rainy season, they grow paddy and in the winter they engage themselves for vegetable farming. The villagers are engaged in small trades, wage employment in the remaining period of 6 months. The village has two SHGs, and Farmers' Club. The SHG group has different names such as 1. Shiva Ajeevika 2. Ram Ajeevika 3. Sita Ajeevika 4. Suraj Ajeevika 5. Tara Aajeevika 6. Deep Aajeevika. Jyoti Kerketta, a member of the 'Deep Ajeevika Self Help Group' was interviewed by the author during the field visit and found that she had planted some trees like Subabul, Sagun, Gamhar, Arjun, etc. on her small plot of land in order to protect local ecology and environment. Now a day her sources of income are vegetable cultivation, paddy cultivation and small poultry. She had attended in the training programmes at KVK, Hazaribag on the capacity building subject which was organized the organisations. As a result she is now confident and empowered to lead her economic responsibilities as well as family affairs independently. Utilizing the inter-loaning facility, she had taken loans from SHG for creating family assets. This investment gave a multiplier effect. She had taken loan of Rs. 5000/-for vegetables cultivation in 2014, which gave her an income of Rs. 18735/- after three years (2014-2017). Thus, we find that she has been benefited heavily from the self-help group as it provides economic help to carry out her piggery and agricultural activities and also provides awareness and capacity building to make her self-empowered and self-sustained.

Table 29

CPRs Social Capital in Latauli Village

District: Khunti	Block – Torpa	
Total Geographical Area (In ha)	1697.87	
Total Forest Area (In ha)	16	
Total CPRs Land (In ha)	24	(Community pastures, wastelands, common dumping, and threshing grounds, watershed drainages, village ponds, river and their banks)
Number of households	218	
Total population	1228	
Adults (above 14 year)	Male : 428	Female : 403
Children (0-14 year)	Boy : 201	Girl : 195
Caste/Tribe – Wise Distribution		
Name of the Caste/Tribe	**Number of households**	**Population**
Scheduled Tribe (Christian)	176	1061
Scheduled Caste (Lohara, Turi, Weaver)	42	267
Total number of literates:		
Adults (above 14 year)	Male : 311	Female : 204
Children (6-14 year)	166	84
Livestock population: (%)	Bovine 50	Ovine 50
Physical products through CPRs		
• Food and fibre items	Blackberry, Jirhul, Kachnar, kusum,mango, pithod, Tamarind	
• Fodder	common land	

• Fuel and timber	asan,bahera, Dahu, dhaunta, eucalyptus	
• Water	Dobha, rivers,	
• Manure	both fertilizer and vermin composed	
CPRs Contribution		
Employment	through making leave plat 13 basket making 3 and collecting forest produce 13	
Income generation	through SHGs activities	
Asset accumulation	poultry	
Sustenance of village Community	subsistence level	
Grazing of animals	on common lands	
Protect new plantation	in process	
Reduce weed infestation	not recorded	

Social Capital Core Factors at work in the village: neighbourhood

Source: Primary Survey 2018.

Latauli village is located in Torpa Tehsil of Khunti district in Jharkhand. It is situated 15km away from sub-district headquarter Torpa and 45km away from district headquarter Khunti. The total geographical area of village is 1697.87 hectares. Latauli has a total population of 1228 peoples. There are about 218 houses in Latauli village. Torpa is nearest town to Latauli.

During the study the author tried to interact with some of the forest dwellers of the village. One of the respondents- Mr. Sebastian of

Lodobari tola said, "Earlier there was a big problem of drinking water in the village but when the natural resource of water (*dadi*) was given a proper structure by Hoffmann Social Service Society (HSSS), Khunti project our problem for water was solved and we started getting good water throughout the year.

When he was asked about the date engraved on the well platform being the year of 2017 which should have been 2013 as the well was constructed that year, he replied, "What was built by HSSS' got damaged by heavy rain last year and therefore we contributed some money from each family and some money  we took from village fund and repaired it and the year engraved on the platform is the year of last repair done by the collective effort of the community which too is an outcome of HSSS's intervention." He told that they have also made a drain type structure to channelize rainwater so that it does not destroy the well again.

He was then asked if the water is still used for the drinking purposes the response was very positive. He replied "Yes we do use. Now a hand pump has been installed and water is taken from both for drinking water purposes. Indeed, a bucket and a piece of cloth (for filtering) is kept always near the well so that anyone who comes to take water may will have no problem in drawing water from the well."

Mengotoli Gudlupiri is another tola of Latauli Village where 14 Munda families are residing inside the forest area where there is no transportation facility. At most vehicles go up to Latauli village of which it is a part. Miss Somari Hemrom D/o Mr. Chamra Hemrom is a physically challenged person by birth and when HSSS operative in the area, the project staffs helped her to get name registered in the disability pension and suggested too other possibilities. Today when on 17th of July 2018 the visit was made to the family by HSSS, Mr. Chamra Hemrom, the father of the girl said, "I am elder to you but you enlightened me and today I am a happy man. You have come at this hour when I am supposed to be having lunch. But your coming has filled me and please keep coming."

The girl who has very rarely associated with the outer world spoke to the HSSS team very boldly. She said, that she was helped by villagers to make her aadhar card and disability pension and that is the reason for which she is able to get the benefits from the government.

The intervention also helped people to get Prime Minister Awas Yojana. HSSS is the first organization to work in this area and they have made a big difference in the life of these poor village folks.

Latauli Khas is also a *tola* of Latauli village where 50 families are residing. All are Mundas and 5 families are *Rautia* among the social groups. There is a big well in the village which was made by the  government but was left incomplete due to some reasons. HSSS motivated the villagers and supported them with a little finance to complete the well. Mr. Santosh Bodra, the former Mukhia of the village narrates how the well was complete, "we ourselves provided stones for the well and have given our labour freely for the completion of the well." This well was the only source of good drinking water for the villagers. When this well was made every family without any discrimination took water for household use. Mr. Santosh Bodra says, "Today this well is very important for us. 16 to 17 families take water from this well. Now there are hand pumps in the village, therefore, those who are close to hand pumps they take water from the pumps but rest come to this well. Time to time we clean the well and if some money is needed for pumping the water out we use village fund."

Just beside the well there is one bucket and a piece of cloth. On asking the purpose of it he replied, "we all use this same bucket to draw water from the well and the same cloth we all use to filter the water".

Table 30
CPRs Social Capital in Hario Village

District: Chatra	Block – Simeria	
Total Geographical Area (In ha)	655	
Total Forest Area (In ha)	8	
Total CPRs Land (In ha)	13	(Community pastures, wastelands, common dumping, and threshing grounds, watershed drainages, village ponds, river and their banks)
Number of households	35	
Total population	175	
Adults (above 14 year)	Male : 51	Female : 50
Children (0-14 year)	Boy : 40	Girl : 34
Caste/Tribe – Wise Distribution		
Name of the Caste/Tribe	Number of households	Population
Scheduled Tribe (Christian)	35	175
Scheduled Caste	Nil	Nil
Total number of literates		
Adults (above 14 year)	Male : 6	Female : 39
Children (6-14 year)	53	26
Livestock population: (%)	Bovine 70	Ovine 30

Physical products through CPRs		
Food and fibre items	Blackberry, Jirhul, Kachnar, kusum,mango, pithod, Tamarind	
Fodder	common land	
Fuel and timber	asan,bahera, Dahu, dhaunta, eucalyptus	
Water	Dobha, rivers,	
Manure	both fertilizer and vermin composed	
CPRs Contribution		
Employment	through making leave plat 13 basket making 3 and collecting forest produce 13	
Income generation	through SHGs activities	
Asset accumulation	poultry	
Sustenance of village Community	subsistence level	
Grazing of animals	on common lands	
Protect new plantation	in process	
Reduce weed infestation	not recorded	

Social Capital Core Factors at work in the village: social ties and collective action.

Source: Primary Survey 2018.

Hario hamlet falls under the Torar revenue village. All families are Christians by religion. The village has a small group of community who managed forest land. The village has two SHGs –Jyoti SHG and Rose 'SHG'. Sohrai Tirkey on the Hario village had joined Jyoti SHG in 2008. Currently, he lives in a joint family comprising of nine members i.e. with her parents, two brothers, three sisters and her sister-in-law. According to her the staff members of JVK had motivated her to join the Jyoti SHG. JVK had explained that "at the time of financial crisis there is no need of asking money from others. Rather you may start saving your own money through SHG and you get rid of borrowing during the time of crisis". Accordingly, she had joined the SHG by opening her account with Rs. 5 per week. She reported that this amount get changed to Rs. 10 and Rs. 20 per week in 2008 and in 2017 respectively. Now the amount is ranged between Rs. 25 to Rs. 50 per week. At present, all the three other sisters have also joined this SHG and she has become the treasurer of the group. According to her, joining the group proved to be very helpful as it changed her life. After attending the awareness capacity building and other training programmes (on livestock rearing, poultry, SRI, and on paddy and vegetable cultivation) now she feels to be self-dependent, empowered and self-sustained. She had taken a loan of Rs. 2000 from the SHG for cultivation purposes in the year 2016. She had spent this amount on purchasing of fertilizer, seed, labour, etc. for cultivation in her land. In 2018, agriculture harvest brought her Rs. 6000 as income excluding the harvest for household consumption and other expenses on social activities. This saved income gave a multiplier effect as out of the saved Rs. 6000 she used Rs. 3000 for vegetable cultivation (cabbage and cauliflower) which brought her an income of Rs. 31,000 at the end of the season. But to her bad luck she had to spend the entire amount in the treatment of illness of some of her family members during the next year as every month she had to spend more than Rs. 2000 on the ill members of her family. As a result the original amount of loan could only be paid back by her by the end of next year. However, she feels herself happy to be associated with the SHG as well JVK, Hazaribag.

Table 31

CPRs Social Capital in Angara Village

District: Chatra		Block – Simeria
Total Geographical Area (In ha)	890.42	
Total Forest Area (In ha)	14	
Total CPRs Land (In ha)	7.39	(Community pastures, wastelands, common dumping, and threshing grounds, watershed drainages, village ponds, river and their banks)
Number of households	84	
Total population	445	
Adults (above 14 year)	Male : 105	Female : 100
Children (0-14 year)	Boy : 120	Girl : 120
Caste/Tribe – Wise Distribution		
Name of the Caste/Tribe	Number of households	Population
Scheduled Tribe (Christian)	84	445
Scheduled Caste	Nil	Nil
Total number of literates:		
Adults (above 14 year):	Male : 135	Female :101
Children (6-14 year)	89	77
Livestock population: (%)	Bovine 77	Ovine 23
Physical products through CPRs		
Food and fibre items	Blackberry, Jirhul, Kachnar, kusum,mango, pithod, Tamarind	
Fodder	common land	

Fuel and timber	asan,bahera, Dahu, dhaunta, eucalyptus	
Water	Dobha, rivers,	
Manure	both fertilizer and vermin composed	
CPRs Contribution		
Employment	through making leave plat 13 basket making 3 and collecting forest produce 13	
Income generation	through SHGs activities	
Asset accumulation	poultry	
Sustenance of village Community	subsistence level	
Grazing of animals	on common lands	
Protect new plantation	in process	
Reduce weed infestation	not recorded	

Social Capital Core Factors at work in the village: reciprocity, leadership

Source: Primary Survey 2018.

Angara village is located in Simeria Tehsil of Chatra district. It is situated 6 km away from sub-district headquarters Simeria and 18 km away from district headquarters Chatra. Chatra is the nearest town to Angara village. The total geographical area of village is 890.42 hectares. Angara has a total population of 445 peoples. There are about 84 households in Angara village.

In the past, the villagers were unorganized. Literacy rate of the village was very low. Food security was a big concern for them. Children were sent to forest with cattle for grazing them instead of going to school. Their livelihood was dependent on grazing cattle and selling firewood. The women folk were engaged mainly in collection of firewood and forest products. Jan Vikas Kendra started thinking on the issues. It started organizing the villagers through formation of SHGs for women and Farmers' Clubs for men. Land leveling and plot bunding was done. Several training and exposure programmes related to 'Forest Rights', agricultural and NRM were undertaken. SHGs were formed. People were given inputs in vegetable cultivation. Some 22 families of Oraon (20) and Munda (2) who were displaced from Khunti and Hatia-dams had given lands to them for their settlement and rehabilitation. Now the community is able to take ownership of the local natural resources. The community has become aware about the importance of health particularly knowledge about herbal remedies for minor 'natural' illness. They discuss the health issues in the open discussion and in the village meetings. The community has deployed a system of 'collective work' (social capital) in agriculture or any emergency situation arises in the community like agricultural processing, repairing of dam, and road, land leveling, etc. The community is capable to resolve the conflicts, (social capital) in the village. If any conflict arises in the community, they call for a meeting and resolve the matter in the community level itself.

Table 32

CPRs Social Capital in Sos Village

District: Chatra		Block – Simeria
Total Geographical Area (In ha)	966	
Total Forest Area (In ha)	13	
Total CPRs Land (In ha)	11	(Community pastures, wastelands, common dumping, and threshing grounds, watershed drainages, village ponds, river and their banks)

Number of households	75	
Total population	544	
Adults (above 14 year)	Male : 200	Female : 184
Children (0-14 year)	Boy : 135	Girl : 24
Caste/Tribe – Wise Distribution		
Name of the Caste/Tribe	**Number of households**	**Population**
Scheduled Tribe (Christian)	40	284
(Sarna)	15	105
Scheduled Caste (Ganju)	15	120
(Bhuiya)	05	35
Total number of literates:	89	77
Adults (above 14 year)	Male : 75	Female : 80
Children (6-14 year)	100	70
Livestock population: (%)	Bovine 65	Ovine 35
Physical products through CPRs		
Food and fibre items	bar, papaya, Jackfruit,	
Fodder	common lands	
Fuel and timber	gamhar, sal, sagwan,asan	
Water	pond, river, and its tributaries	
Manure	vermin composed and fertilizers	
CPRs Contribution		
Employment	through firewood collection	
Income generation	through forest products and SHGs	

Asset accumulation	fishery, poultry,	
Sustenance of village Community	subsistence level	
Grazing of animals	on common lands	
Protect new plantation	3000 trees	

Social Capital Core Factors at work in the village: collective action and networking

Source: Primary Survey 2018.

Sos village is located in Simaria Tehsil of Chatra district. It is situated 28km away from sub-district headquarter Simaria and 43km away from district headquarter Chatra. The total geographical area of village is 966 hectares. Sos has a total population of 544 peoples. There are about 75 houses in Sos village. Simaria is nearest town to Sos.

SOS (Chatra District) is a village of mixed community consisting of ST, SC, Sarna, and OBC population. It is divided into four tolas: 1. Baramia, 2. Sapahi, 3. Bhuniya Tola, 4. Girija Toli. The village has three self-help groups 1. Mahila Samakhya Society (12 members) 2. Suman Mahila Samakhya SOS (11 members) 3. Jyoti Mahila Samakhya (11 members). All were active in their fields. They provide petty loans to the SHG- members from time to time at the time of the needs. JVK has been providing its services in the area since last 15 years. It has provided tube wells, wells and agricultural implements to the farmers of the village under 'Farmer's club scheme'. However due to water scarcity only mono-cropping is practiced by the farmers. The main problems in the village as stated by respondents were: 1. Education, 2. Timely distribution of seeds, and 3. Employability. Here it is observed that the village is surrounded by undulated topography, means upland and medium uplands owned largely by poor people has not served by the flow of irrigation systems. However, lift irrigation is the only alternative. Management of JVK should take a note of this.

Table 33

CPRs Social Capital in Dahwa Village

District: Hazaribag	Block – Sadar Hazaribag	
Total Geographical Area (In ha)	133	
Total Forest Area (In ha)	15	
Total CPRs Land (In ha)	21	(Community pastures, wastelands, common dumping, and threshing grounds, Watershed, drainages, village ponds, river and their banks)
Number of households	35	
Total population	163	
Adults (above 14 year)	Male : 50	Female : 49
Children (0-14 year)	Boy : 43	Girl : 21
Caste/Tribe – Wise Distribution		
Name of the Caste/Tribe	**Number of households**	**Population**
Scheduled Tribe (Sarna)	29	135
(Christian)	6	28
Scheduled Caste	Nil	120
Total number of literates:	05	35
Adults (above 14 year)	Male : 26	Female : 22
Children (6-14 year)	23	13
Livestock population: (%)	Bovine 75	Ovine 25
Physical products through CPRs		
Food and fibre items	Blackberry, Jirhul, Kachnar, kusum, mango, pithod, Tamarind	
Fodder	common land	

Fuel and timber	asan,bahera, Dahu, dhaunta, eucalyptus	
Water	Dobha, rivers,	
Manure	both fertilizer and vermin composed	
CPRs Contribution		
Employment	through making leave plat 13 basket making 3 and collecting forest produce 13	
Income generation	through SHGs activities	
Asset accumulation	poultry	
Sustenance of village Community	subsistence level	
Grazing of animals	on common lands	
Grazing of animals	on common lands	
Protect new plantation	3000 trees	

Social Capital Core Factors at work in the village: collective action

Source: Primary Survey 2018.

Sustaining Water Bodies for Agricultural Practices in Dahwa Village

Dahwa is a small hamlet of village Gurhet and situated in Sadar block of Hazaribag. The area is surrounded by terrene hills and forest. Dhahwa has 45 households and dominated by *Santal* tribe. They are basically farmers and fully depended on monsoon rains due to lack of alternative source of irrigation facility. Many of them do migrate to earn an income to maintain their families during the slack season.

Jan Vikas Kendra implemented Natural Resource Management project in this area supported by Caritas India during the year 2011-2012. The project helped the villagers to dig a water body in their own land. It was a decision taken in the village council. Now, 7 years have passed and the pond has continued to be a boon to the farmers. They have maintained the pond to this date as it sustains their cultivation. The pond irrigates almost 5 acres of land belonging to 7 marginal farmers besides fishery and duck rearing. The pond is also used for other purposes. The maintenance of the structure without any further support from Jan Vika Kendra is a significant indicator of people's realization to work for common good collectively (social capital).

Addition Income through Fruits Plantation in Jamuary Village
The Mission Hamlet is part of Jamuary village in Base Gram panchayat in Katkamdag Block of Hazaribag district. The hamlet is well known for fruit plantation, especially the Mango cultivation. It is a small hamlet, consisted of 12 households and mostly belongs to either marginal or small farmer's category.

Masih Hans, progressive farmers asserted that, before year 2014, many of us used to migrate to different places in search of job, especially when paddy cultivation was over. He also articulated that we don't have any other choice, because it was very difficult to feed family members throughout the year from one cultivation, i.e. Paddy production.

They also explained that earlier we were not aware about the importance of fruit plantation, its process, pest control management and market linkages, etc. Hanry Hans, a farmer told that almost 03 years ago Jan Vikas Kendra implemented a project on Agriculture Development and during this period many of us were skilled on fruit plantation - an alternative source of surplus income. Since 2015 onwards, we have made a plantation of Mango /Other types of fruit trees on wasteland and getting good amount of return every year. Now they asserted that none of us now migrates outside in search of employment. They have also understood about the value addition of each fruit plants and it is increasing every year and adding more income. *Today almost all the 12 families are engaged in Mango & other fruit plantations and getting additional income out of it which has almost put an end to migration. Now the parents are able to give more time for their children and take care of their families.*

Construction of Village Link Road through Collective Action

Hurnali is a Munda dominated village situated under Piri gram panchayat

of Chatra district of Jharkhand. Hurnali is a village located in remote rural area and surrounded by dense forest. Hurnali is still backward due to the lack of basic amenities like drinking water, road, education, health, etc. Tetua Tari is a hamlet of Hurnali, and famous for its strong socio-cultural capital. The people of this village are honest, hardworking and simple. *Tetua Tari* has 14 households. All are Oraons. People are literate only at the primary and secondary levels. They are well aware about their rights and entitlements. Youth and young farmers seem to be very active in village development. The village was not connected by any road linking it to the outside world. They could not transport anything to their village, as even tractors could not reach to the village. Jan Vikas Kendra worked among these villagers for agriculture development and related with fishery activities. One day, the entire village community came together at a common place '*Akhra*' and decided to make 2 kms long road by "*Shramdan* (labour donation). Within a few months, the decision became a reality. Currently, **this road is the only mode for transportation, and linking the village to outside villages and towns to avail various services to the villagers of Hurnali.**

The villagers also have a *PACHA, PERSA* (Support) systems as per which they conduct meetings with all headmen, share day to day problems and try to find solutions together. Tetua Tari hamlet is a finest example of community participation and ownership in maintaining local resources and living together with trust and harmony.

Community Development through *Punch* System at Hardia Hamlet

Badgaon, a Munda dominated village is located in Chope gram panchayat of Simaria block of Chatra district. Hardia is one of the hamlets of Badgaon. Khadia Munda's are residing in the village over the period of last five decades. Alike other tribal groups, Khadia Munda's are mainly depending  on agriculture during kharif season and collection of forest products during dry seasons including daily wage activities.

A few key features of Hardia make them different from others – it's because of existing PACHA (Support) system, active Van Suraksha Samiti, community contribution in preparation of link road & maintenance of pond, etc.

The construction of village link road is a remarkable work performed by villagers with community effort. Speaking to us, they explained that they were concerned every year of the rainwater caused damage to the village road. Therefore, during one of their meetings held in the village Akhra, it was collectively decided that every house will raise a mud wall in front of each house to cut the current of the rainwater flow and thus minimize the damage to the road. Every year, they care for the road and are maintaining it from further damage.

The village has also a **Van Suraksha Samiti** which has been existing in this village well before project intervention. The head of every household is part of this samiti and they take turn in guarding the village forest. They managed to save the trees from any illegal felling. *Community sense appears to be strong among the villagers.*

Maintenance of Pond by Community Effort in Bandgaon Village

The farmers of Badgaon village under Chope gram panchayat have proved themselves to be a changemaker. The villagers have been engaged in

 agricultural activities through regular care and maintenance of a pond (200×100×10 feet) given to them through a project in 1976. The villagers together have maintained the pond and have used it for irrigation, fishery and duck rearing purposes.

The pond is situated at Hardia hamlet. Nearly 34 households of Munda community are residing in this area since a long time. It was gathered from them that they struggled to cultivate vegetables, or sometimes even paddy during a poor monsoon season, or for other purposes. The pond came as a blessing for the villagers. However, the villagers observed that the water level of the pond started getting down from the past few years. Jan Vikas Kendra motivated them, and they decided to deepen the pond by voluntary effort. The villagers worked together and deepened the pond. During the survey it was found that all about 7 acres of land were irrigated through the deepened pond.

Construction of Wooden Bridge by Mutual Contribution of Farmers in Sons Village

Sons, a revenue village in Simaria of Chatra district is situated in a tough terrain, around 46 kilometers from district head quarter of Chatra district in Jharkhand.

The village is surrounded with a dense forest and hills, with poor infrastructural facilities viz. road, drinking water, health and transport, etc.

As reported by the villagers, they had to face hardship while going out of the village having no road (Kucha/Pucca). The toughest time was during rainy season as the rivulet close to the village would get inundated making it almost impossible for kids to reach schools or for sick people to be taken to hospitals.

One day all the villagers sat together and decided to construct a wooden bridge across the rivulet to solve this perennial problem. Every member agreed to make a contribution both in kinds, cash and physical labour. The bridge spanning 30' long was constructed in the year 2015. According to the villagers 10 kms walk has been cut short to just 2 kms to go to school, or market or other places. Collective effort to ease the life for all.

Dissemination of Health and Hygiene through Marches

The young girls of Kathotia village in Katkamsandi block are playing a crucial role in the dissemination of information about personal hygiene, cleanliness, health care, and environment among the village folks.

The "Kishori Swasthya Club" formed and mobilized under the project "Holistic Development through Health Care & Poverty Alleviation" in 20 revenue villages of Katkamsandi has created this possibility.

About 11 members are in the organization of *Kishori Swasthya* Club. They do conduct regular monthly meetings and share their problems on

various issues like personal hygiene, health behavior, cleanliness, environment, nutrition, etc.

They are also, in turn, educating the villagers about all these aspects. The villagers are extremely happy by doing so as their children are able to make such a valuable contribution for the wellbeing of the village.

Sitting of Vigilance Committee on the Problems of Trafficking

A minor girl, aged 17 years belonging to OBC community of Madgada village, was saved and rescued from the grip of traffickers. The incident came into light when a person of the same village informed Smt. Reshma Devi, a member of the vigilance committee, anti –trafficking task force constituted by the Jan Vikas Kendra in its operational villages.

As reported by the villagers, the parents sold their daughter to a trafficker from Haryana on a payment of Rs. 40,000. The stepmother was not caring the girl and she wanted to get rid of her. Both the husband and wife decided to sell her by organizing a fake marriage ceremony at home in Madgada. The villagers came to know the fact and they immediately informed Smt. Reshma Devi, a member vigilance committee about the happening. She rushed to the house and saved the girl from the trafficker. This intervention has generated a community consciousness in the village.

Table 34

CPRs Social Capital in Alaunja Kalan Village

District: Hazaribag	Block – Ichak	
Total Geographical Area (In ha)	298	
Total Forest Area (In ha)	No	
Total CPRs Land (In ha)	3.33	(Community pastures, wastelands, common dumping, and threshing grounds, watershed drainages, village ponds, river and their banks)
Number of households	370	
Total population	1951	
Adults (above 14 year)	Male : 703	Female : 693
Children (0-14 year)	Boy : 311	Girl : 244
Caste/Tribe – Wise Distribution		
Name of the Caste/Tribe	**Number of households**	**Population**
Scheduled Tribe (Christian)	70	411
Scheduled Caste	300	1540
Total number of literates:	Nil	120
Adults (above 14 year)	Male : 335	Female : 300
Children (6-14 year)	266	190
Livestock population: (%)	Bovine 80	Ovine 20
Physical products through CPRs	**Bovine 75**	**Ovine 25**
• Food and fiber items	No	Ovine 35
• Fodder	open grazing	
• Fuel and timber	No	
• Water	river, well, tank	
• Manure	fertilizer	
CPRs Contribution	both fertilizer and vermin composed	

Employment	nonfarm employment, seasonal migration	
Income generation	petty business	
Asset accumulation	data not available	
Sustenance of village Community	pre stage	
Grazing of animals	open grazing on private and common lands	
Protect new plantation	not at all	
Reduce weed infestation	no	
Protect new plantation	3000 trees	

Social Capital Core Factors at work in the village: cooperation with stigmatized people, vertical and horizontal social ties

Source: Primary Survey 2018.

Empowering Villagers for HIV/Aids Prevention and far Beyond: Alomja Kurdh Shows the Way

Alaunja Kurdha village is located in Ichak block of Hazaribag district. The village is known for unity and for its collective action. Currently, the member of HIV/AIDS cases in Jharkhand state is approaching 20018 (Jharkhand State AIDS Control Society estimates). Such a number may appear small compared to Jharkhand's three crore – plus population. However, HIV/AIDS spreads in Jharkhand is a social reality. During 2016, the number of people infected rose to 20018 persons, from 18039 persons in the previous year. In just one year, numbers of people living with HIV increased by 1989 cases; but in the age group of 15-49 years, one out of every 100 persons in HIV/AIDS are positive. The recent sharp rise in people living with HIV clearly indicated that disease has taken root in every corner of Jharkhand. The figure of HIV/AIDS in

Hazaribag district was of 2000 plus. Thus, about 10 percent of the total HIV/AIDS cases are found in Hazaribag district alone. For an in-depth understanding of the situation, a case study of HIV/AIDS victim's family of Alonja Kurdh village of Hazaribag was conducted during the author's visit.

In the afternoon, we met a Turia family consisting of four members –all have been suffering from HIV/AIDS since 15 years. But they live in the community very happily without any stigma. The family does not own any land, except a small hut, and almost invariably works as landless laborers. They earn Rs. 5600 per month through this traditional occupation – basket manufacturing. The level of education is extremely low and culture of poverty in which they live and breathe has left deep scars on their personality and behavior. It is natural, therefore, that any agency like HOLY Cross Community Care Centre, Hazaribag, working for them must need for a long gestation period in which some of the basic *ideas* of modern existence may take root among them, though the NGO has been accompanying them in their life journey under the able leadership of Sr. Britto H.C. and her HIV/AIDS team.

The author met with NGOs, researchers, and government officials in this regard on access to HIV/AIDS eradication campaign, and potential new research on technological change supported by a social theory. Here are victims and community as well as the counselors' reflections on HIV/AIDS programme. They feel that HIV campaign has not yet achieved the target and still HIV disease remains wide spread in the society. They feel that the campaign should not merely target oriented, but social in its dimensions. The emphasis should be on educating the people in its concept and rationale of HIV eradication within the context of the functioning of society as a whole. The author has given an excellent and fascinating account of a day journey with the HIV/AIDS search volunteers. The team has recommended that as the disease spreads to the general public, it is important to combat AIDS on many fronts, from the education of young people to the maintenances of a safe and secure blood supply. Secondly, Counseling also encourages more open discussion on sensitive matters in communities and between partners.

Shift from BCC Model to Empowerment Model

When the Snehadeep Holy Cross Hazaribag (SHCH) Project started in 2005, its structure was based on the behavioral change communication (BCC) Model. As expected, the process of shifting the Project's approach towards empowering one of the most deprived and stigmatized sections of the society, encountered various types of obstacles, both from within the family, community and, more seriously, from outside it. Thirteen years' experience (2005-2018) of the SHCH has demonstrated that the success of any STD/HIV/AIDS intervention project among any poor, powerless and stigmatized group depends heavily on how far its members actively participate in its activities and what roles they play in the Project's structure.

Achievement in terms of beneficiaries attended HIV/AIDS awareness programme and training provided by SHCH to them on income generation programmes during 2017-2018 were as follows:

S. No.	Activities	No. of Beneficiaries
1	Total no. of participants who has attended HIV/AIDS awareness programme at SHGs centre Hazaribag.	46,549
2	Total no. of participants who have attended sensitization meetings with CBO's service providers, health workers.	3673
3	Trainings provided to them on income generation and asset creation programmes.	653

Source: Annual Report of SHCH Hazaribag 2017-18.

Broadly speaking, our visit to 'HIV/AIDS community' at *Alonja Kurdh* village of Ichak block in Hazaribag district, On July 8th, 2017, however, was not primarily related to the fact that Mr. Lakhan Turia, his wife and two sons (17 & 10 years old) who are HIV/AIDS victims and have most vulnerable links in the development chain, require merely sympathy, goodwill for the stigma attached to HIV/AIDS. It is rather related to the fact that they require "counseling, treatment and insurance" that such epidemic will not spread to more in the community.

Table 35

CPRs Social Capital in Banpur Village

District: Ranchi	Block – Angara	
Total Geographical Area (In ha)	846	
Total Forest Area (In ha)	15	
Total CPRs Land (In ha)	31	(Community pastures, wastelands, common dumping, and threshing grounds, watershed drainages, village ponds, river and their banks)
Number of households	215	
Total population	1013	
Adults (above 14 year)	Male : 382	Female : 348
Children (0-14 year)	Boy : 150	Girl : 133
Caste/Tribe – Wise Distribution		
Name of the Caste/Tribe	**Number of households**	**Population**
Scheduled Tribe (Christian)	86	401
(Sarna)	127	601
(Lohra)	02	11
Scheduled Caste	Nil	Nil
Total number of literates:		
Adults (above 14 year):	Male : 246	Female : 194
Children (6-14 year)	112	56

Livestock population: (%)	Bovine 65	Ovine 35
Physical products through CPRs		
Food and fibre items	ber, kusum, mahua flower-dori fruit, kend, jackfruit, blackberry, Char, Guava, Mango, Dahuwa, Khajur (Dates)	
Fodder	green leaves and grass	
Fuel and timber	sakhuwa, eucalyptus, sal, gamhar, Tunj	
Water	river,dobha, tube wells irrigation and drinking wells, ponds	
Manure	vermicompost and fertilizers	
CPRs Contribution	petty business	
Employment	through firewood collection	
Income generation	through SHGs and cultivation, lac	
Asset accumulation	piggery, hotty culture, goatery, duckery	
Sustenance of village Community	depended upon agriculture and forestry	
Grazing of animals	common lands	
Protect new plantation	Afforestation	
Reduce weed infestation	to some extent	

Social Capital Core Factors at work in the village: leadership, collective action

Source: Primary Survey 2018.

Banpur village is located in Angara Tehsil of Ranchi district in Jharkhand, India. It is situated at 20km away from sub-district headquarters-Angara and 30km away from district headquarters- Ranchi, which is the nearest town to Banpur.

Banpur is a village comprising of 13 hamlets. It is a total tribal village with 215 households. The total geographical area of the village is 846 ha of which 362.16 ha are under cultivation. However, only 212.80 ha are being used for cultivation. The village has 2 primary schools. The primary health centre in the village is in Banpur. There are 22 private and 3 public wells, 12 private and 13 public hand-pumps and 1 public and 8 private ponds in the village.

There is a need for more livelihood support programmes in this region to improve the economic condition of the people. More importance needs to be given to income generating activities in the village.

Banpur village is one of the target revenue villages of *Swadhikar* project. Most of the tribal people are marginalised and vulnerable. The area is covered with forests. Agriculture land is sizeable. The Jharkhand government started Public Distribution System (PDS) in the region for the marginalised population.

Matiyas Lakra served as the PDS dealer of the Banpur village. He was engaged as a catechist of the GEL church in the past.

He had a good behavioural attitude in the society. But now a day his behaviour has changed. Some misconduct practices were found in him. Ultimately, the villagers called a meeting and decided to eliminate him and appoint a new one.

CPRs Social Capital Practices

Bicha Oraon belongs to Banpur Village. He is a role model for the villagers. Before the intervention of Catholic Charities in the village, he used to cultivate lac. He did not have the technical idea about the lac cultivation.

 Bicha Oraon started taking an active part in the lac training program. At present, he has expanded to 155 BER & KUSUM trees. When interacted with him, he told that the investment in lac cultivation is around Rs. 20000/-. The women of Banpur have also been involved in this productive work. It was found that changes are taking place in them due to SHG interventions, especially related with agriculture, lac cultivation and livestock.

Table 36

CPRs Social Capital in Saidup Village

District: Latehar	Block – Barwadih	
Total Geographical Area (In ha)	864	
Total Forest Area (In ha)	15	
Total CPRs Land (In ha)	18	(Community pastures, wastelands, common dumping, and threshing grounds, watershed drainages, village ponds, river and their banks)
Number of households	394	
Total population	2147	
Adults (above 14 year)	Male : 733	Female : 703
Children (0-14 year)	Boy : 450	Girl : 261
Caste/Tribe – Wise Distribution		

Name of the Caste/Tribe	Number of households	Population
Scheduled Tribe (Christian)	294	1644
(Sarna)	100	53
Scheduled Caste	No	
Total number of literates:		
Adults (above 14 year)	Male : 653	Female :401
Children (6-14 year)	433	211
Livestock population: (%)	Bovine 65	Ovine 35
Physical products through CPRs		
Food and fiber items	amla, different fruits leaves and flowers, jackfruit,	
Fodder	forest leaves trees and grass	
Fuel and timber	asan, gamhar, sakhuwa, sal, Jackfruit	
Water	rivers, check-dam, dobha	
Manure	fertilizers and vermin composed	
CPRs Contribution		
Employment	agriculture hotty culture, forestry,	
Income generation	SHGs, trade-business	
Asset accumulation	through piggery, forest products	
Sustenance of village Community	25 % sustainability	
Grazing of animals	common lands, waste land and pasture land	

Protect new plantation	more than 5000 plantation	
Reduce weed infestation	to a larger extent	
Reduce weed infestation	to some extent	

Social Capital Core Factors at work in the village: conflict resolution was done and collective action women leadership

Source: Primary Survey 2018.

Saidup village is located in Barwadih Tehsil of Latehar district in Jharkhand, India. It is situated at 20km away from sub-district headquarter-Barwadih and 85km away from district headquarter-Latehar. The total geographical area of village is 864 hectares. Saidup has a total population of 2147 peoples. There are about 394 houses in Saidup village. Latehar is nearest town to Saidup.

Agriculture practices through SRI method were done in this village from 2012. Besides, seed distribution among farmers, seed treatment, nursery bed making, transplantation of saplings, run of Cono-Weeder Machines, and making of pesticides called ARIT-JAL were in process. It has been reported that 34 farmers adopted SRI techniques and the same number of farmers had received food security during the year. Tree plantation was done through SHGs ownership. About 606 types of trees were planted through the SHGs. SHGs were active in fostering vermin compost practices in the village. During the study 38 farmers were found in adopting SWI method for their cultivation. Piglet distribution work was also done, but due to some practical problem it was not completed in due time. So far as organizational structure of this village is concern, there is a farmers' club, youth club, wisdom club, and self-help groups. Their function is to watch NRM, forest protection and regulation of the CPRs, activities.

Broadly speaking, 'Rita SHG' is very active in the village. This SHG has started making *Mahuwa Achar* which is very popular in this area. Women of this village are very active in generating part time employment through CPRs and through cultivation. The SHGs are linked with Banks and Government programmes. Saidup people generally believe in Church inspired development with the protection of indigenous seed species (CPRs), at village and community levels. Munda community was totally banned on making and selling *Haria*. By this process, the villagers have resolved to change the society for the betterment.

Table 37

CPRs Social Capital in Rungikocha Village

District: West Sighbhum	Block – Manoharpur	
Total Geographical Area (In ha)	444	
Total Forest Area (In ha)	13	
Total CPRs Land (In ha)	16	(Community pastures, wastelands, common dumping, and threshing grounds, watershed drainages, village ponds, river and their banks)
Number of households	141	
Total population	688	
Adults (above 14 year)	Male : 283	Female : 205
Children (0-14 year)	Boy : 107	Girl : 93
Caste/Tribe – Wise Distribution		
Name of the Caste/Tribe	**Number of households**	**Population**
Scheduled Tribe (Christian)	141	688
Scheduled Caste	No	No
Total number of literates:		
Adults (above 14 year)	Male :155	Female : 95
Children (6-14 year)	86	43
Livestock population: (%)	Bovine 77	Ovine 23

Physical products through CPRs		
Food and fiber items	amla, different fruits leaves and flowers, jackfruit,	
Fodder	(forest leaves trees and grass)	
Fuel and timber	(asan, gamhar, sakhuwa, sal, Jackfruit)	
Water	(river, well check dam)	
Manure	(vermin composed and fertilizers)	
CPRs Contribution		
Employment	agriculture hotty culture, forestry,	
Income generation	SHGs, trade-business	
Asset accumulation	through piggery, forest products	
Sustenance of village Community	25 % sustainability	
Grazing of animals	common lands, waste land and pasture land	
Protect new plantation	more than 5000 plantation	
Reduce weed infestation	to a larger extent	

Social Capital Core Factors at work in the village: leadership, collective action

Source: Primary Survey 2018.

Note: Detail discussion about Rungikocha village is given with sample village of 'Koenjali', which is given below:

Table 38

CPRs Social Capital in Koenjali Village

District: West Singhbhum	Block – Manoharpur	
Total Geographical Area (In ha)	100.11	
Total Forest Area (In ha)	No	10
Total CPRs Land (In ha)	13	(Community pastures, wastelands, common dumping, and threshing grounds, watershed drainages, village ponds, river and their banks)
Number of households	36	
Total population	173	
Adults (above 14 year)	Male : 58	Female : 53
Children (0-14 year)	Boy : 34	Girl : 32
Caste/Tribe – Wise Distribution		
Name of the Caste/Tribe	Number of households	Population
Scheduled Tribe (Christian)	36	173
Scheduled Caste	Nil	Nil
Total number of literates:		
Adults (above 14 year)	Male : 49	Female : 42
Children (6-14 year)	43	29
Livestock population: (%)	Bovine 77	Ovine 23
Physical products through CPRs		
Food and fiber items	amla, different fruits leaves and flowers, jackfruit,	
Fodder	(forest leaves trees and grass)	

Fuel and timber	(asan, gamhar, sakhuwa, sal, Jackfruit)	
Water	(river, well check dam)	
Manure	(vermin composed and fertilizers)	
CPRs Contribution		
Employment	agriculture hotty culture, forestry,	
Income generation	SHGs, trade-business	
Asset accumulation	through piggery, forest products	
Sustenance of village Community	25 % sustainability	
Grazing of animals	common lands, waste land and pasture land	
Protect new plantation	more than 5000 plantation	
Reduce weed infestation	to a larger extent	

Social Capital Core Factors at work in the village: reciprocity, social ties

Source: Primary Survey 2018.

Rungikocha and Koenjali Villages

Both Rungikocha and Koenjali are tribal villages which come under Manoharpur block in West Singhbhum District of Jharkhand. Rungikocha village has 141 households with a total population of 444 persons. The village is situated at distance of 78 kms from Chaibasa Headquarters. The area is full of rocky waste land. The main agricultural land exists near the irrigation tank/ponds. Both the villages are completely fallen under forest area. The main source of income of the villagers is agriculture, labor, and forest based products. Both area are totally rain-fed and as such the period of cultivation in very less e.g. 4-5 months in a year. Only those families are more depended on agriculture who have landholdings near some water resources. Otherwise the villagers are involved in labor work both agricultural and non-agricultural. The villagers in the area use firewood as fuel for cooking. The women folk share most of the job responsibility in the household than men. They cook and go to forest for collecting firewood, they also go to the market to sale firewood apart from assisting the men in farming and even go as temporary or permanent labor force apart from tending their children and families.

Self-help groups at work

Mahila Samitis were formed in both the villages in the year 2011. Motivated by Catholic Charities Jamshedpur, 16 women from Rungikocha and Koenjali villages came forward and sought membership. The members had started with a weekly saving Rs 10 per week. The SHGs started very well and were functioning very smoothly with a weekly meeting on every Sunday. The groups have deposited Rs 26000/ towards repayment of loan to the Bank Manoharpur.

Problem arouse in 2016, when PDS was allotted to the self-help group of Koenjali village. President of the group was taking care of the supply of rice, wheat and kerosene to the villagers. Then one day an allegation was made on him by the members of the SHG regarding corrupt practices prevailing in the PDS. As a result, the president of this group was in dispute regarding poor maintenance of funds of the SHG and the irregularity in the PDS. This led to the disintegration of the *Mahila Samiti* of Koenjali and also winding of the PDS center allotted to the group.

This situation continued for long. During the study it was found that SHG was not functioning at all. After a lot of discussion on why the SHG needs to be continued for the betterment of the people in general and specially for women folk of the village, the author succeeded in motivating them and the group members had finally decided that in the SHG meeting they would ask the president about the details of deposited fund of the SHG. If she provides the details of amount collected for saving then the group would allow her to continue with PDS responsibility otherwise SHG members would decide in fresh way about who should be given the responsibility of PDS next.

Concluding Remarks

We have given a brief description of the general socio-economic and cultural features of the sample villages (p 144-193) and have shown how CPRs and 'Social Capital', actually at work in these villages. Inter-religion and caste-relations in these villages constitute "vertical ties". They are bound together by 'economic ties' (Social Capital). In the study villages, with their largely subsistence, and not fully monetized economy, the relationship between the different tribal groups take a particular form. The relationship is generally stable, and usually inherited. Overall impacts of CPRs Social Capital practices made by these villages are narrated in the following paragraphs:

Like many other rural people in India and throughout the developing world (Joshi, 1983; Eckholm, 1984; Agarwal. 1986b; Dankelman and Davidson, 1988; Henshal Momsen, 1991; Pathak, 1994; World Resources Institute, 1994), villagers in the sample villages of Jharkhand spend a considerable amount of their time in gathering fuel wood. In sample villages, most households collect fuel wood at least twice a week during the agricultural 'slack season' between November and May when their work loads are lower and the wood in the forest is fairly dry and easy to carry. The Table 39 also shows that many forest trees species have a variety of practical and socio-cultural uses. For the majority of the people in the research villages, however, the most important forest products are fuel wood, construction timber and wood for plough-making. Looking at fuel wood collection first, all households in the research areas use the village forest as their main source of supply. The following tables give the detail:

Table 39

The Different Uses of CPRs (Forest Trees)* in Research Area

Trees	Fuel	House Timber	Furniture	Plough wood	Food	Oil	Medicine	Religion	Fodder
Asan	*	*		*			*		*
Acasia	*	*							
Amla	*	*			*	*	*		
Bahera	*	*	*		*	*	*		*
Bar	*	*	*		*				*
Ber	*	*	*		*				*
Bel	*	*			*			*	*
Bhelwa	*	*			*	*	*	*	*
Bokla	*				*				*
Dahu	*	*	*		*			*	*
Dhaunta	*	*	*	*					*
Dumar	*	*			*			*	
Eucalyptus	*	*	*						
Footkal	*				*				*
Gamhar	*	*	*						
Harra	*								
Jackfruit	*	*	*		*		*		*
Jamun	*	*	*	*	*		*		*
Jirhul	*				*				*

Tree								
Kachnar	*		*		*			*
Karam		*				*		*
Karanj	*				*			
Karonda	*		*		*			*
Kend	*		*	*	*	*	*	*
Koinar	*				*	*		*
Kusum	*			*	*		*	*
Mahua	*	*	*	*	*		*	*
Mango	*		*	*	*			*
Neem	*	*	*	*	*		*	*
Parsa	*							
Pipal	*	*			*			*
Pithod	*				*			*
Piyar	*		*		*		*	*
Putus	*							
Sal	*	*	*	*	*	*	*	*
Simbal	*		*		*		*	*
Tamarind	*				*			*
Teak	*					*		
Tetair	*				*			

Source: Field work research (2018)

For the botanical names of these trees, see Appendix- III

In studied villages (except the following villages such as Sitasal, Bishubandh, Khayerbani, Gangtia, Tilbitha, Rajabari, Murgadanga, Kolebira Mamarla Alaynja Kalan), members of the forest protection committees obtain the large timber that they need for house construction, agricultural implements and furniture from community forest. In some sample villages, by contrast, there are not enough large trees to satisfy all the right-handers' requirements and villagers wanting to undertake major house construction work often have to buy at least some of the wood that they need.

Table 40

CPRs (Tree) Preference Ranking+ in the Research Area

Trees	Fuel	Timber	Food	Oil	Medicine	Fodder
Asan	2	2			11	3
Acasia	9	13				
Amla				2	1	
Bahera		19	14	5	2	5
Bar		17	15			16
Ber		10	12			18
Bel			10		6	10
Bhelwa		20	4		9	
Bokla						
Dahu		18	13			13
Dhaunta		21				11
Dumar		11	11			
Eucalyptus	10	12				
Footkal			9			2
Gamhar		5				
Harra					4	20
Jackfruit		4	3			

Jamun		7	6			9
Karam		9				14
Karanj	7			1	5	
Kend		8	5		10	15
Koinar						17
Kusam		14				20
Mahua		16	8	4	7	19
Mango	8	6	1			8
Neem		22			3	6
Parsa	6					
Piyar		15	2			1
Putri						4
Putus	3					
Sal	1	1	16	3	12	12
Tamarind	5		7		8	7
Teak		3				
Tetair	4					

Source: Field work research 2018

+ *The highest ranking is 1*

In research villages, 75% of the sample households regularly collect various forest fruits. The most popular of these are *kend, piyar, mang jamun, ber dumar, and bel*, all of which ripen between late February and August. Many villagers also eat the dried, newly formed leaves of the *footkal (Ficus retusa)* tree which are collected in late-February. Many villagers also collect the seeds of *amla* (Emblica officinalis) *karanj, bahera* and *mahua* trees to use for oil. *Karanj, bahera* and *mahua* oil are used in the manufacture of soap and *sal* oil is used for cooking. *Amla* is sometimes used as a hair dye and is often found along with karanj oil as one of the main ingredients in hair styling and conditioning. Another useful seed is that of *simbal* tree which contains a fluffy cotton like substance that is used to fill pillows and mattresses.

Table 41

CPRs (Forest Foods) for the Villagers in the Research Area

Trees	Plants Parts	Time Available
Amla	Fruits Leaves	November-December
Bar	Fruit	April-May
Ber	Fruit	July-August
Bel	Fruit	June-July
Dahu	Fruits-Flowers	March-April
Dumar	Fruit	March-April
Footkal	Leaves	February-March
Jackfruit	Fruit	February-March
Jamun	Fruit	July-August
Jirhul	Flowers-Leaves	June-July
Kachnar	Flowers-Leaves	May-June
Karonda	Fruit	September
Kend	Fruit	May-June
Koinar	Leaves	May-November
Kusam	Fruit	April-May
Mahua	Flowers	March
Mango	Fruit	April-June
Neem	Leaves	June-July
Pithod	Fruit	September
Piyar	Seeds	May-June
Sal	Flowers	March-April
Tamarind	Fruit	May-June

Herbs and Mushrooms+	Plants Parts	Time Available
Chimti Sag	Leaves	January-February
Kattay Sag	Leaves	May-June
Matak Sag	Leaves	May-June
Sataur	Fruit	November-December
Suga Sag	Leaves	July-August
Mushrooms	All	February-May

Source: Field work research 2018

+ It was not possible to find out the botanical names for these plants

33% of sample population possesses some 'mainstream' knowledge about herbal remedies for minor 'natural' illnesses (such as coughs, mouth ulcers, fever, dysentery and pain in humans or coughs, sore tongues and sore feet in cattle), so even villagers who do not know about herbal medicine usually have a friend or relative who does. As only 22 of these 22469 villagers of the sample villages were familiar with more than four different remedies, however, most of the more complex treatments are referred to village 'experts'. The best known and most respected of these experts are many who regularly use twenty six different forest plants to treat 'natural illnesses' in both humans and cattle (see Table 42).

Table 42

Silvicultural Knowledges of
Herbal Remedies CPRs in the Research Area

Local Name	Plant Part	Use
Asan	Whole Plant	Fever
Bahera	Fruit	Cough
Bahera	Whole Plant	Wonns

Banana	Fruit	Dysentery
Bel	Fruit	Dysentery
Bhelwa	Seeds	Wound disinfectant
Chiraita	Whole Plant	Blood Purification Dysentery. Fever
Dumar	Fruit, Root	Swollen wounds
Dawai	Seeds	Pain
Guava	Leaf, flower	Dysentery
Harra	Whole Plant	Worms, Cough
Jhibru	Roots	Pain
Kachnar	Roots	Stomach Upset
Kend	Fruit	Dysentery
Kundri	Roots	Vitamins
Lal	Roots	Mouth Ulcer
Lilkant	Roots	Fever, Pain, Stomach Upset
Mahua	Oil	Stomach Upset
Nakbail	Bark	Nose Bleeds
Neem	Leaves, Bark	Fever, Pain
Papaya	Root	Pain
Parsawanti	Leaves	Health And Energy during pregnancy
Ramadatoon	Root	Pain
Sataur	Whole Plant	Dysentery Stomach Upset
Sisam	Leaves	Stomach Upset
Sal	Ash from bark	Stomach Upset, Wound disinfectant

Source: Field work research 2018

* For the botanical names of these plants, see Appendix-III

Table 43

Typical Non-agricultural Products Sold
by Forest Dwellers in Research Villages

Item	Price (Rupees)	Unit of Measurement
Chickens	80-120	Each
Ducks	300-325	Each
Goats	7000-8000	Each
Cattle	15000-25000	Each
Calves	10000-12000	Each
Eggs	70	Dozen
Mats	200	One 1m x 1.5 m mat
Straw	300	Two large basket
Bamboo baskets	200	Each
Lac	300	Kg
Bamboo	400	Per pole
Mushrooms	400	Kg
Mahua flowers	400	Kg
Mango fruits	80-120	Kg
Kend fruit	50	Kg
Tamarind Pods	80	Kg
Ber fruit	25	Kg
Jackfruit	30	Kg
Dumar fruit	25	Kg
Mahua seeds	200	Kg
Karanj seeds	150	Kg
Sal seeds	150	Kg
Karanj oil	150	Liter
Kerosene	60	Liter
Petrol	90	Liter
Karanj cake manure	50	Kg
Farmyard manure	1500-2000	One trench full

Source: Primary Investigation 2018.

For the botanical names of the trees mentioned here. See Appendix III.

Subsistence Strategies in the Research Villages

With the conversion of much forest land for cultivation during the last century, agricultural has long replaced hunting and gathering as the main form of subsistence for most people in the research area. But for many, a history of land alienation and fragmentation means that household food stocks must be supplemented in other ways. As elsewhere in India (Harriss, 1992; Pathak, 1994), some of the most common forms of off-farm employment in the research area include paid employment, business, agricultural labour, casual labour, cash cropping and the sale of non-agricultural produce. Nevertheless, local forests are still very important for meeting subsistence needs (many villagers regularly collect fruit, nuts fuel wood, timber, thatch, leaves for plates and bowls, mushrooms, medicine and even game) and for magico-religious purposes (Kelkar and Nathan, 1991). Degraded forests also provide a potential source of agricultural land for villagers whose field lies close to the forest boundary. Although this is supposed to be illegal (Pathak, 1994), villagers can sometimes come to a special arrangement (for a fee) with the forest guard.

Cash cropping

With respect to agriculture, too, the *Munda, Kharia* and *Oraon* of the sample villages are very enterprising. Most of the families that I sampled grew a variety of cash crops: especially winter vegetables and wheat. The most popular vegetables that are sold as cash crops are peas, cauliflowers and potatoes grown as early vegetables for the Kolkata market. Trucks come to nearby the research areas- markets to collect these vegetables which sell for between Rs. 65-150 per kg compared to the regular price of around Rs. 25 per kg. Also popular are potatoes onions, beans, cabbage, tomatoes, sweet potatoes, radish, ladies finger and aubergine which sell for Rs. 15-25 per kg at local markets. Most villagers use this money to purchase vegetables that they don't grow themselves, good quality rice, clothing, household items or ordinary rice to make up lean season shortfalls.

The sale of non-agricultural produce

Some of the poorer villagers who cannot afford the necessary inputs for winter vegetables and wheat sell non-agricultural produce to help meet their subsistence needs. The most common items sold in research villages include chickens, ducks, goats, pigs, cattle, eggs, mats, straw, manure, baskets and also wood, oil. Mushrooms, fruit and nuts from homestead trees and/or state forests (see Table 43).

Not surprisingly, the Mahli and the Manjhi basket-making communities have the largest incomes from non-agricultural products as they rely on the sale of their manufactured goods, rather than agriculture, for their livelihood. Few Oraons and Mundas are also sufficiently enterprising to make a fair income from selling liquor. In addition, a number of the poorest villagers rely on illegal fuel wood sales for the cash to buy rice during the lean season. Both activities can be quite lucrative, however as shoulder and head-loads of fuel wood fetch between Rs. 18-20 and Rs. 14-16 respectively at the weekly markets and liquor is almost always in demand in areas. Rice beer (hanria) is usually sold for around Rs. 40 per bottle and mahua (distilled from the flowers of the mahua tree which blooms in March) fetches Rs. 80-120 bottle depending on its potency.

Furthermore, livestock scenario of studied villages is presented in tables 14 to 38. The bovine population showed an increasing trend in sampled villages. In bovine, buffalos are stall-fed implying a shift away from open grazing. Since ovine are not stall-fed, an increase in their population mounted greater pressure on public lands. They also damage the new plantations and cause decline in the productivity of grass lands.

The evidences do not suggest bright prospect for CPRs in the study area. There are institutional constraints preventing the offsetting of these damaging and serious trends. Generally, the physical and legal-cum-administrative intervention dealing with CPRs are insensitive to the CPRs perspective.

The CPRs of the study villages, by and large, have come under the strain wherein every member of the society stakes claim in open pool resources and nobody shares the efforts and cost in managing them. As such, we come across over-exploitation of NRM, overgrazing of pasture, encroachment, depletion of waste resources, etc.

Since sheep and goats are mainly grazed in hills, it was considered appropriate to convert the different categories of animals into sheep equivalent. The average numbers of cattle kept by the farmers was higher on small farms as compared with marginal farms.

For successful institutional management of CPRs, the government has launched several programmes. The protection of CPR lands is the main responsibility of the government. The regeneration/plantation, grazing of livestock, fire control and clearing / felling of trees in the forest land are under the forest department. There is also involvement of grass root level institutions and NGOs like SIGN and its partner organizations for regeneration of degraded forest area, conservation and management of CPRs. On the other side, there has been a study increase in human and livestock population in CPRs. Farmers under the Farmer's Club project of SIGN should be educated to go in for improved breeds of cattle. It will reduce the pressure on CPRs and increase the income of the farmers. It is important to ensure the involvement of local people, especially the female of the sample villages of SIGN in the management of these resources. The village communities, SIGN and development agencies also should work coherently in a participatory mode.

Endnotes

[1] Elinor Ostrom (1990) classified organizational rules into three categories constitutional rule, collective choice, and operational rule in order of hierarchy. She opined that change/modification of rules becomes more difficult in the upper hierarchy.

CHAPTER - 5

Major Findings and Policy Implications

This chapter is organized in three sections. Section I conceptualizes the contributions to CPRs Social Capital Theories' and highlights the magnitude of CPRs social capital-linked poverty in Jharkhand. Section II reviews the contributions of SIGN and its nine partner-organizations in the field of 'CPRs Social Capital' thinking followed by the summary of the major findings. Section III depicts the policy implications followed by the recommendations. Now, I start to deal with section I first.

In mountainous regions like Jharkhand, common property resources and social capital (CPRs Social Capital) are important natural resources and play a vital role in the economy, and they help to maintain ecological balance, check soil erosion, meet the demand for timber, farm implements and industry, and provide firewood and shelter to the inhabitant, animal population and wildlife. CPRs Social Capital allows community to take part in resource management and resource ownership without anybody having exclusive property rights over them (Jodha 1995), and motivates tribal community to strive for sustainable development. In hilly agriculture, CPRs enhance and stabilize the income, employment and sustenance of village community by providing multiple products to farming systems (Murty 1994). Both the components (CPRs Social Capital) help in rebuilding relationship of trust, reciprocity and networking and in downsizing the government bureaucracy thereby reducing transaction and overhead costs. This study has been made with respect to tribal Jharkhand in Eastern India and tries to see how the CPRs Social Capital with poverty alleviation thinking stimulates development?

In the past, several studies have been conducted in different parts of the world to find out the role of social capital in the process of economic development at both macro and micro levels. Keeping this in view, the present study has been conducted of SIGN and its nine partner organizations located in different mountainous regions of Jharkhand in Eastern India. The results of the study of SIGN and its nine partner organizations have been divided into two parts, i.e., overall view of the organizations (Chapter- 3) and analysis of 25 sample villages of these organizations including SIGN (Chapter- 4).

SECTION - I

Contribution to CPRs Social Capital Theory with Poverty Thinking

CPRs theory with poverty thinking (Berker, 1989, Bromley, 1992, Ostrom, 1990, 1992) sought to examine how and when CPRs have been successfully managed by users without stable intervention or privatization. A key concept in CPRs theory is 'property' and 'property rights' (see chapter 1). Pierre Bourdieu (1930-2002) developed his theory of cultural capital in social origin to show that social exclusion is a continuous process. According to him, three forms of capital combine; social capital, cultural capital and economic capital. Social capital he refers to the network of useful relationships that can secure material or 'symbolic profits' (Bourdieu, 1986:249): the amount of social capital that an individual can draw upon is thus the sum of the number of people in their network and the amount of capital so possessed. Such capital has the capacity to reproduce in identical or expanded form, becoming part of the structure of society that enables and constrains individual's lives. Putnam (1995:67) defined social capital as 'features of social organization such as networks, norms and social trust that facilitate coordination and cooperation for mutual benefit. However, Putnams' definition is very different from Bourdieu's; whereas for

Bourdieu social capital was held by the individual (Walters, 2002:387), for Putnam it is a collective capacity (ibid, p. 379). These days social capital has been used in various frameworks such as the livelihoods, capitals and capacities, etc. Broadly speaking, social capital, unlike other forms of capital, is not depleted with use but actually increases in value with its use (Ostrom, 1999).

Like physical and human capital, a new form of capital has been recognized by the French Sociologist Bourdieu[1] with the name social capital. It is defined as the aggregate of the actual or potential resources which are linked to possession of durable network of more or less institutionalized relationships of mutual assistance and recognition.[2] Another definition refers to so inclinations that arise from these networks to do things for each other.[3] The World Bank defines social capital as "the institution, relationships and norms that shape the quality and quantity of a society's social interaction".[4] Simply, social capital can be defined as the advantage created by a person's location in a structure of relationships.[5] Social Capital is categories as formal and informal social capital. Formal social capital refers to "to formally defined patterns of behavior, norms of exchange, networks and institutions".[6] On the other hand, informal social capital refers to informal networks like individual, families, groups and kinship. It is easy to measure and estimate the extent of the first kind of social capital while estimation of second type is problematic and complicated.

The interdependence of social capital becomes obvious when social capital is measured using the three generic criteria of productivity, equity and sustainability.[7] These criteria are shown in Chart 1. In the preceding chapters we have observed that how SIGN and its partner organizations have acted upon and practiced towards the criteria of productivity, equity and sustainability since the tenure of their existence (1981-2018).

Chart - 1

Measurement Criteria for Social Capital

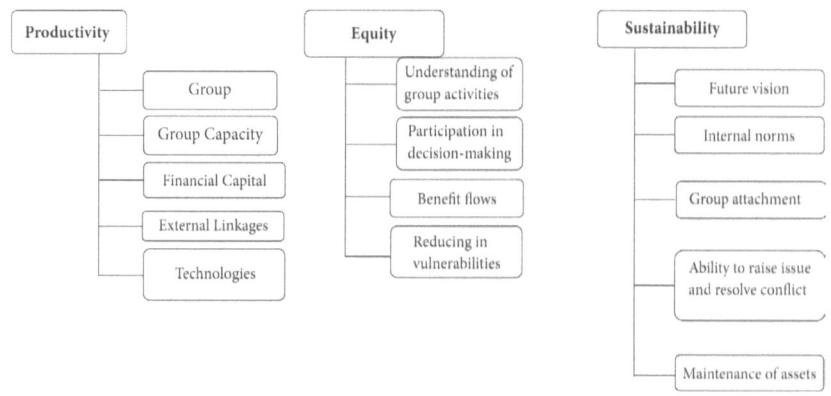

SECTION - II

Contributions of SIGN and its Partners
towards CPRs Social Capital Praxis

This exploratory study of the SIGN and its partners may be concluded by giving a short account of their achievements and major findings of the objective study. Apart from an empirical significance of this exploratory study for social science research at global level; its policy implications cannot be overlooked. We are, therefore, setting below some of the specific issues that the study has highlighted and offer some meaningful suggestions for solving them.

The historical analysis of the development of CPR facilities in Jharkhand shows clearly the scale of governmental neglect towards tribal economy and society (chapter- 4). In the British period, CPR-users did not expect governmental assistance and with plentiful land, forest and water endogenously-developed storage works to meet the needs of the forest dwellers. Since Indian independence successive governments, inconsiderate of the basic needs of forest dwellers, have promoted inappropriate technologies many of which remain unused, and have indirectly, through policy, restrained any meaningful development of CPRs. It is in this context that I have located my analysis of the SIGN and its nine partner organizations including 25 sample villages from five different geographical regions of Jharkhand selected for the field research work.

Ten leading Church- inspired NGOs of Jharkhand covered in the study area (see chapter- 3) are: Social Initiatives for Growth and Networking (SIGN) Ranchi; DSES Dumka; GUK Gumla; VK Simdega; HSSS Khunti; JVK Hazaribag; SHC Hazaribag; CCSSS Ranchi; SVS Latehar and Catholic Charities Jamshedpur. These organizations have an experience of CPRs Social Capital practices and welfare work for the period ranging between 10 -50 years. It was found that these NGOs have recorded different rates of progress in accordance with the quality of leadership, organization, time coverage and the kind of assistance made available to them by different funding agencies. These NGOs, during the past fifty years, have been engaged in various innovative experiments. Some of these have been given up while others are still continuing.

SIGN is known all over Jharkhand and even at national and international levels as a 'lead organization' in tribal rights and heritage, social capital and promotion of CPRs and entitlements. The most popular concept of SIGN 'Awakening Tribal Soul' has become a watchword calling forth people to work for the awakening of tribal folks in Jharkhand on diverse fields of CPRs social capital regimes. Moreover, one of the important activities of SIGN is to help those NGOs which are in need and seeking support for their survival, through peaceful and fair means in society. Nearly 53 such centres in Jharkhand which have been partners or member-agencies of the SIGN till the date of this study. The SIGN has been engaged in providing technical, material and capacity building trainings to these grassroots level NGOs. Not only that, SIGN also mobilizes resources for them to work for 'hungry population' and their rehabilitation, educational support to children (2167), farmers' club and NRM (39 villages, 19 Panchayats, 10 Blocks in Jharkhand), awakening the tribal soul through 1395 workshops covering 207464 plus people among the tribal and *Dalit* communities of Jharkhand.

As a matter of fact, impact of the programmes of these NGOs can be viewed from two angles – (A) Tangible results supported by statistics, and (b) The intangible outcome which can be only observed and felt. On the tangible side, the most important programme of SIGN is Social and community mobilization, trainings and capacity buildings, and educational support to the children, farmers' club formation and NRM, health components, and awakening tribal soul, etc.

I started in the beginning of the chapter that the Christian-inspired organizations are providing a set of potential solutions to some of the most severe problems facing tribal Jharkhand today. These solutions are models of organized, long term viable villages, and all their constituent programmes. At this time the models are few compared to Jharkhand's population. Yet, the destructive effects of the centralized consumerist society are mounting and people all over India are losing faith in the system's ability to right itself, or even to hold together to the end of the country. Tensions are mounting perhaps the evidence of healthy villages in contrast to the experience of the system's failures will move more people to direct their lives towards building alternatives.

The SIGN and other partner development organizations located in Jharkhand State of this book is all are citizens of India, who have chosen to work among the powerless to alleviate poverty and to build a new social order. Poverty in Jharkhand is a painful puzzle: the poor are uneducated, atomized, and own few economic inputs. Economic opportunities do exit, but some more initiatives are required to seek them out, a combination of education and self-confidence to establish them, and some capital to get started and tide one through initial mistakes. The government wants economic growth, but finds it more productive to assist those who are moderately well off. The schemes the government does direct to the most poor are channeled through inefficient and often corrupt bureaucracies, so their effectiveness is limited. There are both similarities and differences in the strategies of the projects we have discussed. All ten organizations make some effort to help the villagers gain access to government programmes meant for them.

The SIGN places a strong emphasis on helping villagers get government schemes, fighting corruption and encouraging government officers to implement their schemes as fully as possible. SIGN through its partner organizations has trained and educated the people in its more than 2693 village areas in such a manner that it has the most participatory and self-sufficient people's organizations. Its programme scope is more modest. SIGN was able to find enough technically skilled staff and advisors and to teach villagers the practical skills for managing the agricultural and NRM works, but that is not unusual. What is special is that SIGN set very high standards for its programmes and built them into its operating procedures. Its work demonstrates that villagers do need to take on new values attitudes in order to run economic programmes efficiently and with priority to the poorest.

However, to view village development as individuals helping individuals is inadequate. The poor are poor because they are powerless, and since they are powerless they are generally oppressed; used or ignored. They are poor as a result of the socio-economic system, and it is run by the powerful for the powerful. Most of them well off people in the service area are fully occupied advancing their own interest and in the process perpetuate the system that supports them. The Christian inspired organization considers their work to be building the villagers' power so they can claim their due from the system.

At first these development organizations set themselves up as advocates of the villagers' rights. Over time they try to help villagers reach a point where they can protect their own rights and advance their own interest within the system. Education is a prerequisite, and legal aid helps, but the villagers' main source of power is their numbers organized through single village and area wide committees. At Gram Utthan Kendra (Gumla) and Samaj Vikas Sanstha (Chandwa), the villages were able to stop most local injustice and petty corruption just by getting organized (collective efforts). They are able to influence government structures at least up to the district level through mass marches and by making common demands. Each project the village committees are able to use the power of numbers strengthen their position in relation to outside economic institutions.

The author concludes that the social effects of SIGN' activities will lead to a sustained use of indigenous resource and knowledge, leading to a stronger position of the tribals in the local area. Economically the programme has positive effects for those who directly participate in the income- generating activities. The wider application will depend on the transfer of indigenous wisdom and silvicultural knowledge with appropriate technology to other social action groups.

However, the author is of the opinion that the social effects of SIGN seem to be sustainable. The economic effects so far are not widespread, but significant for those able to participate in income generating activities through livelihood promotion programme, NRM and training. The social effects of DSES, GUK, JVK, SVS, Catholic Charities, and Jamshedpur will lead to a sustained use of indigenous resources and knowledge (CPRs Social Capital). The long-term environmental effects of these organizations' activities may be such that a further erosion of natural resources is prevented, promoting further revitalization of the tribal community. Moreover, in the social field Snehadeep Holy Cross, Hazaribag has established an alternative participatory structure for its activities. It has achieved a lot also for destitute, deprived and stigmatized sections of the Society. Regarding Vikas Kendra, Simdega, HSSS, Khunti, and CCSSS, Ranchi, organizations, a sound approach is adhered to, though it may be advisable to devote more time to the programme implementation.

Organizational work of these studied NGOs is concentrated on major fields- the foremost being village organization in the form of Mahila Mandals, Lok Samitees, Wisdom Councils, Farmers' Clubs, Yuva Mandals and Van Suraksha Samittees which are an effort to rebuild tribal communities based on community lead and action. They are used to devote people's power as an action of resistance against injustices.

So far as the social field is concerned, crude exploitation and injustices have decreased, but much more has to be achieved in the case of alcoholism. The social distance in terms of cooperation, neighborhood and fellow-feeling with the primitive tribes- Birhors, Sabhors and Paharias and with Dalits has gone to the maximum extent.

These NGOs have registered considerable achievements in the field of health, hygiene, and sanitation. Various water-borne diseases and a number of chronic diseases were prevalent in the area. Malaria visited door to door every year in the past. Now these have been mitigated to a great extent. They have succeeded in controlling the incidence of chronic disease by establishing health clinics, herbal dispensaries, distribution of free medicines and launching health education and training programmes in its service area.

This success was possible due to the readily available help from the UINCEF Jharkhand, CARITAS India, Manos Unidas, Fondazione Fratelli Dimenticati Onlus, District Administrations of Jharkhand and other voluntary organizations at national and international levels.

There has been a gradual depletion of forests, particularly in Simdega, Gumla, Tonto, Karamburu, and Tundi areas of Jharkhand. This has resulted in sever soil erosion, scarcity of water, forest wood and raw materials for the very survival of the tribals of the region. Such degradation has caused poverty and uncontrolled exploitation of resources of the region. Although Mahila Mandals and Lok Samittees, Wisdom Councils, and Van Suraksha Samittees are vigilant towards this problem and have taken up projects for social forestry and Afforestation in order to maintain sustainable environment and cultivation techniques in the study villages and to educate the people to preserve the forest capital for the future generations, it has failed to restructure the tribal economy through voluntary efforts (social capital).

There is no doubt that the management and workers of SIGN have been working in the interest of the beneficiary-partners. But self-interest is still persisting in some of the workers. This ideal is not so easy to realize. It requires a total change of heart, total change in the mental make-up of the workers, and a total change in day-to-day life of workers and management. This change may not occur within a few decades and may take centuries. Really, it is difficult to give it practical shape in the life of workers and even among the leaders of the programme. Thus, it appears that action and contemplation or Praxis cannot be taken as a strategy for the beneficiary-partners themselves.

The study reveals the government helps whatsoever funds are available for the clusters. Therefore, the study NGOs like other developmental NGOs in the country have to rely on the external or foreign funding agencies. Internal sources such as the funds raised from 'savings' or contributions of beneficiaries are negligible. Thus, dependency on external resources for the development is still persistent in almost all the clusters of SIGN and its partner organizations. Thus, less dependency on external sources, as one of the ultimate objectives of SIGN and its partners is not much visible in their service villages/ clusters. Management should take a note of this.

We have drawn attention to the failures of SIGN and its partner organizations and their ongoing programmes but do not wish to imply that the experiments made by the SIGN and its partners have failed. We have also summarized the major findings which have emerged from the study. Any suggestion for covering the unfinished agenda of SIGN can only be made in the light of the existing scenario and the past experience. In this connection, it would be necessary to take into account the goals of development which have been projected by the 'Governing and General Bodies' of SIGN from time to time. It is to be realized that the ultimate aim of all development is not just to create the socio-economic infrastructure such as, generation of employment and creation of organizational assets etc. the destination of all development is man himself. This human factor or the human context is of extreme importance and should always be held as the focal point of all efforts. In this light, some suggestions could be made which may help the management of SIGN to evolve a meaningful programme of action aimed at reconstruction and development of Tribal population in general, and promotion of CPRs Social Capital in particular.

It is important to note that the weak linkages of both the farm forestry and CPRs with the agricultural sector were noticed. Farmers under the 'farmer club' go in for improved breeds of cattle. It will reduce the pressure on CPRs and increase the income of the farmers. It is important to ensure the involvement of local people, especially the females, in the management of those resources. The village communities, partner - organizations of SIGN and development agencies should work coherently in a participatory mode in planning, development, management and benefit- sharing of 'CPRs Social Capital' to avert the proverbial 'Tragedy of Commons'(CPRs).

Some of the most common forms of off-farm employment in the research area include paid employment, business, agricultural labour, casual labour, cash cropping and the sale of non-agricultural produce. Nevertheless, local forests are still very important for meeting subsistence needs (many villagers regularly collect fruit, nuts fuel wood, timber, thatch, leaves for plates and bowls, mushrooms, medicine and even game) and for magico-religious purposes.

My findings reveal that in the study villages a number of changes have occurred. Traditional management systems for CPRs have practically disappeared. This is a side-effect of certain institutional reforms, such as the introduction of land reforms and 73rd and 74th Panchayati Raj Amendment Act. The former led to abolition of a number of levies and taxes on CPRs users, and the latter undermined the traditional informal authority (*Manki-Munda*) of village elders and replaced the formal authority of feudal landlords in the village. But in sample villages I found that the traditional management systems for CPRs are in action to some extent. It was wonderful to see the engineering marvel of self-initiated and indigenously designed watershed works, contour bunds converted into ridge terraces for cultivation of paddy in research villages. In these villages SIGN played a crucial role in educating villagers about the CPRs (forest, water, land, seeds, herbal plants, etc.) and about the village social capital. This encouraged villagers to form their own wisdom councils, cooperatives and self-help groups and promoted to link them with various tribal and rural developmental programmes of local government.

As I have already described that the village panchayats, despite their legal powers, are generally unable to enforce any regulation about 'CPRs'. Broadly speaking, the panchayats in all the sample villages have little interest in CPRs. The study reveals that the default on the part of the panchayats has thus converted CPRs into open access resources with the consequent tragedy. However, the exceptions are that the village elders still have informal authority. It is clear that the social institutions like wisdom council, farmers club, SHGs, *Manki Munda* (social capital) based on trust, reciprocity, and agreed norms and rules for behaviour, have mediated such kind of unfettered private action. New thinking and practices are required, particularly to develop forms of social organization that are structurally suited for CPRs management and protection at the low level. This means more than just reviving the old institutions and tradition. It calls for formation of new forms of organizations, associations and platforms for common action.

The findings of my study suggested that the success of the CPRs management could be measured in terms of two facts: (i) creation of a healthy organizational base which could cover the totality of the CPR users and ensure their full and effective participation, and (ii) orientation of the commoners towards the ideals of CPRs social capital such as measures adopted for the uplift of weaker commoners, elimination of poverty and conflict management, and emergence of self-governance; and self-reliant polity which may be characterized by collective conscience, unity and action.

The analysis of the data both at macro and micro levels on the impact of the programmes on the life and level of living of the beneficiaries reveal that due to agricultural training and formation of Farmers' Clubs, SHGs, Wisdom Councils, Forest Protection Committees etc. have changed the socio economic scenario of the forest dwellers of

Jharkhand. The better quality land has been transferred to marketable crops including vegetables. The contribution from agriculture has gone up and the cropping pattern disclosed a notable shift towards marketable crops like vegetables and floriculture as a result of development of irrigation and agricultural training. Naturally, in terms of the value of production, which among others reflects the quality of the land transferred to non-cereal crops, the change is much more conspicuous. However, not all the beneficiaries have gained the benefits accruing by turning the single crop areas in to double and triple with the help of irrigation facilities. Similarly, the formation of Self-Help Groups and the inter loaning facility have promoted various income generating activities like vegetable cultivation, floriculture, goat and sheep rearing and poultry of the villages. The capacity buildings through various activities are also taking place for empowering women for the future sustainability of the groups. Although the group members feel that their work load has increased they are happy and don't mind putting the extra effort as they don't have to work for anyone else as labourers but they are working for themselves. However, not all the SHGs are doing well in terms of regularity in meetings, savings, decision making and changing the group behavior as required for achieving a sustainable status. Similar findings highlight the significance of group structure and processes for the effectiveness of Women's Self-Help Groups (Kumar, Suar, and Mishra, 2018).

Peoples' perception towards SIGN's contributions has been perceived differently by different section of the society. They have not only viewed it differently, but have also suggested certain measures for strengthening the SIGN functioning in a better way. Most Rev Late Bishop Charles Soreng had viewed in this regard and said "The basic Philosophy of SIGN has been one of "harmony with nature and society". He further said, SIGN under the able leadership of Fr Christu Das has been doing well. A "Parable of Jesus" who has given each of us some talents and wisdom and wants us to earn return on them. Jesus gives us through these parables the massage that it is our duty to make the best the resources God has entrusted to us. The author here feels not qualify to judge on this lasting statement as articulated by Late Bishop Soreng rather, would wait till exegetes can answer this statement.

Mr. Birbal of Manav Vikas Organization, Hazaribag said that poverty exists in the society due to deforestation. Community forest management systems, largely if not entirely, fail in Jharkhand. The role of SIGN seems to be insignificant in this regard. On the contrary, Dr. Prabhat Kumar Verma, an agricultural scientist of KVK, Hazaribag was of the view that SIGN has been serving among the exploitative society in the mountainous regions of Jharkhand since a decade. Since then SIGN has done a commendable work in the field of poverty alleviation through organizing Farmer's Clubs and through building social awareness in the society but it has done a very little work in the field of CPRs. Professor Ramesh Sharsan, Vice Chancellor of Vinoba Bhave University stressed the need for the execution of the 'Fifth Schedule' in the 112 of schedule blocks of Jharkhand. He made a plea to undertake the food for work programme in the tribal area in order to protect food security and malnutrition. Dr. (Sister Grace Toppo, the Principal of Inter-College, Ranchi was impressed with the work performance of SIGN. Although she was honest enough to say that she has got not an opportunity to see the action- oriented villages of SIGN, but she has learnt a lot about the work culture of SIGN. Mother General Linda Mary D. S. A. of Ranchi voiced a similar opinion and said that without up-gradation of moral values in the Society, social capital cannot be institutionalized. She remarked SIGN is itself a social capital. Therefore, SIGN should be linked more with social harmony and dignity. Dungdung Gladson, a well-known writer and social activist of national repute said "SIGN is mainly known as a resource and an institution. SIGN has also been deeply concerned about the degradation of the ecological foundations essential for sustainable agriculture".

SECTION - III

Policy Implications and Recommendations

Management practices of 'CPRs Social Capital' are not solved by more government or privatization but through self-governance. The study emphasizes the importance of communications and also civic education. It also needs to shed its romanticization of traditional knowledge systems, adopting instead of more 'demand side' populist awareness of the linkages between technical a socio-cultural knowledge systems; particularly tribal people's aspirations about development. At the same time, it needs to be sensitive to local variations in knowledge possession and control over resources and be aware of the role that different local sectors and power structures can have in assisting or preventive development goal from being met. Therefore, governments need to work with NGOs like SIGN to create social cohesion (social capital). However, most bureaucracies around the world are not equipped to think or function like that but that is the way of the future. This study is designed to serve as an introductory reference for future scholarly work.

The livelihood and occupation of tribal has a strong bond (social capital) with their culture and tradition and they do not consider it separate from their way of life. In other words, we may say that communing is a way of life and the roots of sustainability lie in the 'CPRs'. Therefore, any policy programme devised for CPR users should take into consideration their cultural background and should not be imposed from outside. They should be trained and promoted in their traditional skills and local knowledge on making products so that they do not feel being imposed and take interest in that and put their heart and soul in their production and promotion. Keeping this background in view the following points are being suggested in terms of recommendations for smooth functioning of SIGN and its partner organizations as well as for the policy implications, in general.

1. The responsibility of social development rests equally with the people, private entrepreneurs and government. Since the *Adivasis* are the weakest and most vulnerable link in the development chain, it is necessary to push the socio-economic programmes for them with a greater sense of sincerity, commitment, patience and sympathy. It is a good that SIGN and its partner organizations are doing well in this direction. However, if they feel necessary, separate workable action plan for the indigent tribal community maybe prepared and executed with the help of funding agencies.

2. Indigenous varieties (CPRs) both in agriculture and forestry are rapidly disappearing (chapters 1, 3 and 4), through the introduction of high-yielding varieties of grains and mono-culture plantations. The author recommends that all possible efforts are made to prevent further loss of species and varieties both in agriculture and on forest lands. The increased use of irrigation and high yielding varieties results in increased use of chemical fertilizers and pesticides. The ill effects of such usage animal health have to be taken into consideration by all partner organizations of SIGN. The author recommends that all attention is given to prevent the environmental risks because of the use of chemical fertilizers and pesticides. The author also recommends that wherever possible the organizations might take up advocacy role regarding the reduction of harmful chemical inputs. The role of SIGN and its partner organizations would be praiseworthy in this regard. For this, the study recommends that all partner-organizations should undertake steps to improve the soil conditions in the project area by incorporating green manuring composting and other sources of soil improvement.

3. The author further recommends that improved rainwater harvesting techniques together with water conservation measures be introduced and implemented in all project areas. Main emphasis should be given to construction of check dams, overflows, community wells and contour cultivation, combined with measures to reconstruct a proper vegetative cover of the barren soils, including intensive reforestation.

4. The upgrading of indigenous species which are more drought and pest resistant is of importance. Jharkhand is still rich in indigenous species (e.g. 47 different rice varieties are known) while at the same

time indigenous species are rapidly declining. The author recommend that each concerned partner organization experiments at least with a small number of indigenous species in combination with ecologically sound farming methods.

5. The author furthermore recommends that in risk prone areas where rainfed agriculture is practiced, mixed cropping be used. Efforts should be made to reduce the use of chemical fertilizer and pesticides to the lowest possible level. Gradual reduction of chemical fertilizer obviously has to be balanced with an increased application of organic manure.

6. It is also recommended that more attention be given to the organization of marginal farmers and landless laborers (women and men) in order to uplift their social position in the society. At the same time their awareness and skills related to sustainable land use and water management has to be increased. The author is of the opinion that the creation of local off-farm employment opportunities is of utmost importance, it could arrest to some extent seasonal migration.

7. All partner organizations have improved the professionality of their staff over the years. Although expertise in various specific fields was high, overall expertise in relation to land use planning, ecological agriculture or agro-forestry issues should increase. The author recommends that the concerned organizations develop a systematic human resource development plan including staff training activities so as to further develop the professional expertise of its staff in relation to land-use planning, low external input agriculture or forestry. The author also recommends that SIGN favors project proposals which include staff training in the mentioned fields.

8. All nine organizations are providing training in specific skills like cultivation practices, food processing, weaving, carpentry, masonry, etc. The author is of the opinion that the first task of partner organizations who are involved in sustainable agriculture is to provide training and extension in soil conservation techniques (e. g green manuring, mixed cropping, composting, Afforestation), water conservation techniques

(e. g. water harvesting, building, check dams) and the use of improved traditional varieties. The need for training in other income generating activities is felt and all nine organizations are carrying out training activities in various fields. Apart from the positive results visible in all organizations, the author sees the danger that too many training activities in too many different fields are undertaken, given the organizational and professional limitations of the respective organizations.

9. The findings recommend to the partner organizations that project proposals include budget items on development of staff related to management training, training and expert advice in sustainable agriculture. It recommends both to SIGN and to partner organizations to conduct research and studies on the following subjects:

> a. The role of women in agriculture and the change that affects their position
>
> b. How do the various development programmes affect women?

Women seem to be under-represented in most partner organizations except Catholic Charities Jamshedpur. Here most of the programmes are being managed and supervised by the women folk. The necessity to employ more women in their staff is clearly understood by the partner organizations, as the majority of the beneficiaries are women. However, it may not be easy to find women with the required expertise, who are willing or allowed to work in the far off project areas. In-service training seems for most organizations to be the only solution for the time being. The author recommends those organizations who have difficulties in recruiting women to investigate the possibility to recruit "trainees" instead of "staff-members". As stated above Catholic Charities Jamshedpur, Snehadeep holy Cross Hazaribag, Samaj Vikas Santhan Chandwa, and Gram Utthan Kendra Gumla organizations have quite successful with this approach.

10. Snehadeep Holy Cross Hazaribag has completed 13 years of its service to the deprived and stigmatized section of the society. Now time has come to shift its approach from behavioral change communication model to empowerment model. This will help to encounter various types of obstacles faced by the SHCH both from the family, community and more seriously from the outsider.

11. SIGN working in the study villages can start an experiment of 'value based education' amongst the commoners. Education should be free and linked with rural setting training and productive manual labour correlated to agriculture, dairy farming, mechanics, and masonry work for low-cost housing. It should not be attached with diplomas, degrees and the desire for a subsequent service, but with the development of the child's personality and values (character building) and his social and environmental awareness, and ability to learn and earn in the village setting with a scheme *'Vriksha Sanskar'*. Under this scheme, each of the village schools would be allotted land on which the tribal children would plant and raise 250 mango trees, bordered by teak trees. The produce of these trees will be utilized towards meeting the food needs of the children and the cost of running the schools. The plan would work as follows. 4 acres of land would be reclaimed for each of the schools from nearby uncultivated government owned forest land. Then, with the planting of each tree costing 425 rupees, the children and teachers, in units of one teacher and 25 children each will be given responsibility for 10 mango saplings and 5 teak trees. Of the 425 rupees 125 will go towards nursery cost Rs. 30/- towards manuring cost and the remaining Rs. 275/- to the child for his labour. The teacher and the children will raise these trees and after 5 years the trees will bear fruits. Of this, 10 percent will go to the children and 90 percent to the village education *sabha*, which will be constituted in each of the villages. Once the trees start bearing fruit, their produce will fully meet the teacher's wages and the other cost of running the schools, thereby enabling the funding agencies to withdraw the financial support it presently gives. After the trees become old they will provide fuel, fruit and timber. This is the proposed plan for 'value-added education' for the marginalized children and socially excluded children. This is a broad idea which should be given the shape of a detailed project. This scheme will, of

course, require the support of government machineries, NGOs and other corporate venture.

12. Moreover, the commoners should adopt a *Chakriya Vikas Paranali* (CVP) or the system of cyclic development, which aims at fighting poverty in tribal areas through sustainable development process. The principle of CVP is to establish a *'sustainable society'* through a cyclical system of investment in the un-irrigated and wastelands for rural self-reliance. It envisages a onetime capital investment in land to ensure generation of employment, intermediary benefits and income to the villagers in rotational cycle of seven to eight years. The process of "detaining, retaining and utilizing rain water, as it falls and where it falls is the first principle for regeneration of wastelands and successful management of land and related resources. The second important ingredient is to make the process of decentralisation at the grass-root level planning in order to take all decisions from planning to the implementation. All the workers of the CVP actively participate in Eco-service appraisal and preparation of master plans. The management of land is strictly on water shed basis. Under the CVP, the uncultivable wastelands belonging to different owners will be pooled together to constitute an economically viable unit of at least 8-12 acres of land. The CVP envisages equitable distribution of economic gains both to the land owners and the landless. The system of distribution of intermediary benefits and final income from the pooled based land will be as under: (a) 10% for the village welfare fund; (b) 30% for the land owner; (c) 30% for the CVP workers; (d) 30% as the capital for reinvestment in the village. All the CVP workers would be recruited from village and the entire work related to the treatment of land would be done by workers who are referred to as 'sustainable development practitioners in CVP terminology.' The above model of sustainable development for 'sustainable tribal society' may be adopted by the working partners to start with a few selected villages among the studied partner organizations of Jharkhand on an experimental basis. So far as capital investment of this test model is concerned, initially local government and NGOs may spend a considerable amount for this purpose.

13. The focus of intervention should be to improve forest dweller's income and strengthen their livelihood, food security at least twice or thrice from their present level. Strong linkages between input supply system like credit, technology on one hand, and market and rural infrastructure on the other have great potential to break the impasse and as such should be considered as a key to improve the resource productivity in these villages. These in turn have the potential to improve the tribal income and lead the society towards sustainable development, which is reflected from the figure given below:

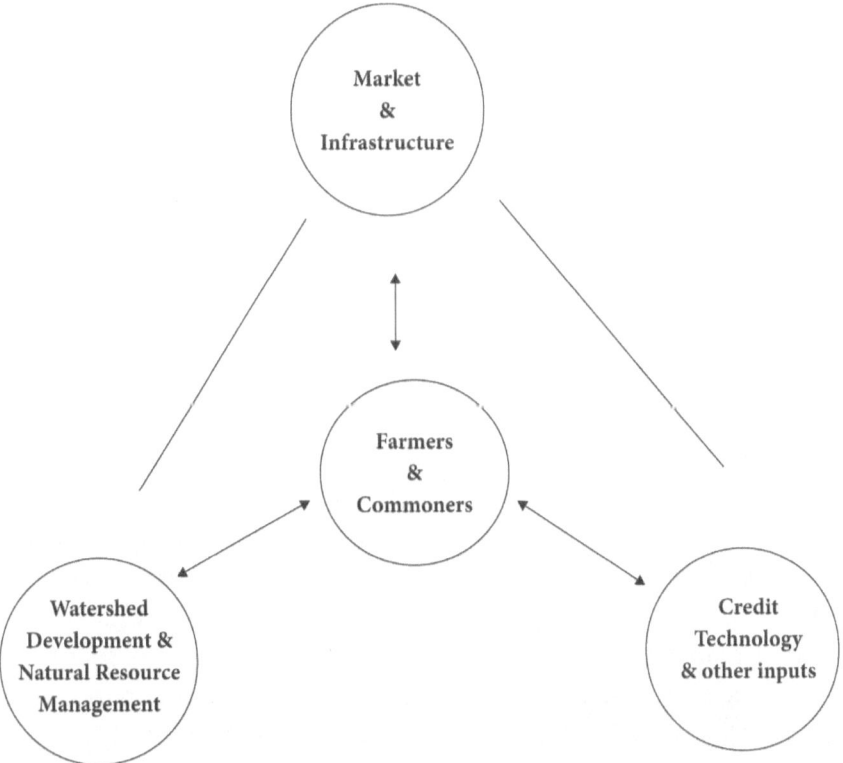

Figure – 4

14. Government - model of sustainable development seems to be unsustainable because it is not possible to fund forever on social welfare progammes to achieve the high HDI as proposed by UNDP (composite index) that measures progress in three basic dimensions of human development: (i) good and healthy life measured by life expectancy index', (ii) knowledge variable measured by education index, and (iii) decent standard of living measured from Gross Domestic Product (GDP) or income per capita index (while tolerating low growth rate, high cost, poor labour productivity, and inadequate investment). An economy can be considered sustainable only if it can maintain its essential programmes and discharge its credit responsibility without increasing debts. If such an economy cannot increase its revenues to meet its rising commitment, or becomes dependent on sources of funds over which it has no control in deployment, then clearly it is unsustainable proposition. Government, NGOs and even corporates who are engaged in protection of commons should realize this and try to involve the commoners in their own development so that their dependency on any authority is gradually reduced and they begin to strive for their own betterment.

15. There are many avenues lying in the tribal villages of Jharkhand, tangible or intangible, which can be mobilized for alternative sources of CPRs social capital and theses can be mobilized for reconstruction of the tribal village and the well-being of the society. The alternatives are as follows: (i) waste and pasture land; (ii) *gairmajurwa aam and gairmajuwa khash land;* (iii) use of idle manpower; (iv) orchards & forestry; (v) minor forest products; (vi) reservoirs and canals; (vii) common tanks; (viii) mobilization of skilled persons; (ix) mobilization of women men power; (x) proper mobilization of youths; (xi) donations; (xii) revolving fund of *gram sabha kosh*; (xiii) creation of capital through charitable shows like drama, street plays and songs etc. (xiv) contribution within the village (xv) collection of revenues from the weekly or bi-weekly tribal *haats;* (xvi) rent from the immunities for community use; (xvii) donation of one day labor or one day's wages in a month to the '*gram sabha*', (xviii) tolls, and (xix) assistance from the government, SIGN and other NGOs etc. In fact, the above avenues may be the real mapping of CPRs and social capital assets of any forest-dweller settlements. The SIGN and its partner organizations can mobilize these resources at maximum extent in order to increase an additional income to the families in their service area.

The micro study from Shiikaripara and Dumka blocks in district to Manoharpur block West Singhbhum district (one of the 25 sampled villages of my study) shows that the sampled farmers have used a total of 42 insecticides (see Tables 14 to 38). This increase in pesticide use is neither sustainable nor desirable. Most food production has been based on high- input and resource – intensive farming systems at a high cost to the environment, and as a result soil, forest, water, air quality and biodiversity continue to degrade. This is a serious matter for the management of SIGN and its partner organizations working in almost all districts of Jharkhand. The question is how to reconcile their basic philosophy of "to maintain environmental harmony in the operational area" with the practice of chemical pesticides with a high dose in their service area in spite of launching a several projects like formation of Farmers' Clubs and composition of vermincomposts, etc. This issue may be reconsidered seriously by the SIGN and its partner organisations.

There is no doubt that as the present stage of Jharkhand's integrated development, the contributions of 'CPRs Social Capital' towards rural development, in general, and tribal development, in particular has an important role to play in our economy. In this regard, CPRs through community based management systems has been playing a constructive role in mountainous dwellers and indigent communities' life and in adding to national output by producing essential forest consumer goods (like different uses of forest trees and timbers; forest foods for the villagers, silvicultural knowledge of herbal remedies and typical non-agricultural products, etc.); creating wage employment and generating additional income through CPRs produce with social Capital thinking, such contributions are the net addition to the total state and national output, in absence of these, the Jharkhand state and the country as whole would have lost much in terms of total output of essential consumer goods, demographic dividend, asset creation and income generation, which have potential to enhance the prosperity and quality of life of the people living in the remote, rural and forest fringe areas of Jharkhand. In this regard the role of SIGN and its nine partner organizations working in different geographical settings in Jharkhand at both macro and micro levels are praiseworthy and commendable.

Endnotes

[1] Bourdieu, Pierre, The Forms of Capital.

[2] Bourdieu, Pierre, http://www.viet-studies.org/Bourdieu-capital.htm.

[3] Putnam, Robert, Bowling Alone: The Collapse and Revival of American Community.

[4] World Bank, Social Capital Initiative.

[5] Wikipedia, The Free Encyclopedia.

[6] Morris, Mathew, Social Capital and Poverty in India; IDS Working Paper No. 61.

[7] Mukherjee, Neela, Measuring Social Capital.

Bibliography

Agarwal, A. (1994). Rules, rulemaking, and rule breaking: Examining the fit between rule Systems and resource use. In E. Ostrom, R. Gardener, and J. Walker, *Rules, Games, and Common-Pool Resources*. Michigan: University of Michigan Press.

Agarwal, B. (1997). Environmental action, gender and equity, and women's participation. *Development and Change*, 28, 1-44.

Agarwal, B. (2001). Participatory exclusions, community forestry, and gender: an analysis for south Asia and a conceptual framework. *World Development*, 29(10), 1623 – 1648.

Baland J.M., Platteau, J.P. (1995). Does heterogeneity hinter collective action? Cahiers de la Faculte des Science Economques Sociales No. 142.

Baland, J.M., Platteau, J.P. (1996). *Halting Degradation of Natural Resources: Is there a Role for Rural communities?* Oxford: FAO and Claredon Press.

Baland, J.M., & Platteau, J.P. (1998). "Divisions of the commons: A partial assessment of the new institutional economic of land rights." *American Journal of Agricultural Economics*, 80(3), 644-650.

Barkow, J.H., Cosmides, L., Tooby, J. (Eds.), (1992). *The Adapted Mind*. New York: Oxford University Press.

Barth, F. (1992). Towards greater naturalism in conceptualizing societies. In A. Kuper (Ed.), *Conceptualising Society*, London: Routledge, 17 -33.

Blomquist, W., Schalger, E. (1998). Individual and institutional heterogeneity and the resolutions of CPR dilemmas. Paper presented to IASCP 7th Conference, Crossing Boundaries, 10- 14 June, Vancouver.

Bourdieu, P. (1986). The forms of social capital. In J. Richarson (Ed.), *Handbook of Theory and Research for the Sociology of Education.*, Westport, CT: Greenwood Press, 249- 262.

Bromley, D. (1993). Common property as a metaphor: Systems of knowledge, resources and the decline of individualism. *The common property digest* 27, 1-8. Hyderabad: Winrock and ICRISAT.

Bromley, D. W., Cernea, M.M. (1989). The management of common property natural resources: some conceptual and operational fallacies. *World Bank Discussion Papers,* No. 57.

Bromley, D.W., Chapagain, D.P. (1984). The village against the centre: resource depletion in south Asia. *American Journal of Agricultural Economics,* 66(5): 868 – 73.

Castle, E.N. (1998). A conceptual framework for the study of rural places. *American Journal* of *Agricultural Economics,* 80, 621-631.

Cernea, M. M. (1987). "Farmer organization and institution building for sustainable Development." *Regional Development Dialogue,* 8, 1- 24.

Chambers, R. (1997). *Whose Reality Counts? Putting the First last.* London: Intermediate Technology publications.

Coleman, J. (1988). "Social capital and creation of human capital." *American Journal of Sociology* 94, S95- S120 (Suppl.).

Coleman, J. (1990). *Foundation of social theory.* Boston, MA: Harvard University Press.

Coleman, J.S. (1987). Norms as social capital. In G. Radnitzky, P. Bernholz (Eds.), *Economic Imperialism: The Economic Approach Applied Outside the Field of Economics.* New York: Paragon.

Coleman, J.S. (1988). Social capital in the creation of human capital. *American Journal of Sociology.* 1994, S95-S120.

Collier, P. (1998). Social capital and poverty. *The World Bank Social Capital Initiative Working Paper, Rep. No. 4.*

Collins, C.J., & Chippendale, P.J. (1991). *New wisdom: The nature of social reality.* Sunnybank, Queensland: Acorn Publications.

Costanja, R., d' Arge, R., de Groot, R., Farber, S., Grasso, M., Hannon, B., Limburg, K., Naeem, S., O'Neil, R., Parvelo, J., Raskin, R. G., Sutton, P., & de van den Belt, M. (1997). "The value of the world's ecosystem services and natural capital." *Nature,* 387, 253-260.

Dayton- Johnson, J., Bardhan, P. (1998). Inequality and conservation on the local commons: a theoretical exercise. *Working Paper,* Berkeley: University of California, Department of Economics.

De Moor, Tine. (2007). Avoiding tragedies. A Flemish common and its commoners under the pressure of social and economic change during the eighteenth century. *Economic History Review.*

Ellis, F. (1998). Household strategies and rural livelihood diversification. Journal of Development Studies, 35(1), 1- 38.

Elster, J. (1989). *The cement of society: A study of social order.* Cambridge: Cambridge University Press.

Etzioni, A. (1995). *The spirit of community: Rights responsibilities and communitarian agenda.* London: Fontana Press.

Frank, R. (1997). Melding sociology and economics: James Coleman's foundation of social theory. *Journal of Economic Literature,* 30, 147-170.

Fukuyama, F. (1995). *Trust: The social values and the creation of prosperity.* New York: Free Press.

Fukuyama, F. (1995). *Trust: The Social Virtues and the Creation of Prosperity.* New York: Free Press.

Gambetta, D. (Ed.) (1988). *Trust: Making and breaking co-operative relations.* Oxford: Blackwell.

Granovetter, M. (1985). Economic action and social structure. *American Journal of Sociology.* 1991, 481-510.

Grootaert, C. (1998). Social capital: the missing link? *The World Bank, Social Capital Initiative Working Paper, Rep. No. 3.*

Gupta, A. (1985). Socio-ecological paradigm to analyse the problem of poor in dry regions. *Eco-development News,* 32, 71-75.

Hardin, G. (1968). "Tragedy of the commons." *Science,* 162, 1243-1248.

Heiner, R.A. (1983). The origin of predictable behavior. *American Economic Review,* 73, 560-595.

Hoffman, E., McCabe, K.A., Smith, V.L. (1998). Behavioural foundations of reciprocity: experimental economics and evolutionary psychology. *Economic Inquiry,* 36, 335-352.

Huxley, E. (1960). *A new earth: An experiment in colonialism.* London: Chatto and Windus.

Jewitt, S. (1996). Agro-ecological knowledge and forest management in the Jharkhand, *India: Tribal development or populist impasse?* Unpublished doctoral dissertation, Newnham College, University of Cambridge, Cambridge.

Jodha, N.S. (1990). Common property resources and rural poor in dry regions of India. *Economic and Political Weekly,* 21, 1169 – 1181.

Keohane, R., Ostrom, E. (Eds.) (1995). *Local commons and global interdependence: Heterogeneity and co-operation in two domains.* London: Sage Publications.

Kothari, A., Pathak, N., Anuradha, R., & Taneja, B. (1998). *Communities and conservation: Natural resource management in South and Central Asia.* New Delhi: Sage Publications.

Kumar, R., Suar, D., & Mishra, P. (2018). Characteristics of the Effectiveness of Women's Self-Help Groups. VOLUNTAS: International Journal of Voluntary and Nonprofit Organizations, doi: 10.1007/s11266-018-9995-9.

Kumar, Suar, and Mishra, 2018.

Lawry, S.W. (1989). Tenure policy and natural resource management in Sahelian West Africa, Research paper No. 130, Land tenure Centre, University of Wisconsian-Madison.

Molinas, J.R; (1998). The impact of inequality, gender, external assistance and social capital on local level collective action. *World Development,* 26(3), 413-431.

Narayan, D., Pritchart, L. (1997). Cents and sociability: household income and social capital in rural Tanzania. *Policy Research Working Paper,* no. 1796, Washington D.C: World Bank.

Nee, V., Ingram, P. (1998). Embeddedness and beyond: institutions, exchange, and social Structure. In M.C. Brinton, V. Nee (Eds.), *The New Institutionalism in Sociology.* New York: Russell Sage Foundation,19-47.

North, D.C. (1990). *Institutions, Institutional change and Economic Performance.* Cambridge, UK: Cambridge University Press.

North, D.C. (1998). Economic performance through time. In M.C. Brinton, V. Nee (Eds.), *The New Institutionalism in Sociology.* New York: Russell Sage Foundation.

Olson, M. (1965). *The Logic of Collective Action: public Goods and the Theory of Groups,* Cambridge, MA: Harvard University Press.

Ostrom, E. (1990). *Governing the Commons: the Evolution of Collective Action,* Cambridge, UK: Cambridge University Press.

Ostrom, E. (1998). A behavioural approach to the rational choice theory of collective action. *American Political Science Review,* 92, 1-22.

Ostrom, E. (1999). Coping with tragedies of the commons. *Annual Review of political Science,* 2, 493-535.

Ostrom, E., Gardner, R., Walker, J. (1994). *Rules, games, and Common Pool Resources.* Ann Arbor, MI: University of Michigan Press.

Palmer, I. (1976). *The new rice in Asia: Conclusions from four country studies.* Geneva: UNRISED.

Platteau, J. P. (1997). Mutual insurance as an elusive concept in traditional communities. *Journal of Development Studies*, 33(6), 764-796.

Pretty, J. (1995). *Regenerating agriculture: Policies and practice for sustainable and self-reliance*. London: Earthscan Publications.

Pretty, J., ward, H., (2000). Social capital and the environment. World Development, 29(2), 209-227.

Putnam, R. (1993). *Making democracy work: Civic traditions in modern Italy*. Princeton, N.J.: Princeton University Press.

Robinson, L.J., Siles, M.E., (1997). Social capital and household income distributions in the United States: 1980, 1990. Department of Agricultural Economics, Michigan State University, Research Report no. 595 and Julian Samora Research Institute research Report No. 18.

Rowley, J. (1999). *Working with social capital*. London: Department for international development.

Rudd, M.A. (2000). Live long and prosper: Collective action, social capital and social vision. *Ecological Economics*, 34, 131-144.

Sally, D. (2000). I, TOO, Sail Past: Odysseus and the logic of self- control. *Kyklos*, 53(2), 173-200.

Sarin, M. (1996). From conflict to collaboration: Institutional issues in community management. In M. Poffenberger and B. MacGean (ed.), *Village voices, forest choices: Joint forest management in India* (pp. 165-209). Delhi: Oxford University Press.

Shah, T. (1991). *The dynamism of India's village co-operatives: A survey of issue and new agenda for research*. Anand, Gujarat: Institute of Rural Management.

Shiva, V. (1998). Western Science and Destruction of Local Knowledge (Eds.), The post Development Reader, London: Zed Publications.

Simon, H.A. (1996). *The Sciences of the Artificial*, third ed. MIT Press, Cambridge, MA.

Simon, H. (1985). Human nature in politics: the dialogue of psychology with political sciences. *American Political Science Review*, 79(2), 293-304.

Singh, K. & Ballabh, V. (1997). *Co-operative management of natural resources*. New Delhi: Sage Publications.

Singh, Katar, Ballabh, V., Palakudiyil, T. (1996). Introduction and Overview, in K. Singh (Ed.) *Co-operative Management of Natural Resources*. New Delhi: Sage Publications.

Taylor, M. (1982). *Community anarchy and liberty*. Cambridge: Cambridge University Press.

Uphoff, N. (1986). *Local Institutional Development: An Analytical Sourcebook, with cases.* West Hartford: Kumarian Press.

Varughese, G., Ostrom, E. (2001). The contested role of heterogeneity in collective action: some evidence from community forestry in Nepal. *World Development,* 29(5), 747-765.

Vedeld, T. (1997). Village politics: Heterogeneity, Leadership and Collective Action. Doctor Scientiarum thesis No. 13, Department of Land Use Planning: Agriculture University of Norway, Aas.

Vedeld, T. (2000). Village politics: heterogeneity, leadership and collective action. *Journal of Development Studies,* 36(5), 105-134.

Wade, R. (1987). The management of common property resources: Finding a co-operative solution, *World Bank Research Observer,* 2(2), 219-234.

Wade, Robert (1988). *Village Republics: Economic Conditions for Collective Action in South India, Cambridge,* Cambridge: Cambridge University Press.

Williumson, O. E. (1994). Transaction cost economics and organisation theory. In N.J. Smelser, R. Swedberg (Eds.), *The Handbook of Economic Sociology,* Princeton, NJ: Princeton University Press,.

Woolcock, M. (1998). "Social capital and economic development: Towards a theoretical synthesis and policy framework." *Theory and Society,.*

Woolcock, M. and Narayan, D. (2000). Social capital: Implications for development theory, research, and policy. *The World Bank Research Observer* 15(2).

World Bank (1998). *World Development report. Knowledge for development.* Oxford: Oxford University Press.

Index of Acronym

CPR	Common Property Resource
CPRs	Common Property Resources
CPrRs	Common Property Right Resource
VHND	Village Health Nutrition Day
PRI	Panchayat Raj Institutions
IDCE	Intensified Diarrhoea Control
	Fortnight Inter-departmental Commons of Forestry
PESA	Panchayati Extension Schedules Area
KVK	Krishi Vigyan Kendra
NRM	National Resource Management
HDI	Human Development Index
UNDP	United Nations Development Programme
GDP	Gross Domestic Product
ICFM	Indigent Committee of Forest Management
NSSO	National Sample Survey Organisation
JFM	Joint Forest Management
ATSEC	Action against Trafficking and Sexual Exploration of Children

SDC   Social Development Centre

SIGN   Social Initiative for Growth Networking

UNICEF   United Nations International Children's Emergency
                 Fund

SPWD   Society for Promotion of Wasteland Development

HYV   High-yielding Variety

STAG   Skill Target Academic Growth

DSES   Dumka Social and Educational Society, Dumka

BCC Model   Behaviourial Change Communication Model

PDS   Public Distribution System

GUK   Gram Utthan Kendra

HSSS   Hoffman Social Service Society

SHCH   Snehadeep Holy Cross, Hazaribag

CCSSS   Catholic Charities Social Service Society

MAP 1

ACTIVITIES COVERED BY
SIGN AND ITS PARTNER ORGANISATIONS

INDEX

🏠 Food self reliance through integrated livelihood initiatives and NRM

🔷 Strengthening the civil society in order to enhance their standard of living through NRM

🍴 Social and community mobilization for improving child health system

▶ Inclusive, integrated and sustainable community development project

▲ Tribal heritage and rights

■ Education support to children

★ Malaria eradication project

🔺 Capacitating parents of poor children on agricultural and livelihood practices

MAP 2

LOCATIONS OF DIOCESES IN JHARKHAND, SIGN AND ITS PARTNER ORGANISATIONS

DIOCESE

- RANCHI ARCH-DIOCESE
- HAZARIBAGH DIOCESE
- KHUNTI DIOCESE
- GUMLA DIOCESE
- JAMSHEDPUR DIOCESE
- SIMDEGA DIOCESE
- DALTONGANJ DIOCESE
- DUMKA DIOCESE

PARTNERS

1. CC RANCHI
2. JVK HAZARIBAGH
3. SHC HAZARIBAGH
4. HSSS KHUNTI
5. GUK GUMLA
6. CC JAMSHEDPUR
7. VK SIMDEGA
8. SVS CHANDWA
9. DSES DUMKA

MAP 3

NO. OF VILLAGES COVERED BY SIGN
AND ITS PARTNER ORGANISATIONS

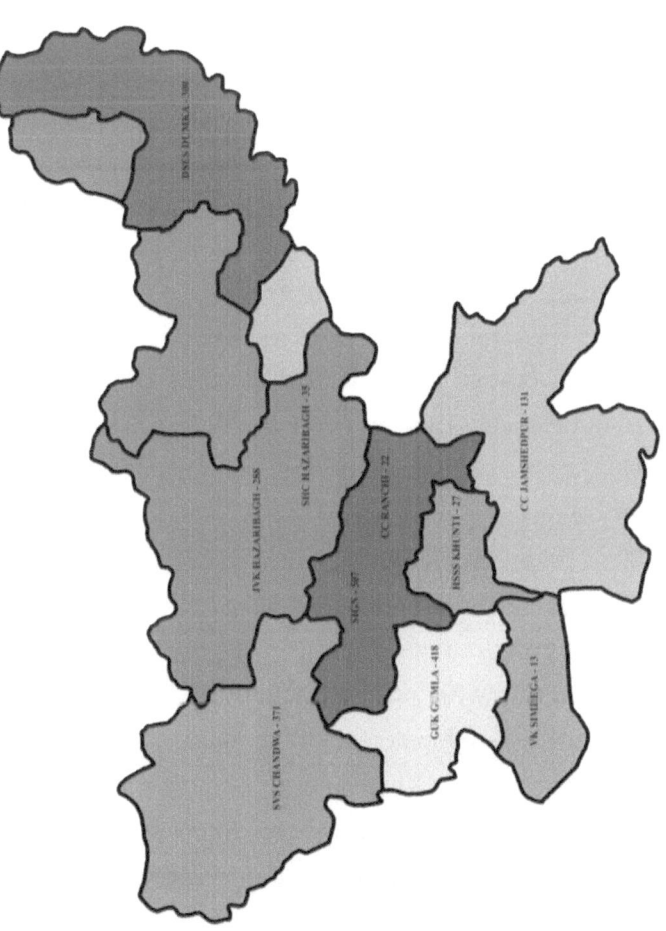

Other Select Publications of the Author

2019   Cultural Capital Deficits and Development: What Should Bihar State and Society Do and Why?

2016   Beyond Business: Mapping the CSR and Sustainable Development Initiatives of TATA Steel

2008   Social Research Methodologies in Action Vol. I & Vol. II (eds)

2007   Christians of Tribal Origin in Jharkhand: Its Implications on Demography and Development

2005   Social Empowerment Through Development Interventions (Innovative Experiments at the Grassroots) Ed.

2001   Alleviating Hunger: Challenge for the New Millennium

2000   Jharkhand Vikas: Challenge and Opportunities (Hindi)

1999   Status of Harijan Women

1998   Harijan Women in the Votex of Change

1997   Decentralised Production Management: Its Implications In Rural Industralization

1997   Voluntary Action and Rural Reconstruction

1994   Tribal Development and Voluntary Action

1991   Economics of Khadi and Village Industries

1987   Voluntary Efforts for the Development of Musahars

1987   Lifeways and Thoughtways of Musharas in Bodh Gaya Region of Bihar

1986   Samanwaya Ashram in the Service of Harijans

1983   Atrocities Committed on Scheduled Castes

1976   Naxalites and their Rehabilitation

1973   Resource Mobilization for Economic Development in Gramdan Villages of Bihar